CHILL RUN

RUSSELL BROOKS

CHILL RUN

By Russell Brooks

13-Digit ISBN (print version): 978-0-9867513-4-9

Acknowledgements

I'd like to thank these individuals for which this novel would not have been possible.

My sponsor: Brooks-Latouche Photography
My editors: Victory Crayne, Lisa Martinez
My book formatters: Signe Nichols of FirebirdEbooks.com and Carol Webb of Bella Media Management (who did an excellent job with the cover design).

My family: Stanley and Cynthia Brooks, Gordon Brooks and other immediate family members.
Special mention to my lawyer Howard Barza who helped me fight the good fight for truth and justice.

Fabien Dépres, Jerry D. Simmons, Jane Ubell-Meyer, Jeff Rivera, Ron Muka, book bloggers, the Rainiacs, and everyone that helped to spread the word.

Preface

Some of you may notice typos in the dialogue between some of the charac-
ters. What may appear to be typos actually reflect the broken English dialect
that is typical among people of Caribbean descent and also among French
Canadians. This was intentionally done and should not be interpreted as
carelessness on behalf of the author nor the editor.

Prologue

Eddie Barrow, Jr. didn't remember feeling the bullet tear into his shoulder. From where he lay on the hardwood floor, the ceiling spun in and out of focus. *God, I can't even lift my arms and legs, let alone move my wrists.* The bullet may have been small, but he felt that it had blown a hole in him the size of a golf ball. Now a chunk of his shoulder was gone. It was surely splattered on the wall somewhere, oozing towards the floor and leaving a trail of blood and tissue.

Eddie could barely open his eyes, but he heard several voices all at once. It wasn't too long after, that he felt himself lifted onto a slightly softer surface and tied down. The frost gnashed into his cheeks and chin as he felt a wintery wind-chill seconds after being wheeled outside. He caught glimpses of men and women in burgundy jackets, shouting orders and calling out words in French that he barely caught. Eddie soon felt himself being jerked upwards and hoisted into the belly of the ambulance, the doors slammed shut.

The warm air inside was a welcome relief as it chased away the chill on his face. This was followed by the jarring, unpleasant screaming of the siren. Although he was strapped in, he still rocked from side to side as the ambulance raced off.

Through partially opened eyes, he saw one of the burgundy jackets—a woman in her forties—staring down at him.

"Ca va?" *You're doing all right?* But Eddie was too weak and drowsy to answer. He guessed that's what morphine did to a person. "Soyez fort, mon grand. On est presque là." *Be strong, buddy. We're almost there.* He felt the patting on his forearm from the paramedic, which gave him some comfort.

It was only supposed to be a stupid and harmless publicity stunt. No one was supposed to die. How was he supposed to know that he'd be involved in the biggest investment-fraud scandal in Canadian history? As of now, three people were dead and his best friend had been shot. He'd dreamed of making it big in the world with his first novel. For now, he'd settle to live long enough to see tomorrow's sunrise.

Chapter 1

Montreal, Quebec. Four days earlier.

This shit-storm of a day has to end!

There wasn't a pleasant thought in Eddie's mind at the time, as puffs of vapour disappeared nearly as fast as he breathed out. He unbuckled his seatbelt and got out of his car, pulling his wool hat over his ears leaving the tips of his cornrows hanging out the back.

He deliberately parked two blocks away from the strip club so that no one there would know that he drove around in a piece of crap. Not only was it old, had rust stains on the bumper and around the wheels, but lately it had started backfiring. He was sure an art dealer would claim that bird drop stains would increase its value. Boy, how he regretted giving $4000 cash to that salesman. He should've known the man was a snake.

But the car was the least of Eddie's problems. Earlier in the day he'd lost both his girlfriend and his job. His roommate and best friend, Corey, still hadn't paid his share of the rent. This had been going on for weeks, and every time Corey kept telling him that he'd pay him.

Bullshit!

Corey always kept blowing his money on liquor and video lottery terminals. Corey had spent the last three weeks integrating with the other lowlifes at the strip joint his girlfriend, Jordyn, worked at as a barmaid. Eddie knew that she must be getting fed up with him. It was a miracle that she put up with his crap for so long. Eddie figured that it was the thick skin Jordyn developed from serving winos and other lowlifes every night.

He splashed his way through the mixture of gray, inch-high slush and gravel that covered the sidewalk. He couldn't believe that it was already November—meaning that there was another four to five more months in this freezer box. *Why'd my parents leave Barbados for this? What the hell were they thinking—giving up the hot sun, and the beach, just so that I could be born in this?* After all, the Barbadian economy's strong enough, there's no damn snow to shovel and no icy roads and sidewalks to throw him down. And he didn't have to put the snow tires on the car every year—a law that was recently enacted in this province.

Eddie didn't make it five feet inside the joint when a human cement truck blocked him.

"Ton identification," said the bald-headed bouncer.

Eddie made a face. "What?" He'd only been asked the same question by this bastard the last dozen times he'd come to this strip joint.

"I said, hi want to see your *hidee.* You make me repeat in *henglish,* so show it."

"Boy, move aside. You've seen me come here before. You know I'm twenty-four."

"Rules are rules. I want to see your *hidee.*"

Screw my ID, I don't have time for this. "Man, move aside. I'm not in the mood."

"Patrick." A young woman's voice came from the bar. Eddie glanced around the bouncer and saw Jordyn behind the bar counter. He gazed at her, forgetting about the cement truck. Corey sure knew how to pick them. It must have been so easy for him since the best ones were always attracted to him. But Jordyn was somewhat unique, being born to an Italian father and a Jamaican mother. There wasn't a place that Corey went with her where they didn't draw stares. She preferred her dark hair to be in locks, showing off her Caribbean roots. And her arms were just as toned as Michelle Obama's, which she loved to expose. Eddie didn't recall her ever having mentioned playing any sports while in high school, but she sure knew how to take care of herself.

She finished wiping off a glass with the towel and put it back beneath the counter. "Come on, stop teasing Eddie and let him in."

"You heard the woman. Move your ass," said Eddie.

Patrick grumbled. "You're lucky you 'ave friends that work here."

"Yeah, and you're lucky I ain't a foot taller with the same steroid supplier." That's when two gorilla-sized hands grabbed him by the collar.

"Hey!" Jordyn's yell would've put every female police officer to shame. "Let go of him."

Eddie narrowed his gaze as he looked into Patrick's crimson-colored face as he was released. Eddie then shot him a smirk, as though to say, "*You can't mess with me.*"

"Eddie," Jordyn yelled again. "Get your ass over here and stop antagonizing him."

Eddie's mouth dropped as he looked at her. "What did I do?"

"Don't give me that puppy dog stare. Get your ass over here. Now!" She emphasized the *now* with an index finger pointed downwards at the empty barstool that was beside where Corey slouched over the counter.

Eddie walked over, lowering his head, too embarrassed to look at the winos that stared at him. *Damn, why'd she have to go dissing me in front of everyone?*

There wasn't any music playing at the moment, which was unusual since the jukebox was usually blaring. Then again, there weren't any strippers performing at this time—meaning that they were either in the back smoking or giving private shows. At the bar, sat the four regulars that he saw each time he passed by. Now Corey was becoming one of them. Three weeks was all it took for him to blend in.

Eddie walked up behind and stared at his best friend. He wondered if Corey knew that he was standing next to him. Eddie slapped him on the back of his bald head, jolting him up and making him nearly fall off his barstool.

"Get up. Where's the money?" Eddie's Barbadian accent erupted.

"Damn, why you have to lash me so?" Corey answered, rubbing the back of his head.

"You were supposed to leave the money for me, remember? Where is it?"

"Money for what?"

"The rent. You *do* remember what that is, don't you?"

Corey sighed and mumbled into his arm. "I'll get you the money, don't worry about it."

"Don't give me that shit again," Eddie yelled, only to lower his voice when he saw Jordyn give him a cold stare. "I came home from work half hour ago to find nothing but bills on the table—and not the type you can buy things with. You ain't in Trinidad. You think we can survive without electricity in this cold weather?"

Corey's head dropped back down into his arms on the counter. "I'll come up with the money. Don't worry." Corey then fumbled for the glass, grabbed it, and stretched his arm out across the counter banging the glass twice. "Baby-girl, pour me another one."

"You ain't getting one," Jordyn replied as she cleared the counter of some empty beer bottles. Yup, she still had some of the Italian-sister attitude.

Corey looked up at her. "Oh come on, just one more for your boy."

"I said, no. You've had enough." She then narrowed her eyes, clearly annoyed. "I don't even know why I bothered giving you those two drinks earlier." She then looked at Eddie. "Let me pour you one. It'll help calm you down."

Eddie shook his head. "I'm good."

"Suit yourself." Jordyn swiped some tip money off the counter and dropped the bills and coins into her pocket. Eddie missed the clinking sound of coins, something he wished he had more of at this moment.

"Will you talk to Corey, please? He's had a rough day," asked Jordyn.

Who the hell am I, his psychologist? Eddie sat down on the stool next to him. "Let me guess. You got fired again, didn't you?" Corey groaned and looked away from him.

"Goddamn it! When are you going to stop this nonsense? I ain't here to bail your ass out for the rest of your life. You owe me at least eight hundred in rent back-payments now. You're pulling me down with your *Canadian Idol* trauma. But I ain't going to put up with this much longer. You hear me?"

"What happened to your friend?" asked one of the regulars.

"He auditioned for Canadian Idol last year when they were in town," Jordyn answered. "He was good to go up until he stood in front of the judges and saw that the British guy—I can't remember his name—paid a surprise visit."

"I know who you're talking about," he slurred.

"He was so freaked out that he lost his concentration," Jordyn said. "It was a complete disaster. Long story short, his audition was broadcast on national TV last summer and he's been named the worst singer ever. He can't walk down the street without someone recognizing him."

"Poor kid," the man said covering a cough with his hand. "So can I have another drink?"

"No."

"How about a lap dance?" Jordyn flashed her middle finger to him before she walked away.

Eddie then leaned closer to Corey. "You got to let this go. If you can't pull yourself together, you're on your own. You'll be lucky if Jordyn doesn't leave you too." Corey groaned and put his head back down on the counter. *Whatever. In one ear and out the other, as they say.*

"Hang on a few minutes, guys. Marie-Eve just arrived to take over my shift," said Jordyn referring to the other barmaid who just walked in. Marie-Eve pecked Eddie on both cheeks and ran her hand across the top of Corey's head as she walked by. Jordyn disappeared behind a set of swinging doors. When she re-emerged a few minutes later, she was wearing a fake fur coat, carrying her purse in one hand with Corey's jacket hanging on the other.

Eddie watched the way the blackness of her coat reflected the light. She only wore fake fur, and he was always careful not to bring up any animal abuse cases around her because she'd rant for hours about it. Jordyn put Corey's jacket on the bar stool next to his. "Help me get him up?"

Eddie looked down at Corey, who was still hunched over the counter. "Sure, anything." He then slapped Corey on the back of the head—jolting him out of his nap.

Corey refused Eddie and Jordyn's help in walking to the car. He slid into the backseat, while Jordyn sat with Eddie up front. The car backfired once before Eddie drove off. All Eddie could think of was getting a new car.

A half hour later they were in the Notre-Dame-de-Grace borough and were parked in front of their favorite Jamaican restaurant. It wasn't anything flashy, just a simple hangout in the basement of an old two-story brick building—with a hair salon and a video rental store upstairs. The car backfired again, just before they all got out.

"When are you going to trash this car?" asked Corey—a lot more sober—as he shut the door.

Eddie shot him a look. "The money you owe me would've helped me pay for the repairs. Did you ever think about that?" *The nerve of him, telling me to trash my car.*

"I told you not to buy any car from that guy. He's a crook. Besides, you're better off buying a new one."

Jordyn was the first to walk down the narrow steps and open the front door, jingling the bell attached to it.

"Guys, keep it down," she said as she held the door open for them.

"Hold that thought, baby-girl," said Corey as he rushed past her to the back of the restaurant. Eddie figured all that beer he'd been drinking earlier was finally making its way out.

There wasn't anyone inside the cramped three-table dining room except for Robert—Flick's son—who leaned on his elbows by the cash register, flipping through a magazine.

"Junior, is that you?" Flick's unmistakable Jamaican-accented voice came from the kitchen, just as the sound of sizzling blasted. The smell of exotic spices leaked into the dining area, guaranteeing any visitor's mouth to water.

Eddie walked up to Robert and bumped fists with him as he looked towards the kitchen. "What's going on, boss? How you know it's me?"

"Whenever your car backfires, my clients all run for cover. Can't you see the place is empty?"

Eddie and the others sat down at a table. He never knew Flick's real name. It was sad how he served the best Jamaican food in this part of town, yet he couldn't get many customers. Things went downhill for him when he lost his wife to cancer three years before. The financial strain was catastrophic to the point that he nearly lost his restaurant. Being in this location was all he could afford.

Robert came over and placed some plastic table mats and silver utensils for them. Eddie took off his winter hat and gloves, shoved them into the sleeve of his jacket and hung it on the back of his chair. He sat on one side of the four-person table facing Jordyn, who did the same with her jacket.

"We got jerk chicken and rice tonight." said Robert.

"I'll have that with a Sorrel. A large one." said Eddie.

"Corey and I'll have the same," said Jordyn.

Robert left them and Jordyn turned to Eddie. "So what's going on with you today? You were quiet on the way over."

Eddie sighed and leaned back in his chair. She always knew when something wasn't right with him. Such as, the week that led up to the day that he moved out of his parent's house. They were sitting at this very table. She and Cory were drinking Trinidadian beer while he had an Irish Moss. It was the first time he cried in front of them, being unsure where he was heading in life. His father didn't support the idea of him wanting to be a novelist. What did his dad know? All he wanted were the same things all West-Indian parents wanted of their children—that they either became teachers, doctors or lawyers. But a novelist? Please.

"Vanessa left me and I got laid off," said Eddie.

"What? You're kidding," said Jordyn. Just then they heard the toilet flush in the chicken-coop of a bathroom in the back of the restaurant.

Corey—appearing to be much more sober than before—approached their table, hung his jacket on the empty chair beside Jordyn, and sat. He then noticed Eddie's long face. "What happened?"

Eddie broke the bad news to him. Corey's torso dipped forward. "Your girl left you *and* you got laid off? No way."

Eddie put his elbows on the table and dropped his head into his hands. "I decided to drop by her place this morning before work only to find out that she wanted her apartment key back."

"Did she at least tell you why?" Jordyn asked.

"She didn't have to. I knew that she was cheating on me."

"You found another man's underwear in her laundry basket, didn't you," said Corey.

"No, there was a used condom in her bedroom. I saw the wrapper next to it—and it *wasn't* a brand I normally use."

Jordyn fell back in her chair with her hand covering her mouth. "Whoa, wait a minute. You go to her place, she tells you it's over. And you do what, search her place?"

"In a way, yeah."

"How'd you know that she was cheating on you? I mean, before you found the condom." Corey asked.

"Last week I came by and saw a juice glass on one of the night tables in her bedroom."

Corey shrugged his shoulders. "So?"

"It was on the table that I normally sleep next to. Not the one she usually leaves her drinks on."

"Damn, you're good," said Corey.

"So did you bring it up this evening?" asked Jordyn.

"Of course I did. She told me that I was paranoid. So I barged past her, walked into her room, emptied the trash on the floor, and sure enough, found the condom wrapped in a bunch of tissue paper along with the condom wrapper."

"What did she say then?" asked Corey.

"Not much. So I threw her key on the floor and left. I guess I ain't good enough for her. I'm just some wannabe writer that works in a bookstore and can't even get a book deal or sell my last ebook online. Nothing was ever good enough for her."

"Oh, I almost forgot," said Corey as he reached into his coat pocket and handed Eddie two envelopes. They were opened. "These came for you today."

"You opened my mail?"

"One's from an agency. The other's from a publisher."

"Thanks. Maybe you can tell me what they said."

"Oh you'll want to throw them out. They didn't like what you sent them." All Eddie got in the last two months from agents and publishers that he had queried were rejection letters and emails. He tossed the envelopes back at Corey. *Those were the last two I queried. Now what? I guess I can turn it into an ebook and then sell it online.*

Jordyn got up, walked around to Eddie and hugged him, pecking him on his forehead. "I'm sorry about what happened. You didn't deserve that." Corey came over and did the same, mocking Jordyn. Eddie shoved him away before Corey had a chance to fake-kiss him on the forehead. He wouldn't cry this time. Not over Vanessa, not over the rejection letters. *Just be strong.* That's all he could tell himself.

Just then, Jordyn looked up at the television that sat on a shelf on the wall. She turned to Robert. "Can you turn up the TV?" When Eddie looked up, the volume was being raised. He assumed Robert must have used the remote control from where he stood. It was entertainment news and they were talking about some pop singer he didn't care for.

"The singer just signed a twenty million dollar book deal in which she will tell all. From the sex tape scandal, to her New Years Eve Party bar fight, to getting back in the music studio..."

What the fuck? Eddie turned to Robert, "Man, turn that off. I'm tired of hearing such nonsense."

"Damn! Twenty million!" echoed Corey.

Eddie shot Corey a glance. "Go ahead, rub it in. Never mind that she can't sing, and sells millions of albums. All because of what? Because she behaves like some high-priced-ho? Now *she's* got the book deal and I don't. Give me a break."

Robert brought over their meals and set them down before them.

Eddie dove into his food when Corey said to him, "You know? Maybe that's what you need to do."

Eddie swallowed and looked up at him. "Need to do what?"

"Maybe you need to do what the stars do in order to get book deals or sell more books—do something scandalous."

Eddie chuckled. "Boy, you crazy."

Corey shook his head. "No, I'm serious. How often does a celebrity put out a book that *doesn't* make it to the bestseller's list?"

Eddie thought about the question before he answered. "Hardly. Now what does that have to do with me?"

"You've written a book. No one knows who you are. That's why publishers don't want you."

"Maybe it's because my stories aren't any good. Maybe I should try to figure out what I'm doing wrong or just write another book."

"Please. Do you think that blonde bimbo got a book deal because of her writing skills? She can't even sing and she's got record deals. Lately, her record sales hit a slump. Next thing you know, she films herself being humped several times and leaks it to the internet. Now, everyone's talking about her again, and the scandal's helped to boost her album sales. It ain't got nothing to do with talent. 'Cause we all know that she ain't got none."

"Corey's got a point there," Jordyn said as she ate her salad. She put down the fork and looked at Eddie. "Remember a while back when New York State Governor Eliot Spitzer got caught with a call girl? Guess what happened to the call girl?"

"What?"

"After the scandal broke, the call girl got a job as a sex advice columnist for a major newspaper, I can't remember which one. Oh yeah, it's also boosted her singing career. Maybe if you did something scandalous, you'd be able to sell yourself to agents and publishers a lot easier."

"What, you mean like getting naked on film?" Eddie chuckled as he shook his head. "I can't believe I'm hearing this from you two. You expect me to film my black ass and broadcast it all over the internet. Besides, millions of people are already doing that."

"Ah," Jordyn pointed a finger upwards. "But what if you did it with a celebrity, or an important public figure? Think. What if you were caught with someone who stood to lose everything?"

"I hear you. But it's *those* people who'll bask in the limelight. No one cares who they got nasty with. I'd only be helping *them* get book deals," said Eddie.

"That's why it's important for you to build a back story. Imagine if everyone knew about your problems. Such as, your girlfriend cheated on you, your parents don't even support you, and you got laid off. No offence, but you're also driving a piece of crap with four tires and a steering wheel. True?"

Eddie nodded. "Yeah, in a way."

"There you go," said Corey. "Enough people will feel sorry for you, and the media's going to feed on that."

Eddie finished off his meal, leaned back to stretch and yawn, covering his mouth.

Corey pushed his half-empty plate to the side.

Jordyn glanced down at it and pointed her finger towards his plate. "Are you done with that?"

Corey looked at her and without a word, slid the plate over to her.

Eddie's eyes widened. *Damn, she's had quite an appetite lately.*

"So what do you think?" asked Jordyn.

Eddie shrugged his shoulders. "About what?"

Corey sighed. "Come on, bro. We're trying to help you. Don't you want to be better known as an author?"

"Not *that* way I ain't. Besides, how would I ever get close to a celebrity? I don't know any, and neither do you."

"Actually," said Jordyn as she wolfed down some of the jerk chicken and wiped her mouth with the napkin. "I never said this to anyone, but I'm a femdom."

"You're a what?" Eddie cried out.

Corey and Jordyn hushed him. "Keep your voice down."

Eddie glanced over his shoulder at Robert, who momentarily looked up from the magazine he read, obviously due to Eddie's outburst. Eddie looked back at Jordyn while he lowered his head closer to the table. "You're a dominatrix? Like one of those freaky girls that dress up in vinyl and lash people with whips?"

"Yes. And don't you dare tell anyone."

"Why the hell would you do something like that?" He then looked at Corey. "Did you know about this?"

Corey shrugged his shoulders. "Yeah."

"And you're cool with the fact that your woman sleeps around with Lord knows who?"

"Whoa, just a minute," Jordyn pointed her finger at him. "I'm not a prostitute, so let's get that straight. I entertain my clients by humiliating them. There's no sex involved."

"'Cause that's my territory," said Corey patting his chest.

"I didn't know you were so freaky," said Eddie.

Jordyn leaned closer to him. "It's just work. Do you think I want to serve drinks for the rest of my life to a bunch of lowlifes who have nothing better to do than get drunk and stare at my ass all the time? No. I want to own my own coffee shop someday. The banks are giving me a hard time loaning me the cash, so I have no choice."

Her words hit him like stones the way she spat them out, jolting him to the back of his chair.

"Anyhow," she said, a bit calmer. "Getting back to what I was saying before. I would do my thing once a week. Some of my male friends are doing the same thing too. You'd be amazed at some of the clients we've had."

"Not to mention the cheddar that she brings home in one night," Corey added.

Eddie wasn't as interested in the money as he was in knowing who her clients were. He stretched his neck forward with his eyes dilated. "Who?"

"All types of people. You'd get your regular Joe and Jane who are living out their fantasies behind the backs of their spouses and families. Sometimes we get couples—gay and straight. At times, we'd get your typical grandma and grandpa."

Eddie made a face. The images of geriatrics struggling to zip up their leather or PVC outfits over their adult diapers came to mind. *Ewww!*

"Then you'd also have real celebs, pro athletes and even politicians."

"No way," said Eddie.

"Yes way," said Corey.

"And this weekend, one of my colleagues will be hooking up with a very high-profile individual who lives south of the border."

"Who is it?" asked Corey.

Jordyn glanced briefly over at Robert and lowered her voice even more. "I'm not really sure yet. But from what I was told. She's the CEO of a Fortune 500 company, and she'll be in town for a conference this weekend."

"You lie."

"It's no lie, Eddie," Jordyn replied. "The guy that's doing the job owes me a big favor. I'm sure that I can arrange to have you substitute for him."

"What, like being a...a *pinch* dominator."

"Well, yeah. A *maledom* is the correct term. But you can put it that way. Geez, it's amazing how guys always use sports analogies when it comes to anything remotely sexual."

"Do you know what she looks like?"

"Not right now."

"Then you can count me out."

Corey turned to him. "Why's that?"

"How am I supposed to get freaky with someone when I don't even know what they look like *before* I meet them?"

"Man, don't stress yourself over that," Corey answered. "If she's the CEO of some Fortune 500 company, then she's got to be loaded with cash. She probably goes to the spa once a week and has her own personal trainers to keep herself looking like a twenty-year old."

"And what if she don't?" countered Eddie. "What if she's out of shape and looking twice her age?"

"Then she'll probably be so desperate that she'll pay more to have her session with you," Corey answered.

Eddie jerked back in his seat. "That's easy for you to say."

Jordyn shook a fist. "Will you calm down."

"I am calm," said Eddie raising his voice.

"Yo, man, keep your voice down," said Corey.

Eddie inhaled, and then exhaled. This was way too much for him. What made them think that he'd be so desperate that he'd sink to such a low level? "Man this is way too unbelievable for me."

Jordyn grabbed Eddie's forearm. "Relax. It's not such a big deal."

"So you say."

"Listen," said Jordyn, "You're not having sex with her, you just have to make her live out her fantasy. The guy you'll be substituting for is close to your physique—he's about five-foot-eight, one-hundred-and-fifty to sixty pounds. He's a bit more muscular than you but I think you'll still get away with it. Oh yeah, I'm told that the client prefers men of color, so you're in luck."

"I don't care, 'cause I ain't doing it. This is the stupidest idea I've ever heard," Eddie stood up.

Corey's mouth dropped open as though he was surprised. "What are you talking about? What do you have to lose?"

"It doesn't matter. It's a stupid idea. I'm going to the bathroom." Without pushing the chair back in, he walked to the back—passing Robert—who tried his best to hide his smile.

The bathroom was more of a powder room minus the fanciness of one. One of the floor tiles was missing, and the toilet seat shifted to the left when you sat on it. Closing the door required one to force their entire body into it.

When Eddie was done, he washed his hands, dried them, and then used the hand sanitizer that was on the shelf.

He then looked at himself in the mirror. *Were they for real? How could I expect to get a book deal from doing the dominator thing? Man, that shit only worked in the movies.* Maybe that's what he should write about next, so long as he got his current project off the ground. Who was he kidding? He's not Jordyn. So what, if she could do stuff like that and not think much of it? That's her. And how could Corey enjoy being around her knowing that she's spanking some naked old geezer who had more spots than a leopard?

On his way back to the table Eddie stopped at the cash register. "How much for the meal?"

"Nine-eighty-five each," Robert answered.

Eddie took out his wallet and found a creased five-dollar bill. He then pulled out a few coins from his pocket and sighed. He turned to Corey and Jordyn. "Can you guys spot me a Toonie?"

Jordyn was about to grab a two-dollar coin from her purse and toss it to him. She sucked her teeth, "Keep your money, Eddie. I got this one." She walked over, pulled out two fresh twenties along with a crumpled five, and placed them on the counter. "Keep the change."

Just then, the bell on the front door jingled as it was pulled open. A slight gust of cold air followed. After Eddie turned to see who it was, he looked away, rolling his eyes with a sigh. "Look who's here."

But Jordyn had already seen him and lowered her head. "Oh God."

It was Theo. He was close to Eddie's height and build with dreadlocks hanging out from his winter hat. He was also Jordyn's ex.

"What's up, Flick?" said Theo louder than he needed to. He was always starved for attention.

"Hey," Flick's voice came from the kitchen, above the sounds of frying food. Flick must have been up to his arms in his cooking that he hardly had time to leave the kitchen to greet his customers.

Although Eddie, Jordyn, and Corey paid no attention to Theo, he still saw them.

"What's dis? Me gal come to me favorite hangout spot to find me?"

"You wish," Jordyn said without looking at him.

Eddie swore that this guy was going to push their patience one day. He already had to separate Corey from him after a fight at a nightclub. The bouncers eventually physically threw all of them out.

Theo then looked at Corey. "And she bring along she singing boy toy." He then laughed.

Eddie watched as Corey was about to take a step towards Theo. He immediately blocked him, mouthing the words, "No you don't."

Corey didn't say anything.

"Dem judges tore you up. And dat British dude? Lord have mercy! Did you know you're on *YouTube*? I had to send that video to my friends and family in Jamaica."

Jordyn spun around to face him. "You didn't."

"Of course, *mon*. I couldn't keep dat to me-self. I also emailed it to my friends in St Lucia, St Vincent, and Grenada. You're a hit. I mean your video's got over seventy *tousand* hits in just two weeks. I mean dat video must have made it half way past England by now."

The nerve of this guy. He still couldn't get over Jordyn leaving him for Corey. Shit, that was over two years ago, and he still had it in for Corey.

Corey played along with a fake laugh. "Yeah, I'm glad you found that video funny."

Eddie tapped Corey's arm, hoping to draw his attention away from Theo. It didn't work.

"Yeah, mon. Nuff respect." Theo was about to bump fists with him.

"Good, now get the fuck out of my face," growled Corey. Theo dropped the smile and raised his hands in surrender as he backed off.

"What's dat I hear?" Flick's voice echoed from the kitchen.

Shit! Now Corey's done it. Eddie's first two inner fingers shot up to both his temples. Saying the wrong thing in his franchise was a sure fire way to get Flick out of the kitchen, no matter what he was doing. Flick was out by the cash register seconds later, shaking a large wooden spoon. He was in his sixties, but still had the agility of a forty-year old. "I told you youngsters before that I don't want to hear *any* foul language in my restaurant, do you understand me? I ought to put ten lashes across your behinds with dis spoon."

"Yes, and we're so sorry. It won't happen again," said Jordyn, waving her hands quickly, as though she was surrendering for all of them.

"It better not." Flick pointed the spoon at each of them, one at a time.

"For sure, sir. It won't happen again," Jordyn repeated. Flick then retreated back to the kitchen, mumbling something to himself. Eddie then signaled to Jordyn to walk on.

Eddie looked at Theo, who was clearly trying to hold back a laugh. Theo then lifted his gold chains from under his jacket, letting them dangle out in the open as he turned to Jordyn.

"You know my number when you're ready to come home to a real man, right?"

Jordyn ignored Theo as she walked past him.

Corey eyed him as he walked away, which prompted Eddie to nudge him forward. He wasn't going to break up another fight between the two of them, and get them banned from his favorite restaurant.

Eddie zipped up his jacket by the time he reached the top of the stairs, took out the car keys, and pondered what just happened. Leave it to Jordyn to always be there to bail him and Corey out of a sticky situation. When his eyes fell on his car, he thought again about what Jordyn and Corey had suggested. *Could this really work?* Then images of half-naked old people in PVC came to mind. He made a face in disgust. *Hell naw!*

Chapter 2

Laval-sur-le-Lac, Québec. Three days earlier.

Serge Lamont tugged on the mutt's leash as it stopped to sniff at something in the snow. It was the only way of showing the Saint Bernard—Marc-Antoni—who's boss. The dog ought to appreciate having him as his master, after he put down $1600 in loose change two days ago in veterinarian fees. How the hell can one mutt cost so much? There was a fee for the heart *Doppler*, another for routine checkups, the cleaning of the nails, ears, and teeth. There was even a charge for the office call. How the hell do they justify charging for an office call? These crooks would've charged him for owning his own dog if they could get away with it.

The backyard of his two-storey mansion was big enough to hold a small roller coaster and a Ferris wheel. Some people would've just let the dog run around in the yard on their own every morning. Not Lamont. He needed to get out and catch the crisp morning air. It was the only thing that woke him up, something that coffee couldn't do as it did for others. He left his wife, Chantal, in bed. It was close to the end of the school semester. For her and the other university professors, they'd be psyching themselves up for the midterm exam period.

Outside was quiet, which was normal for the Laval-sur-le-Lac district where he lived. There was hardly any chirping from the birds this time of year since they were all down south, most likely nesting in either his beachfront condominium in the Florida Keys or the other in the Dominican Republic. He pictured the palm trees blowing in the ocean breeze. But all he saw ahead of him were a few pine trees. Surrounding them were a larger number of conifers whose stiff, leafless branches were bent downward from the weight of the ice that covered them.

Lamont pulled up his scarf over his exposed neck and zipped his jacket up over it. Wisps of vapor clouded in front of his mouth as he breathed, only to disappear less than a second later. But he liked his morning walks with Marc-Antoni. Even when the temperature dipped below minus twenty Celsius, he wouldn't back away. After all, how else could he remind the neighbors who the top brass in the neighborhood was if he couldn't be seen regularly? Like him, most of his neighbors also worked in the financial sector. One of them was a Member of Parliament. But they were all in his pocket, since most of them had investment portfolios in his company. Those who weren't, it didn't matter, since he was a major shareholder in some of the companies they worked for.

When he took over as chairman of Borealest Investments fifteen years ago, Lamont helped take the company out of Montreal and brought its presence across Canada and as far south as Houston, Texas. Sure, the economic crisis a few years before hit his company hard. But then again, who wasn't? His company stayed afloat while others went belly-up.

This all started when a couple of greedy and arrogant assholes down in the US screwed things up for everyone. Now the rest of the world was paying for it. And it didn't make things easier for his company, which had lost millions more than he and his partners had let their investors know. Hell, he didn't even know where and when it all started. Sure, he had pocketed some of the money, but then again who wasn't nowadays. There were also a few bad decisions made here and there awhile back. Now the shit kept pouring slowly into the fan.

Marc-Antoni kept weaving back and forth in front of him—his nose inches from the sidewalk-less road. What was he sniffing for anyway? Lamont was sometimes envious of a dog's senses. They could smell better, hear better and could even sense trouble around them. Maybe had he had a dog's senses, he could've predicted the impending financial crisis.

Ahead, two joggers ran towards him.

As they ran by they said, "Bon matin, Monsieur Lamont, ca va?" *Good morning, Mister Lamont. How are you?*

"Ca va, merci," *I'm well, thanks,* he replied with a nod.

Mark-Antoni pulled impatiently on his leash, as they were meters away from the park by the Lake of Two Mountains. This is where Lamont would normally let go of the leash and let the mutt run about on his own. He looked around and saw that they were alone, so he let the mutt go free. He didn't need to be reprimanded by some overzealous city employee. But it shouldn't have been a big deal anyways since Marc-Antoni never wandered too far off from Lamont.

He looked both up and down one last time to be sure that he was alone. Satisfied, he walked up to the lake and stood close enough that he heard the water lapping a few feet away. In a few more days the ice chunks would freeze together and form a new surface. A few weeks after another dumb ice-fisher will be on the news after having fallen through the ice. Even despite the numerous public warnings about the dangers of ice fishing on this lake, people still did it.

He reached into his jacket pocket, took out his mobile phone and dialed a number. Lamont heard the other phone ring twice.

"Oui," came a reply.

"I thought that I should give you a call this morning."

"And?"

"I had another lengthy talk with our friend. I did my best to negotiate but nothing's changed. It's really unfortunate. So you'll have to kill him."

Chapter 3

Dollard-Des-Ormeaux, Quebec.

Eddie stopped his car right behind the green sedan his parents had purchased. It was a decent upgrade from the old station wagon his father used to drive. But there weren't any more family road trips to Toronto or New York, where he and his sister, Denise, would be fighting in the backseat. Why was it that he was the one that always got spanked while Denise always got away with everything? Now that he thought about it, Denise was always favored over him for everything. She got to stay out late at night, got to go out of town with her friends—the list went on. She'll surely be the talk at the dinner table this evening. Denise will go on about Harvard Med School all evening just to prove that she's accomplished something that he didn't. Of course his dad will then go on about how everyone else in the family was a success and Eddie wasn't.

Eddie sighed. *What the fuck am I doing here?* He then remembered that the fridge only had a jug of water, a half-empty jar of mayonnaise, a few slices of bread and some ham. He received his final rejections to his novel in his email account. He didn't even bother filling out job applications online. Just turning on his old junk-box of a computer took nearly five minutes. Seeing Corey passed out on his bed for most of the day among piles of dirty laundry blocking his bedroom door didn't help the ambiance either.

He got out of his car—which didn't backfire for a change—and walked up the driveway to the front door of the split-level cottage. There was a time that he nearly burnt it down when he was six years old, when he lit a fire in the woodstove with a bottle of cooking oil. This happened while his mother, Monica, was upstairs in the kitchen. Boy, he could still feel the stinging on his backside from the spanking his father, who had to rush home from the pharmacy where he worked, gave him. The front door was pulled open from inside before Eddie could ring the doorbell. It was his Aunt Beverly, who was visiting from Barbados.

She stretched out her arms and pulled him in the house, hugging him. Aunt Beverly was one of those rare people that did not have much change in appearance due to their age. She must've been pushing close to seventy and she still had the same slender form as far as he could remember. No visible gray hairs nor wrinkles and she still had her strength, the way she gripped him. His father often commented that she ought to eat more to put some meat on her bones, to which she would tell him she'd be happy to take some of his fat to burn it off since he wasn't able to.

"Hey, Junior, how are you? My goodness, you's a big man now. I see you still wearing the necklace I gave you."

"You know I am." She released him and he showed her the flash drive that hung from it. "It's never far from me."

"Just make sure you don't lose it."

Eddie closed the door behind him and took off his jacket and winter hat. "How was the flight? You got in okay?"

"Boy, I tell you that these airports overdo it with the security. I arrive here at the airport and I catch this man letting his dog sniff my bags. Boy, I tell he off fast enough."

"They're part of airport security. You can't go about cussing these people."

"Well I ain't know that. We should've been warned about these things before we got off the plane."

"I just hope that you didn't cause a scene."

"Of course she caused a scene," yelled his father from the kitchen. "And guess who had to bail she out."

"Don't you two start again," yelled his mother from the bedroom upstairs.

"I ain't know what's wrong with the women in your family," said Edward, Senior. "I come to pick she up and instead, wind up having to clear she from an assault charge."

Eddie turned to his aunt. "Don't tell me that you hit the security guard?"

"I just gave him a little slap. But how was I supposed to know he was security?"

"Your so-called *little* slap ended up costing me an extra fifty dollars at the car park. All of a sudden you want to be Zsa-Zsa Gabor," said his father.

Eddie headed to the living room away from the argument. Lord, those two were always at each other's throats, like Israel and Palestine. It would calm down a bit and before the end of the evening, they'd be fighting again. He sat down on the living room couch, when he heard his father come out of the kitchen. When he turned, he saw him with a steaming plate of flying fish—his favorite. Eddie wondered why he didn't learn to prepare that or any of the other meals his parents made. The only things he hasn't learned to screw up were white rice, spaghetti, and defrosting frozen food in the microwave.

Edward stood at six-foot three and could've been mistaken for a football linebacker instead of the pharmacist he was. Many first-time clients that went to his pharmacy with a prescription still mistook one of his employees as being the head pharmacist—even after twenty-seven years.

"What's going on, Son?" His voice was a powerful base that boomed in the background of the church choir. It also used to make him cringe as a child, seconds before the belt came out whenever he misbehaved.

"I'm doing well. No complaints."

"That's good to hear. Where's Vanessa?"

"She's busy this evening. But she says hello." *Please don't bring her up anymore.*

"Oh that's too bad. We set an extra seat at the table for her. Well, I guess there's next time."

Don't count on it. When Eddie looked at the dining room table, he saw all of his favorites. Among them was a separate dish of white rice—since he couldn't stand rice and peas. There were also the steamed vegetables, sweet potato pie, diced carrot and raisin salad, and green salad. It was everything that caused his stomach to growl like a pack of wolves. He knew that there was a bottle of wine sitting somewhere on the stand in the corner.

Denise was next to come into the dining room, followed by their mother.

"When did you get here?" asked Denise.

"Nice to see you too." Eddie didn't think that Denise even bothered to hear him.

"Hello, Junior," said Monica as she walked over and kissed him on the forehead before she took her seat at the head of the table. "I hope the car didn't give you any problems this time."

"None at all," Eddie answered.

"Beverly, hurry up, the dinner's getting cold," yelled his father.

"Hang on, I coming."

"I ain't hanging on. When I was a little boy and the food was being served, I'd be the first one at the table."

"Yes, and I also heard that you were always sent away because you never washed your hands."

Edward sat down at the other head of the table. "Man, I should've left she ass at the airport."

Monica slapped the edge of the table. "Edward! Don't you dare say that about my sister."

"Is that old demon talking about me behind my back again?" said Beverly as she came into the dining room and sat beside Denise.

"Don't mind he, Bev. No need to raise your blood pressure over him," said Monica.

"Damn right," quipped Edward. "'Cause I ain't got time to carry you to the hospital tonight."

Beverly turned to Denise. "Go boil some water for me. I'm going to show your father how *us* women do things in Barbados."

"Enough!" Monica blasted.

Oh gosh, here they go again. Eddie rested an elbow on the table and held his head in his hand.

"I swear you two are getting worse every year," said Monica. She then turned to Eddie. "Would you like to say grace?"

Eddie nodded and they all bowed their heads as he blessed the meal. Soon after, the food was shared. Eddie couldn't believe that he actually missed his parents' cooking. And he knew that there was some coconut bread and some rum punch for dessert.

As expected, all attention was on his sister. It was Harvard this, Harvard that. For Pete's sake, she wasn't even starting Med School until January, so why were they bringing this up now. Couldn't they just spend one evening together where his sister's accomplishments didn't dominate the dinner conversation?

Monica turned to Eddie with the fork in her hand. "I heard on the radio this afternoon that Pages & Print is going out of business."

Now why'd she have to bring up my former employer? "They're not going out of business, Mum," said Eddie. "Just a few stores are closing."

"But what about *your* store?" Denise asked.

Eddie cleared his throat. "It's still open."

"For now, that is. How much longer it'll stay open? We'll see," his father said.

"Hold on," said Eddie's mother as though something just dawned on her. "Where's Vanessa?"

"She couldn't come." *Could they stop bringing her up?*

"Oh? Why not?"

"She just couldn't come. She had things to do."

"I find that strange. She always liked your father's cooking."

"I have some more in the fridge," said Edward. "I was saving it for you to carry home. It should save you the trouble of poisoning yourself with junk."

"Dad, I'm eating very well."

"Come to think of it," said Monica. "You're looking a little thin. I thought you'd be looking like your father."

"That's because Dad's genes skipped his generation," said Denise as she glanced at her mother. "If you gave birth to another son, maybe *he'd* look like Dad."

Eddie looked at Denise. "Or you can lose the weave and you'd look like Dad."

Before Denise could respond, Monica put her hand out. "Enough. Besides, I'm way past the age to have more children," said Monica.

"Praise the Lord for that," Edward added as he glanced at both Eddie and Denise. "'Cause the two of you were expensive enough."

Monica shot a glance at her husband, but he ignored her as he kept eating. "Genes or no genes," she continued, "you still look as though you've lost weight."

"I said I'm fine." *Could they give it a rest already?*

"Okay, I was just letting you know I cooked some extra food for you to carry home," said Edward as he held the knife and cut into the fish. "Just make sure that ruffian, Corey, don't eat it all. I still can't figure out why you chose him as a roommate."

"Corey's my best friend and we help each other out, plain and simple."

"Oh yeah?" laughed Edward as he put down his utensils. "Then why didn't you stop him from going on that Canadian Idol show and making a fool of himself?"

Eddie sighed as he put down his fork and stared at his father. "Dad, please stop."

"Dad's got a point," Denise giggled. "Corey was just plain awful."

Eddie curved his eyebrows as he shot a glance back at his sister. "I've seen worse, trust me. And it took courage doing what he did."

"Whatever. If you want to call that courage," said Denise as she waved her fork. "Joining the army and fighting in Afghanistan, that's courage. Walking a tightrope without a safety net, that's courage. Trying to sing on national TV when you *can't* sing, that's just dumb." The entire table erupted in laughter except for Eddie and Beverly.

"Corey is very good at what he does. He can play the piano, he composes and writes songs, and he *can* sing. None of you know him so stop talking about him like that."

"You know something?" said Beverly. "I think they were too hard on him. That English judge didn't have to be so nasty, labeling him as the worse singer ever. That was just wicked."

"Wait, they show Canadian Idol in Barbados, too?" asked

Monica.

"No, I saw it on the computer at Missus Watts's house. I went next door to borrow some flour when all of a sudden the children were laughing. So we went to see what it was, and that's when I saw Corey. They were even talking about it on the radio."

Goddamn it. Theo's email thread must have snaked its way into Barbados. At least someone at this table has shown some common sense. "Listen, everyone. I don't want to hear another word about this. Corey can't even leave the house without someone recognizing him on the street and making fun of him. Since that audition, he lost his passion for music, and he hasn't been himself. I think he's suffering from depression and I'm very worried about him."

"That's why I keep telling you to get yourself back in school," said Edward. "If you get yourself an education, then you can go further in life. I became a pharmacist, your mother—a nurse, your aunt—a teacher, and your sister is going to be the family's first medical doctor."

"Don't forget, Dad, I got a full scholarship to Harvard," Denise added.

There she goes boasting again.

"You see, Son?" Edward said. "That's what hard work gets you."

Jesus, he never knew when to quit. You'd think that he would've figured out why I moved out in the first place. Dinner conversations used to be more pleasant. Not anymore. He looked away from his father and back down at his plate. He ate the last of his rice.

"How's the new book coming along," asked Beverly. Edward chuckled to himself as he helped himself to another portion of sweet potato pie, mumbling something under his breath.

Eddie closed his eyes as though it would help him to block out his father's chuckling. "It's finished. I'm querying agencies and publishers now."

Denise looked up at Eddie. "So, does anyone want it yet?"

Screw you. You'd already know if someone wanted it. It's not enough for her to boast about her achievements, she has to trample me too. "A few agents are considering it right now."

"I thought you said earlier that some publishers had asked for the whole manuscript," Monica said.

Shit, she was right. "Yes...both have...I mean two agents are considering representing me while some publishers had requested that I send them the complete manuscript."

"That's great. So when will you get an answer?"

"In a few weeks."

"And if they pass on it, what are you going to do? Try and sell it online for two dollars like your last two?" asked his father.

What's this, a double-team? "I'll keep at it, rewrite it, and send it off again. That's what you do in this business."

"I hope you get through," said Beverly. "Just try to learn as much as you can and move onto the next step."

"Thanks," said Eddie as he turned to his aunt. "It's good to know that I have a family member that supports me."

"Don't get your father wrong," said Monica. "Times are tough right now and we just don't want to see you wasting your life away."

"Listen to your mother," said Edward. "I don't see much of you young people reading. You're all watching TV, listening to music, or playing on the computer."

Eddie felt the back of his throat tighten. No amount of swallowing could ease the pain as the anger built up deep down in his gut and bubbled upwards. "Why are you assuming that I've written a book exclusively for my age group? I've been writing and rewriting this story for the past four years and not once have you asked to read any of it." His father remained silent and shook his head while forking more food. He finally had the big guy against the ropes for a change. He kept his sister in his peripheral vision, just waiting for her to make a counterattack. But he knew she wouldn't dare. This was between him and the big guy.

When his father finished swallowing, he looked back at Eddie. "Listen. Your mother and I sacrificed a lot to put both you and your sister through private school and onwards to ensure that you have a leg up on the competition who'll be trying to get into the best universities. You think the youngsters from all those wealthy families are fooling around and working at these little dead-end jobs? No, they're out there studying. Your sister understood this, and that's why *she* has the scholarship."

Oh Lord, again Denise and her goddamn scholarship. "And what about—"

"Why are you talking? You can't see I'm not finished?" His father had a thick index finger pointed at him.

Eddie bit down hard to avoid himself from trembling. The finger that his father used to point at him came from the same hand that used to spank him. *Wait a minute. Why am I being scared? This is why I'm always on the ropes, because my father always instilled fear in me.*

Edward's eyes narrowed as he spoke. "You quit school, left this house on your own, and got that little job at the bookstore. Now you're living from paycheck to paycheck, running around like a hamster in a wheel. Running around and not going anywhere— that's you. You squandered everything that your mother and I invested in you. Once you decide to do something meaningful and stop writing nonsense, then I'll help you." He then finished off the last of his sweet potato.

The tightness at the back of Eddie's throat suddenly went away. He felt his pulse beating hard in his neck, something he never felt before. It was bad enough to be kicked when he was down. But now his dad had crossed the line. *I stood up to Patrick at the bar, why shouldn't I stand up to you?* "Dad, all I have to say to that is that I can respect you all the way. You came from nothing and you became a pharmacist. You faced an uphill battle to become what *you* wanted."

His father didn't appear to hear what he said. He wasn't landing his punches. "And that's why you are *so* wrong, in *every* way." Eddie felt the shock and awe around him at the table as everyone simultaneously stopped eating. There was about five seconds of coughing and throat clearing.

He finally landed a heavy blow, the audience gasps.

"What?" Edward's deep baritone voice shook the room, but Eddie wouldn't allow that to faze him.

"You heard me. You're wrong. You had a goal, pursued it, and got it. Now I'm trying to do the same. You're only proud of Denise because she's doing something that *you* want." Eddie turned to his sister. "Face it. You'll do anything to please everyone, just so that they can say nice things about you. That's what makes me better than you, because I can steer my own path, not have someone else do it for me. You're not fooling me by pretending that you care about my book. You don't think I overheard your phone calls when I used to live here? Telling everyone how I was in dreamland? Oh yeah, I heard quite a bit." Denise's mouth dropped open and her hand went up to her chest as she looked at their father, then their mother, as though she was expecting them to come to her rescue.

"Young man, you watch your mouth at this table," yelled Edward as he slammed his fist on the table, shaking some utensils to the floor.

I ain't scared of you anymore. You can't do anything more to me that hasn't already been done. Eddie stood up and looked down at his father. "Guess what, you don't have to worry about me doing that little dead-end job at the bookstore anymore, because I was laid off this morning."

"What?" said Monica.

"Jesus Christ," said Edward as he put his elbows on the table and let his head fall into his hands.

Eddie looked at his mother. "Oh yes, and it gets better too. The real reason why Vanessa's too *busy* to be here this evening is because she's *busy* rolling around in bed with someone else. Anyone would think that she was *your* daughter because apparently she doesn't think that I'm good enough for her either."

Knockout punch.

Eddie looked at his mother, who had her hands cupped over her mouth. His sister and aunt remained silent and his father had his head buried deep in those large hands of his as he shook his head.

It didn't appear as though his adversaries would regain consciousness and the victory bell sounded. Eddie stepped behind his chair and pushed it back under the table. "I gone. And trust me...I ain't coming back this time." He let go of the chair, walked to the front room, put on his winter clothes and left. There wasn't a peep from anyone as he shut the door, and it was completely silent outside. He got in his car, started it up, and drove off as quickly as possible. Never mind that the engine was frozen and would likely stall. But he didn't care, he didn't want anyone in that house to come out and call him back. He didn't want their apologies or sympathies because it was over as far as he was concerned. Corey and Jordyn were his family now and were the only ones that gave a shit about him.

A few minutes later, he was on the main boulevard and was less than three hundred meters from the entrance ramp to the Autoroute. The shopping mall was to his right and the entrance was coming up shortly. Why was the shopping mall calling him all of a sudden? It was closed and the parking lot was empty, save for the white lamps that kept it lit all night long. Fuck that, he was finished with this neighborhood. It stunk of well-to-do snobs who scoffed at little guys like him who only wanted their fair chance at getting ahead in this world.

The tightness in the back of his throat came back again, causing a large uncomfortable feeling to rise up deep within his gut, climaxing with him screaming out as loud as he could. He jerked the steering wheel to the right, spinning his car sideways across the black ice. He then stomped down on the gas pedal, causing the tires to spin on the road's surface—the smell of burning rubber flooded the inside of the vehicle. Other cars behind him stopped while a few drivers laid on their horns.

"Fuck off," he yelled at them. He knew they couldn't hear him, but he wouldn't be disrespected anymore. His car finally inched forward and skidded across the ice into the mall's parking lot. He raced along, spinning the car around in circles at random. He didn't care if the police came, let them arrest him. Things couldn't get any worse. When he got dizzy from spinning his car, he stomped down on the brake pedal—causing the car to skid a few feet before it stopped. He allowed both arms to fall on top of the steering wheel and his head followed soon after. The sniffling was impossible to prevent, and the patter of tears that fell onto the leather car seat between his legs soon followed. When he looked up a few moments later, the snow was falling. And a quarter of the windshield was already covered. He continued to stare at the windshield, and a few minutes later it was a bright white, only illuminated by the tall lamp that was close by.

Eddie wiped his face with his jacket sleeve and stepped out, leaving the car door open and the engine running. He walked a few paces away from his car, observing the foggy vapor that came from his mouth. It must have been about minus five degrees Celsius, yet the cold didn't bother him. Maybe it was from the tantrum he just threw. The ground around him faded from shiny black to powdery white as the snow sprinkled around. He had heard that five to ten centimeters was expected by the next day. The snowplows would be out later tonight.

There used to be a time when he would rush to the garage and grab the small plastic shovel while his father grabbed the bigger metal one, and they would shovel the driveway together. They would then use the excess snow to build a fort...no, not his father again. Got to shut him out, he wasn't his friend, nor did Eddie love him.

Eddie grabbed the side of his head with both hands and squeezed inwards as though to block out his childhood memories. Got to think of good memories...

Yes, it was earlier in the evening—nightfall came earlier in November, unlike in the spring and summer—the snowflakes had been thicker than they were now, clumping as they fell to the ground. He had been on his way home from school. Despite the numerous warnings that he'd been told, he'd still taken a shortcut through a certain park that evening, to not risk missing his bus. It would've been a half hour wait before the next one came.

Soon enough, two guys had followed him and shortly after, he was running for his life. He didn't have to see their Swastika tattoos, just being called a Nigger was enough reason for him to haul ass. He was halfway through the park when he had slipped on some black ice, taking a nose-dive onto the pavement. He'd known that he should've stuck to the grass, but who else would have had the time to rationalize? Never mind the stinging he'd felt on the side of his face after he scraped it against the wet surface. It was a matter of just getting away as fast as he could once he'd heard the stomping of boots getting louder.

He was up on his knees when he'd been grabbed by the back of his collar and thrown forward onto the concrete. Then, the swift kicks to his chest, thighs, and ribs came. His thick winter jacket had absorbed most of the attacks, which was the only reason why he didn't have any visible bruises later that evening. He'd curled up into a fetal position, folding his arms across his face to protect it, staving off the rest of the blows.

The kicking suddenly stopped and Eddie heard a scuffle. Trembling, he'd peeked out with one open eye from behind his gloves and saw one of the skinheads crashing into the side of the park bench a few feet away, as though he'd been thrown into it. Eddie quickly sat up and was in time to see the other skinhead charging someone that Eddie couldn't see properly. The attacker wasn't tackled so easily, but instead he'd grabbed the skinhead and forced him head-first into his knee. He'd then pulled him up, formed a fist, and smashed it into his face three times before the skinhead went down, crying out.

Eddie watched as both of his attackers had stumbled to get their footing on the slippery surface as they had run away. He'd looked over his shoulder to see them gone within seconds. When he had looked back in the direction that he faced, their attacker walked towards him. The park lamp that shone behind him made it impossible to see his face, which was obscured by the dark. All he'd seen was someone that was tall, slender, and wore a bulky bomber jacket. The stranger then extended a hand out to him. Eddie was hesitant at first, but he'd taken a chance and had reached out for the stranger's hand, grabbed it, and was helped to his feet.

"You okay, bro?" the guy had asked. *Oh my gosh! Was that a Trinidadian accent?* He was half a foot taller than Eddie was, and was also black. Eddie had held back a smile, and wondered how many more black people lived in this neighborhood. He'd straightened himself out slowly, as he felt some pain in his legs and ribs where he was kicked. "I...I'm still hurting a little. But I think I'll be all right."

The guy had smiled and chuckled. "You're *Bajan*." Bajan was slang for Barbadian.

"I was born here. My parents are from Barbados." *My accent must be as strong as everyone says it is.* "You're Trini?"

"Yup, born and raised," the guy smiled. "My mother sent me to live up here with my aunt last summer." He'd then extended his hand. "I'm Corey."

"I'm Eddie," he'd answered as he shook his hand. He then bent down to pick up his nap sack.

Looking back, he couldn't believe that was over twelve years ago. How could everyone talk about his best friend negatively? They only chose to see his failures while ignoring his achievements, especially the fact that he probably saved his life that evening. Now Corey was flat on his back—broken and discouraged—yet Eddie still looked out for him. And aside from Jordyn and Aunt Beverly, Corey was the only other person that gave a damn about him succeeding as a writer.

To his left, he spotted a phone booth beside the mall entrance. He ran back to his car, slammed the door, turned on the windshield wipers to clear off the snow accumulation, and drove over to the phone booth. He then pulled open the ash tray, pulled out a few dimes and nickels, got out—leaving the door open—and ran to the phone. After throwing in thirty-five cents, he dialed Jordyn's cell number. The phone rang twice before there was an answer.

"Jordyn, it's me. Where are you?"

"I'm at your place with Corey. What's up?"

"I've been doing some thinking about what you and Corey told me the other night. I want to talk some more about it. Can I meet you in about half hour?"

Chapter 4

"So that's it, you ain't talking to them no more?" Corey spun the empty beer bottle on their kitchen table.

"I'm done with them," said Eddie.

The mouth of the bottle stopped and pointed opposite Corey. "For real?"

"You heard me."

Corey got up from the table and went to the couch where he turned on the video game console. "I don't think that was such a good idea. I mean, they're your family."

"Yeah, and they treat me like an outcast, except for Aunt Bev. I can't take them anymore. I don't know why you're defending them. They don't think much of you either. They're accusing you of keeping me back." Eddie looked at Corey expecting an answer, but none came. Of course he didn't answer. Corey knew that he was right.

Eddie then turned to the sounds of the creaking floor, as Jordyn came out of his room holding her cell phone. She wore nothing but a football jersey and panties. It was a pretty sight that Eddie didn't mind. But she had done it often, considering that they had already seen each other in their underwear.

"So, what you get?" asked Eddie.

Jordyn sat at the table next to Eddie, in the same chair that Corey had vacated. "You're in luck. My colleague broke his leg yesterday. I've talked him into letting you replace him."

"Just like that?" Eddie asked.

"As I said, you're in luck. He mostly deals with high-profile clients."

"How high profile?"

"High enough that he'll be able to buy a house in a few months."

"Damn."

"That's some serious cheddar he bringing home, ain't it?" Corey added as his video game character landed a triple combo attack to his opponent.

"Do you know who the client is?" asked Eddie.

"I wasn't told much except that she's the CEO of an American cellular phone company," Jordyn answered.

Corey nodded in their direction without taking his eyes off the television. "Ain't that the same woman you were telling us about the other night?"

"I'd imagine so." Jordyn put her mobile phone on the table and turned to Eddie. "I can't tell you more right now. But I was just told that the she's into bondage. So guess what, you get to tie her up and whip her."

Eddie leaned closer to Jordyn. "You mean, all I have to do is spank her and I'll get paid for that?"

Jordyn raised a hand to face level as though to signal to Eddie to wait. "There's more. You'll have to wear a leather outfit and let her give you a blow job. And you have to be forceful."

Eddie leaned back in his chair as he took a quick breath. *No, don't act like a pussy now, you wanted this.*

"Anything wrong?" asked Jordyn.

"I'm good." No he wasn't. "How are we going to plan the whole thing?"

"You'll meet her in her hotel suite this coming Saturday. During that time, an anonymous phone call would've been made to the press."

Corey then turned to them. "You both get caught in the act, and your faces are splashed across the tabloids, TV, the internet, and that's that." That's all the time it took for his on-screen character to suffer a knockout blow. "Damn, he got me."

They all turned to the ringing sound that came from beside the couch. Corey paused the game, reached over, and grabbed the wireless phone. "Yeah?" He then looked over in Eddie's direction.

Eddie mouthed the word, *who?*

"Oh hello, Beverly, how are you? I don't know if Eddie's home. Let me check his room."

Eddie shook his head.

"No, he's not here. Would you like to leave him a message?"

Jordyn got up from the table and went to the fridge. She took out some sliced ham, bread, and mayonnaise and shut the door.

"Sure, I'll let him know. Take care." Corey pressed the off button and looked up at Eddie. "Your aunt wants you to know that she stands behind you, in everything that you do, and not to let your parents upset you."

Eddie went to the fridge, opened it, and grabbed a soda can. "Yeah, that's good to know."

"She also said that she wanted to send you some money. She said that she would call back later to get your bank info so that she could deposit the money without your parents knowing," said Corey. "You see, not everyone in your family's against you."

"You should call her back and accept the money," said Jordyn as she clinked the sides of the mayonnaise jar to scrape the last bit onto the knife. "At least it'll help you both with the groceries. You're fridge is practically empty."

Eddie cracked open the can and took a swig. He then rested it on the edge of the table. Why was she the only one that came through for him? Beverly never changed, even when he was a child. Whenever his parents couldn't take him to the park or to the movies, she was the one that always stepped up—whenever she was visiting.

He then turned to Jordyn. "I'll think about it."

Jordyn rolled her eyes and threw the empty mayonnaise jar into the recycling bin in the corner. "Hey, it's your life."

Eddie sank into the back of the couch. "So what do we do next?"

Jordyn put the last few slices of bread and ham back in the fridge and returned to the table. "We'll have to coach you. Are you up for a little spanking lesson?"

"Sure." *How bad could it be?* "By the way, who's this acquaintance you keep talking about?"

Jordyn paused as she looked to him, then to Corey. That's when she sighed. "It's Theo."

Eddie's jaw hung open as he stared at Jordyn, who closed her eyes and let her head drop to the table. He then looked at Corey, who was also staring at her. Now he knew for sure that he did not hear wrong.

"You want to run that by me again?" asked Corey.

Shit, even he didn't know.

Jordyn looked back up, elbows on the table, as she rubbed her temples. "I know how it sounds, and I'm sorry."

Corey looked away and sighed. "I don't fucking believe this."

Neither can I.

Corey looked back at her. "How could you keep something like that from me?"

"I said I'm sorry," Jordyn pleaded.

"I'm sorry to hear this too," said Corey. "I thought you left Theo because he was selling dope?"

"That's not why I left him. And he isn't selling dope. He just smokes his weed," said Jordyn.

"Then why *did* you leave him?" asked Corey.

"Because he's an asshole. *Duh!*"

"How long did it take you to figure that out?" asked Corey.

"As long as it took me to meet you. There, are you happy?"

Corey was quiet for a few seconds as though he were fishing for something to say. He then pointed a finger at Jordyn. "He's not making you do things with him, is he?"

"No, he's not."

"He better not. 'Cause if he is, then I'm going to kick down the door to his house and go *Uma Thurman* on his bitch-ass."

Kill Bill. It was one of Corey's favorite movies.

"For the last time I'm not sleeping with him. As I told you before, I want to own my own coffee shop. I'm only doing this because I need the extra cash."

"Then get another job," said Corey.

Eddie placed his hand on Corey's shoulder. "I wouldn't be telling someone else to get a job if I were you."

"I'm not going to be doing this forever," said Jordyn.

Eddie covered his eyes with the base of his palms, as though trying to absorb all these things about Jordyn that he never would have suspected. He then put them down as he looked at her. "This is Theo we're talking about. Your ex-boyfriend and Corey's arch-nemesis."

Jordyn stood up from the table. "Do you guys think that this is easy for me? It's not. I can't stand Theo any more than having to work with him. I'm very close to saving up the money that I need. And I swear that once I have it, it's over."

"Yeah right," said Corey.

"What's that supposed to mean?"

"Nothing. I'll take your word for it."

Jordyn sighed loudly and stormed off to the bathroom, slamming the door behind her.

Great. Now these two were fighting, thought Eddie. There wasn't any way that this plan would work with his only two friends splitting up. Or, more to the point, Eddie wouldn't go through with it if it ended that way.

He got up from the kitchen table, walked to the bathroom and knocked on the door twice. "Jordyn?"

"What?" She was still less than pleasant.

"You okay?" Eddie asked.

"What the hell do you think?"

"I was just wondering. Did you tell Theo why I'm doing this?" There was silence. Eddie then heard the tap running at full blast on the other side of the door. "Are you sure that you're okay in there?"

"Christ! I said I was fine. And no, I didn't tell Theo why you're doing it."

"She didn't have to," Corey chimed in from the couch. "He ought to know by now that you're broke. Guess what, Ed. He now owns you too."

Eddie turned to Corey. "Theo's living a secret life too. I doubt that he'd blackmail me knowing that we could *out* him."

Corey shrugged his shoulders. He was halfway involved in his video game.

"I'm curious, Jordyn," asked Eddie.

"What?" she barked.

"When I get caught with Theo's client and our faces wind up in the papers, how would that affect Theo's business if the word got out?" There was silence on the other side of the door. The bathroom door suddenly swung inwards as Jordyn exited and stood face-to-face with Eddie, to the point that their noses nearly touched. Her face then lit up with a grin.

"It could potentially damage his reputation as being someone who's discreet with his clients. Especially if a certain ex-girlfriend of his were to tip off the media of his involvement."

Eddie turned to Corey, who had put his game on pause as he stared back. He appeared to be more anxious at getting this plan started. Eddie then turned back to Jordyn. "How soon can my maledom lessons start?"

Chapter 5

Downtown Montreal. Thirty hours earlier.

T he leather thong, pants, and vest that Eddie wore now, were less comfortable than when he'd first tried them on. The day before he had gone with Jordyn over to Theo's place. Of course the asshole couldn't resist belittling them, showing off both of his forty-inch high-definition flat screen televisions equipped with stereo surround sound. Then there was his black BMW that sat in the driveway. To add insult to injury he made Eddie refer to him by his professional name—Master Tiger.

Eddie couldn't believe that it took him an entire two-week's work to match what that creep earned in under two hours. The small house that Theo rented in Dorval—a twenty minute to half hour's drive from downtown Montreal—wasn't much, but it still made Eddie and Corey's apartment look like a refugee dwelling. Theo's home had two bedrooms on the main floor and a basement. Although he'd said that he rarely held sessions at his place, he obviously had company come over from time to time. Leave it to Jordyn to notice the lipstick on a wine glass that was left on the corner of the kitchen counter. Based on the scent and its color, she knew that whoever had visited Theo earlier that day had expensive tastes.

These thoughts were interrupted as Eddie unzipped his jacket and scratched his chest. God, this outfit was a pain in the ass to wear—literally. The thong was giving him a wedgie.

Corey, who was at the wheel of Eddie's car, glanced over at him. "You all right?"

"Does it look like I'm all right? You ever wear something like this before?"

Corey laughed. "Come on, it can't be that bad."

"Dammit, you always say that."

"No, I don't."

"Boy, you making sport." *You really must be kidding me.* He then pulled on the seat of his pants and rolled down the window, allowing a chill to blast through the car.

"Are you crazy? Roll up the window," yelled Corey.

"It's hot in here."

"No it ain't."

"Where I'm sitting it is. I'm sweating. I think I'm about to pass out."

"You're not going to pass out, so calm your ass down. And roll the window back up."

Eddie rolled up the window slightly. "Why couldn't I have waited to get to the hotel first before putting these clothes on?"

Corey remained silent, as though in deep thought. "You're right, you could've done that."

"How does Jordyn do this? How can she stand wearing this shit?" asked Eddie, still fidgeting in his seat.

"She wears PVC. She won't touch leather, remember?"

"Leather, PVC, whatever. Why didn't she come along?"

"She's tired. She thinks she might be coming down with something."

"You think? Anyone would get sick from sitting in your bedroom for more than a minute."

"What's that supposed to mean?"

"You're room stinks, that's what I mean. I poked my head in there a few days ago and couldn't even open the door. All your nasty socks and draws were on the floor."

"My socks don't smell that bad."

"You'd kill a skunk in your room. You ever wonder why Jordyn insists on you going to her place?"

"Yeah, because her place is bigger, and it's easier for her to get to work than from our place."

"Corey, please. If she wanted to knock boots with you bad enough, she'd come to our place."

"Yeah, I'm sure you'd love listening to us make love from your room."

"Shut up. And what's with Jordyn's appetite? I find that she's been eating a lot more lately."

"She signed up at a gym a few weeks ago, so she's always hungry after a workout. Why you ask?"

"It's just something I noticed."

"You're always *noticing* stuff."

"What's the matter? I'm not allowed to notice stuff anymore?" Eddie rolled down the window the rest of the way, undid the seatbelt, and stuck his head out to catch the breeze. *Hell yeah! That felt so much better.*

"What the fuck?" Corey grabbed Eddie by the lower part of his leather jacket and pulled him back in. "Are you trying to get us arrested?"

"I'm cooking in this thing. Look how much I'm sweating. I'm going to have to shower again."

"We're almost there...just keep your draws on."

"Draws? I wish I was wearing some. At least my ass could breathe a bit." Eddie tugged at the seat of his pants again. "Who's the idiot that invented this outfit? I'll bet he never tried it on."

"Fuck, man! Am I going to have to listen to you complaining all night?"

Corey was right. He must have been a pain in the ass to ride with. After all, Corey could've been home making out with his girl, but he chose to drive him to the hotel, and even wait for him. Ever since Corey rescued him from the skinheads that snowy evening twelve years ago, he'd always been there to help him get through his most challenging times. It was probably his way of showing Eddie his gratitude for being there for him through his current dramas.

A few minutes later they pulled up in front of l'Hôtel Mont-Royal. Eddie looked out and saw the Canadian, Quebec, and American flags hanging above the veranda. Gold-colored lights also sparkled on the infant pine trees that were on either side of the entrance that was fit for royalty. It then occurred to him that neither he nor Corey thought of picking up a Christmas tree for their apartment. Then again, what would be the point—they never spent Christmas together. Corey would be with his aunt and her friends...come to think of it, since he wasn't talking to his parents anymore, he'd most likely be spending Christmas with Corey.

Corey nudged Eddie with his elbow. "Are you getting out? Are you okay?"

Eddie looked up and down the hotel's façade and sat back in his seat. Everyone that came in and out of the revolving door wore expensive fur or wool coats, topped off with fancy hats. Whether it was fur, fake fur, or wool coats. He was sure that most of them had million dollar checking accounts, sailed around in their yachts in the summer, and probably would've even dined with Presidents, Sultans, or even the Queen at some point in their lives. What the hell was he doing here? He sank a bit low in his seat, as though to hide.

"Hey. You okay, buddy?"

"I'm cool," lied Eddie.

"You don't look so. Don't tell me you're having second thoughts. You can't back out right now, not after what Jordyn went through to get this for you."

"I...I just don't think that I can walk through the lobby."

"Why not?"

"Don't you see who's in there? It's full of rich people. They're all going to know that I don't belong there."

"No they won't. We're in the middle of a financial crisis, I'm sure they're all too busy thinking about how much money they're losing from their Swiss Bank Accounts, *Bluetooth* funds, stocks, and whatever. They won't even have time to notice you. Besides, you're wearing a three quarter length jacket. Your leather outfit is hidden, so no one's going to question you."

"It's a three-quarter length *leather* jacket, first of all. Secondly, it's Blue *Chip* funds."

"Whatever. Anyways, both regular and rich people wear leather jackets too, don't they?"

"I don't look like a rich person in this car," said Eddie. "Drive around the block."

"Fine." Corey sighed as he checked his blind spot before he pulled out. "It's all in your head. Just pretend that you're Simeon Wolf. He wouldn't be scared would he?"

Eddie looked back towards the revolving door. "Simeon Wolf's a fictional character I created."

"So what? Here's your chance to act out his part. Didn't you always say that there has to be some aspect of reality when you write fiction? Well here's your chance to prove it by pretending you're him. I'm sure he's been in situations like this several times. He couldn't finish the mission by acting like a pussy, right?"

Eddie looked back at Corey. He never thought of it that way. *Pretend that I'm Simeon Wolf. And he's undercover to get information from someone that's connected to a terrorist organization.* "You're right. I got to be Simeon Wolf, not Eddie Barrow." He then formed a fist and hit his chest twice in rapid succession to psych himself up.

Corey handed him a mobile phone. "You're going to need this."

"Where'd you get the money for a phone?"

"Don't worry about it. It should have enough minutes on it."

Of course, he stole it. He took the prepaid mobile. "I'll call you when I'm ready." He got out, grabbed the small expandable spinner suitcase from the back seat—courtesy of Theo—and shut the door.

Corey leaned closer to the passenger door window that Eddie had left open. "I'll be close by. Remember to text Jordyn once you're in the room."

A text message should've already been saved in the phone and was ready to be sent to Jordyn's with the push of a button, alerting her to call the media. "I will." Maybe when this was all done he could afford to buy a new mobile phone to replace the one that Corey accidentally dropped in the toilet a few weeks ago. Only *he* would think of texting at the same time as taking a leak. Eddie heard Corey drive off as he walked up to the revolving door, dragging the luggage behind him. He nodded to the doorman, who nodded back with a tip of his hat. He almost stumbled as he went to push the revolving door, only to realize that it revolved automatically.

He walked in and was soon on a red carpet that extended from the entrance to the clerk behind the check-in counter that was fifty meters away. On either side of the aisle were sofas that formed U-Shapes around low glass tables with either newspapers or magazines on top. A few people occupied the sofas and were too busy to notice him. So much the better. There were also protruding rectangular columns that were separated by what appeared to be various paintings—oil or something else Eddie wasn't familiar with. It was all too classy for him.

Eddie remembered that he was to use his pseudonym. *So I'm Simeon Wolf now.* He looked both left and right as he walked up to the front desk. There were about a dozen people in the lobby as expected, even at this hour. Behind the counter were eight clocks. It was 9:55 PM here in Montreal, whereas in Chicago it was 8:55 PM. Los Angeles, 6:55 PM and down to the last in Tokyo, where it was 10:55 AM the next day. A young woman around his age, dressed in a blazer with the hotel's coat of arms on her breast pocket, looked up from her computer and smiled at him. "Bienvenue à l'Hôtel Mont-Royal. Vous avez un reservation?" *Welcome to the Mont-Royal Hotel. Do you have a reservation?*

"J'ai venu collecter une envelope laissé par la cliente de la chambre 514." *I came to pick up an envelope that was left here from the occupant of room 514.*

"Un instant, s'il vous plait." She left the counter and disappeared through a door. She returned a few moments later and handed him an off-white-colored envelope. "Voila."

"Merci," *Wolf* replied with a wink and walked towards the elevators, pulling the suitcase behind him. There, that wasn't so hard. Shit, he could've gotten her number if he wanted to. That's what Wolf would've done.

There were five elevators on either side. Their doors were brass-colored and he could see a perfect reflection of himself in them. He pressed the button to call one and stared at his reflection. They were so spotless, unlike the mirrors in his apartment. There was a *ding* sound behind him and he turned to see one of the elevator doors open. He stepped inside, hit the fifth-floor button, and the doors closed.

He didn't even know why he kicked up such a fuss about people gawking at his clothing in the first place. All that mattered was doing what it took to satisfy his client and getting this publicity stunt moving. By all accounts this woman would be a perfect target. Besides, it should be a breeze. He, Corey, and Jordyn had found her picture from her company's website last night—he could handle her. He didn't know how tall she was, but she appeared to be in her forties, had short dark hair, and was slender. Corey figured that she worked out regularly and therefore must have stamina. That was all right with him. She could suck his dick anytime. In fact he wouldn't mind fucking her either, if it ever came to that. But it was only going to be a one-night stand, something he never did before. *Oh come on, Ed, you're Simeon Wolf. He gets pussy all the time and doesn't give it a second thought. It was all about the mission.*

The doors opened and he stepped into the hallway with his luggage. A gold-plated sign showed an arrow indicating that room 514 was to his left. Not a creak was heard beneath him as his feet sunk into the soft, carpeted floor.

The room was one shy of being the last on, and it had a set of double doors. Wolf opened the envelope he was given and found a plastic key card and a small note. The note read, COME IN AND RING THE BELL THAT'S ON THE TABLE, TO LET ME KNOW YOU'RE HERE. YOU CAN WAIT FOR ME IN THE SECOND BEDROOM UNTIL I FINISH TAKING MY BUBBLE BATH. YOU'LL KNOW THAT I'M READY FOR YOU ONCE YOU HEAR THE BELL RING.

Dayum! She's pampering herself up for me too. That brought a smile to his face.

Wolf swiped the card key through the lock and let himself in. He dragged the spinner luggage with him and closed the door. He swallowed as he became fixated on the cleanliness of his surroundings. The bed was bigger than the one his parents slept on. It also had thicker coverings, along with five pillows. He turned to the sound of splashing and saw the bathroom light through the cracks of the bathroom door. She was in there right now, so where was the bell? He looked back towards the bed and saw it sitting on a plate on top of the night table, along with two bottles. He walked up to the table, leaving the suitcase along the way, and picked up both bottles. They were massaging oils.

He put down the bottles and rang the bell a few times.

She didn't respond.

He put it back onto the plate, grabbed the spinner suitcase, and made his way to the double doors on the opposite side. He let himself into the other room, closing the doors behind him. He let out a sigh of relief and slid himself out of the jacket, burning his flesh as it clung to his sweat-soaked skin. He walked over to the window, opened it, and stood there for a moment to let the cool air blow on him like a boat's sails in the breeze. *Lord, that felt so much better. I wonder if I'll have time to take a shower.* Highly unlikely since the lady's probably drying herself off right now and would be ringing the bell at any moment.

He stripped down to his leather G-String and threw the pants on the bed. He took out the cell phone from the jacket pocket and sent the text message that was saved in the *drafts* folder in the phone, and then tossed it on the bed. Jordyn would call the press in twenty minutes. Jordyn had timed his routine. In about thirty minutes, he should have his client bound up in a compromising position right when the press should arrive at the door. He went into the bathroom, yanked one of the towels off the rack, dried himself off, and tossed it by the sink. *I can't believe anyone would find this thong comfortable.*

He went back into the suite, grabbed his suitcase and lifted it onto the bed. He opened it, took out a black leather flogger whip, and a collar-to-wrist leather back restraint.

He then rehearsed in his head how the events over the next half hour would play out. It was all about the performance—an act—that's all. First, Eddie would open the doors wide with outstretched arms and stand there—giving the appearance of being dominant. He'd then slap the tip of the whip in his palm a few times.

He heard the bell ring in the neighboring suite. It sent a tightness up his spine as he scrambled to put the leather pants back on. He found himself out of breath by the time he hung the restraints around his neck and stood in front of the double doors with the whip sticking out of the back of his pants.

The bell rang again, a second time, as Eddie froze with both hands on both door handles. *Damn, she's impatient. Just remember you're Simeon Wolf, not Eddie. This is a woman of power that wants to be dominated by a young black man. I stood up to my father the other night. This should be a breeze.*

He then pulled the doors opened with his eyes closed and breathed in. He exhaled slowly and stretched his arms out as he stood in the center of the threshold. There was soft saxophone music playing in the background, and it set the mood, especially for him. He turned his head towards the direction of the bed and opened his eyes slowly...then into a quick dilation as he gasped. A nearly-naked man lay on the bed.

Chapter 6

"Oh yes, I'm going to love being punished by you a lot more than the other guy," said the man. He wore nothing more than a tight leather bikini with a leather mask covering his entire head except for the lower part of his face. The bikini would've been more visible had it not been for his protruding hairy gut that hung over it. Eddie looked up at his face, hoping it would prevent him from throwing up. Instead he got a huge grin in return. *What the hell's going on here? Where's the woman CEO? What the hell did Jordyn get me into?*

"Please, don't leave me in suspense. Come on over and punish me."

Control yourself, Eddie. Don't do anything stupid. Just be Simeon Wolf. He wouldn't flinch in a situation like this. Remember, it was all about the mission. Sure, he wouldn't have been so distracted from it, if only he knew who the hell this guy was. He's obviously someone with a lot of money who chooses to be anonymous. *I'll be fine as long as he keeps his hands off me. I'll make sure that the restraints are real tight on him.*

Eddie walked normally, then slowly—remembering the way that he had practiced with Jordyn and Theo—while lowering the fly of his pants. Eddie's eyes slipped to the man's bikini and saw that the flagpole was stretching the leather. *Jesus Christ that was nasty.* He immediately looked back up into the man's eyes. *Just keep looking into his eyes and nowhere else, and you'll make it through.*

He pulled out the leather flogger from where he had tucked it, and slapped the palm of his other hand gently as he stopped short, a foot away from the bed. The man got onto his knees and faced him. If he tried to get any closer Eddie'd use the flogger to keep him at bay. But this was already off to a bad start. He'd already forgotten what to do next.

Just keep your cool. I'm the one in control. Just come up with something. "So... how uh...how naughty are you today...I mean... how have you been?" *Jesus Christ that was bad. He just blew it.* His ex would've fallen off the couch laughing had she been watching him.

"Pretty bad. Very, very bad," the man answered quickly, as though he were in a rush to be punished.

Eddie walked slowly up to the bed, being mindful of the buffer zone he wanted to keep between himself and the client.

The man fell on his hands and began to crawl towards Eddie like a dog running for a treat.

"No!" Eddie yelled, more out of panic than as an instruction, throwing both his arms up towards the client. The client—visibly startled—backed away immediately.

Eddie breathed a sigh of relief, but was quickly mindful of not making it sound too obvious. From where he was, he stretched out his arm as much as he could, pushing the flogger out to let the tip of it brush the man's forehead back and forth. The man lifted his head as though to sniff the strands like a dog.

Come on, think of something. "Tell me. What naughtiness have you been up to?"

"I'm cheating on my wife," the man quickly replied.

Shit, you even tricked a woman into marrying you? "Is that right? That gets you one lash." Eddie took a short step forward and gave him a light slap on his arm. "That's not what I want to hear. I want to hear real naughtiness. It's time for these." Eddie took the restraints and dangled them in the air.

"Oh yeah, baby, tie me up."

Baby? That ain't right. "You'll call me *master*, I'm not your baby. Now turn around."

"I'm sorry, master. It won't happen again," the man turned around. Eddie paused at the sight of his ass—or, more or less, a lack of one—that the leather bikini could not properly cover. Eddie wished that this would end quickly. *How the hell could Jordyn do stuff like this? Shit, there was no way that Corey had any idea what Jordyn really did. Ugghh!*

He'd have to do this quickly. He stepped closer to the client, keeping his eyes on the back of his neck. He then grabbed the collar end of the restraint and clipped it around the man's neck. A strap extended and had a pair of hand cuffs on the other end. He grabbed the man's hands roughly, locked them in the cuffs, and stepped back. Now he was officially his prisoner. Eddie pursed his lips as he whipped the man on his ass once. Eddie knew that he'd be in the shower for a full two hours later on, using all the soap in the house that he could find.

"Oh yeah," said the man.

That was weak. Should I slap him harder? Wait a minute, I'm Simeon Wolf, torturing a prisoner for information. "Tell me who you are." One whip, slightly harder.

"I'm Tony Bevins. Governor Tony Bevins."

Eddie paused as his mouth fell agape. *Holy shit. A Governor?* "From which state?"

"New Hampshire."

"Tell me, Governor. Have you been misusing tax dollars?"

"Yes, master. This hotel suite, all courtesy of the citizens of New Hampshire."

Another slap across his cheeks. "That's naughty, very, very naughty." This was obscene. *I'm going to enjoy exposing you, you son-of-a-bitch.* "Are you gay and keeping the truth from your wife?"

"I sure am. She doesn't suspect a thing. She's my personal lawn ornament."

Eddie squeezed the handle and slapped him even harder. The Governor screamed out loud. This one must have hurt him, and his ass was already red from the lashes.

Did Vanessa see him the same way? Is this what she told her fuck-buddy right before he rode her ass—that Eddie was nothing more than her own lawn ornament?

He leaped onto the bed and shoved the Governor face down

into the pillows. He then flogged him three times, gritting his teeth. "You cheat on the woman that supports you. You squander tax dollars. What other dirty secrets are you keeping from me?"

Bevins's voice was muffled. Simeon Wolf grabbed the back of the collar and heaved him up onto his knees while he wrapped the whip around his neck and squeezed. "I asked you a question. What other secrets are you keeping from me?" Everything was garbled. *What the hell, he's wheezing. Shit, I'm choking him—he can't breathe.* He wasn't angry with Bevins, he was angry with himself and taking it out on Bevins. Eddie loosened the whip from around his neck and yanked it off with a snap. He backed off the bed, falling onto the floor—pushing himself backwards with his hands as though he were trying to get away from a reviled object. He hit the wall until he became aware the Governor was hunched over and coughing, while Eddie breathed loudly with a tremor. *What the hell did I just do? I was hurting this man. I nearly choked him to death.*

"Master, where are you? Please come back. I'll do anything you want me to...anything."

"Shut up."

"Yes master, anything you say."

"No, I mean it. Shut up!" Eddie then threw the whip to the floor, got up, and stomped away with his hands on his hips. He then sighed and turned to the Governor with one hand to his forehead. "I can't do this."

Bevins tried to look over his shoulder, but couldn't turn all the way. "What? What do you mean?"

"You heard me. I can't do this. This ain't me." Eddie walked over to Bevins and undid the handcuffs and the collar restraint. "I'm sorry."

"Sorry about what? What the hell are you talking about?" He was clearly getting annoyed.

Remembering that his cell phone was in the other room, he walked over to the guest phone, picked it up, and dialed Jordyn's number. He waited a few seconds before he heard the voicemail lady speak. *Dammit!* He slammed down the phone, hoping that Jordyn had problems getting through to the press. Why would her phone go to voice mail? She couldn't have turned it off.

"Hey kid," said Bevins as he yanked off his mask, revealing tussled black hair over a round face with bulldog-type hanging cheeks. "You better come straight with me."

"Okay, you want the truth, fine. I'm not a male dominatrix, or master, or whatever I'm supposed to be. I was supposed to get caught with you so I could become famous. You're being set-up. It's just a damn publicity stunt. There, are you satisfied?"

There was silence as Eddie stared at the Governor. He felt relieved getting it out of his system. He just didn't know if that was such a good idea. Bevins stared at him with his mouth closed, it seemed, to hide clenched teeth as his face became red. The man was definitely pissed, and Eddie felt himself drifting backwards.

"You son-of-a-bitch." Bevins lunged at Eddie.

Eddie turned to run, but he felt a hand grab his leg, sending him tumbling to the carpet. He was grabbed and then forced over onto his back as, at least two-hundred-and seventy pounds, pinned his legs—preventing him from kicking. Eddie let out a wail but not much got out as a big palm silenced him.

"You keep quiet, you little bitch," said Bevins in a loud whisper. "So you think you can blackmail me, huh? That's what you're trying to do? You think you can take me on? What's the matter? Did your daddy kick you out of the house because you're a queer, is that it?"

Eddie didn't answer but he felt the wetness damping his eyes as his cries became more muffled.

"You think it's easy for me? Do you think the people would accept me as Governor if they knew that I was into kinky stuff? That I'm a queer? You don't have a clue what goes on, do you, kid?"

Through the tears that slightly clouded his vision, Eddie saw the Governor's facial expression change. He wasn't angry anymore. Now he appeared to be sad. The tear that fell from his right eye onto Eddie's neck came at the precise moment that the Governor took his hand off his mouth, allowing him to gasp for air. Bevins then got up off him.

Eddie sat up, not bothering to wipe the tears off his face, as he watched the Governor waddle over to the bed and sit down, letting his head drop in his palms.

He couldn't believe this. This is probably the most powerful man he's ever met, and he comes out of the closet to him. And his wife doesn't even know. How could she live with him all this time and not suspect anything?

He then wiped the tears off his face with the back of his hand as he watched Bevins get up and walk over to the dresser. When he opened the doors Eddie saw that it was actually a liquor cabinet. Bevins grabbed a bottle with clear liquid that Eddie assumed was vodka, or white rum, and closed the doors. From inside he also grabbed the ice bucket—which was already filled—and then walked over to a round table where there were two liquor glasses and a floral vase in the center. He scooped some ice from the bucket into the two glasses and then rested the bucket on the carpet beside his chair. "Hey, kid. Come on over and have a drink with me."

This man wants to get me drunk.

"Look, I ain't going to rape you if that's what you're thinking. So come on over."

Okay, maybe he was telling the truth. He watched Bevins leave the glass and bottle on the table, disappear into the bathroom, and come back wearing a white bath-robe.

Shit, it's about time that he covered up. He looked decent for a change.

Once Bevins was seated, Eddie got up and joined him at the table. Looking at the table, he wondered if guests played cards or dominos. Probably neither. Had he been staying here, he'd be slamming the dominos all night on this table with his friends. Bevins gestured with a hand for Eddie to sit.

"So what's your name, kid?"

Eddie found it odd. He'd lost his three minutes of power. "Eddie."

Bevins poured him a glass and then sat down. "Eddie, huh? How old are you?"

"Twenty-four."

"Don't bullshit me, son. You look barely over eighteen."

"I ain't lying to you. I ain't got reason to do so. You want me to show you some ID?"

"Nah, don't worry about it," said Bevins, shaking his head with a single wave of his hand. He took a gulp, and put the glass back down on the table with a clank while exhaling loudly with an *ahhh*. "I'll take your word for it. Say, you got one of them island accents. Where are you from?"

"I was born here. My parents are from Barbados."

"Barbados, huh? I've been there a few times. I should've known you had Barbadian heritage once I saw that round, bubble ass of yours. I wonder why the hell your parents would leave such a beautiful island to come live up here in the cold. Besides, down there, there isn't any snow to shovel, no heating bill to worry about. The economy's just as good down there as it is here."

"I've always wondered the same thing." Eddie took a sip of his drink, swallowed, and felt the burn in his chest. The fumes rushed up into his throat so fast that he nearly dropped the glass on the table, as his other hand slapped over his mouth, covering his wild coughing. He stood up too fast, clumsily knocking the table and tipping over the flower vase, the bottle, and the drinking glasses. Alcohol spilled all over the table—soaking the flowers—and poured off onto the carpet.

"Damn, son, this is some strong shit you're drinking," said Bevins as he caught the liquor bottle before it rolled off the table. "I'll go get a towel." He got up and went to the bathroom. He came out with a towel and stopped in front of the fridge. "We can chase that with a soft drink if you want."

Eddie nodded as he caught his breath. Bevins opened the door, grabbed a can, closed the door, and then walked back to the table.

"So why are you trying to get famous?" Bevins said as he removed the vase from the table and wiped it. He then poured himself another full glass and a partial glass for Eddie.

Eddie opened the can and drowned out the liquor in his glass with it. "I don't know why I let my friends talk me into it. I'm a wannabe novelist who has self-published two books no one wants. We figured that if I was caught doing something newsworthy, then I'd be able to convince agents or publishers that I could sell my book on name recognition." He then looked down at his outfit. "I normally wouldn't be caught dead wearing these clothes. And I'm not even gay."

That's when Bevins burst out laughing.

It ain't that funny.

Bevins downed his glass, exhaled loudly with an *aahhhh*, slamming the glass on the table. Eddie was surprised that it didn't break. He wondered how he inhaled the drink so quickly, while he was only able to sip his.

"You got balls, son. I'll give you that much." Bevins then pointed to Eddie's chest. "What's that you got around your neck? It looks like a flash drive."

Eddie looked down and noticed that the tip was partially visible above the front of his collar. He took it out and held it. "Yeah, I like to keep my work close to me at all times."

Bevins snickered. "That's an idea I had once. You and I think alike in some ways. It ain't too late for you." He then looked away, down to the floor, shaking his head. "Don't go screwing up your life the way I have."

The phone call...it suddenly came back to him. Eddie suddenly slapped the heel of his palm to his forehead. "Oh my gosh. I got to get out of here."

"Why...what's wrong?" Eddie looked at him. Bevins' speech was beginning to slur. Come to think of it, he's drunk. "Listen. The press are on their way to bust us. I need to get out of here."

Bevins laughed again.

What's wrong with you? "Are you listening to me?"

"Yeah, so what, let them come, I don't care. Get your fifteen minutes of fame. So you might as well sit back down."

Eddie got up and walked off. "You're on your own, I'm out of here."

"Wait, don't go yet," Bevins slurred almost pleadingly, but Eddie picked up the leather restraint and whip.

"Hey kid!" Bevins yelled.

Eddie turned to him. He felt his chest lock up on him as he stared at the Governor, who was waving a drunken finger to Eddie's vacated chair. He pondered as to whether Bevins would become violent and attack him again. Then again, the man was drunk, he'd probably stumble and fall the moment he stood.

"There's something I need to tell you. Please, I'm begging you."

He's begging me? "Why? What's wrong?"

"I got to come clean. Trust me, kid, I want to change. I mean, I did my part to help us out. But I can't do this anymore."

Help *us* out? "I told you I ain't gay," Eddie fumed. Why didn't this guy get it? "What's this you're talking about? You can't do *what* anymore?"

"I can't live this double life anymore. My marriage is a sham and my wife doesn't even know about me. I've lied to the American people by screwing around with other homos like us at the expense of their tax dollars."

How many times I got to tell him that I ain't...oh whatever, he ain't even listening.

"I'm even involved in a scam to bilk millions out of investors up here in Canada and other countries."

Oh gosh he's rambling...wait a minute. "What did you just say?"

Tears started to roll down Bevin's face. "I'm a fraud. One my golfing buddies, Serge Lamont, you heard of him?" The Governor looked up at Eddie briefly before waving him off. "Naw, of course you haven't. He's got a fantastic golf swing, but he's a world-class prick. He's the CEO of an investment firm. It used to be worth billions. He's got clients up here, down south, even a few hot shots in Europe. I've got a stake in it too. The only problem is that client investment portfolios have lost more money than the company's been reporting."

Eddie started walking back towards him. Was he hearing right, or was he making this up? "What are you saying?"

"We've been robbing people, damn it!" he yelled, causing Eddie to hold his spot. "Investors have lost thousands, some of them millions, of dollars and they don't even know it. It's all because Serge, myself, and a few others thought we could funnel some cash into our own pockets over the years without anyone ever finding out. It goes high up."

"Why are you telling me this?"

"I need a clear conscience, kid. It'll only be days before clients start asking questions and then federal regulators get involved.

We're in too deep to turn back now. I was going to come clean anyways. You might as well be the first to know. You can find it in Darwin's grave. In fact you can find it *all* there. You won't believe the shit that I've gone through lately that Serge isn't even aware of." Bevins dropped an elbow on the table and held his forehead. He then wiped his face. "So you can add that to your fifteen minutes of fame. I don't care. You can do whatever you want with it. I ain't going to be around much longer anyways."

Eddie faded back a few steps. His hands went up to both sides of his head as though to block out the rush of thoughts that poured in. This was the mother-load, even bigger than what he came here for. Holy shit, the media would eat this up. This could be the story of the decade, and he was smack dab right in the middle of it.

Then it hit him. *Did I hear right? Was that a suicide reference?* Naw, Eddie couldn't do this. Not this way. He dropped his hands to his side and turned to head back to the adjoining suite when he heard a loud banging at the door. Whoever it was appeared to be impatient and had banged over six times in rapid succession. Eddie turned back to Bevins. "I got to hide." Eddie said this in a whisper. But Bevins was now slouched over the table. Eddie bolted to the second suite, shut the double doors behind him quietly, and locked them. Wait a minute, what was he doing? This was his chance at exposing himself with the Governor in front of the media crew that was gathered out in the hall. Why the hell did he run away for?

From where he was, Eddie heard another set of loud knocks.

"I'm coming, keep your pants on," came the Governor's voice.

Eddie quickly packed his suitcase and zipped it shut. He then threw on his jacket, not even bothering to zip it up, wondering what to do next. Bevins was a mess, he couldn't just go outside and expose himself to the journalists that were waiting—ready to pounce on him. Eddie knew he couldn't bring down the Governor like this. Okay, the man's a criminal, but doing it this way? He wasn't sure anymore. But he was sitting on the biggest fraud confession, maybe in the country's history. He should be calling the RCMP or the FBI. Shit, this was huge.

He ran to the light switch and turned them off. The room was completely dark, with scarce light coming from the crack between the double doors. He then zipped the suitcase shut, pulled it off the bed and put it on the floor. He then heard voices and stayed still. He turned to the double doors. There was talking in the next room, as though there was a conversation. *Why would the journalists be so quiet? Something wasn't right.*

He walked quietly to the double door and peaked through the crack that separated them. He saw Bevins talking to someone, no, there were at least two other voices.

"Were you expecting company?" said a man that Eddie couldn't see. He spoke with a French-Canadian accent.

"You just missed them about ten minutes ago," Bevins answered.

Bevins kept it up between them, as though he was stalling for time.

The same person then asked Bevins, "So what's it going to be?"

"I've made my decision and I ain't changing it," answered Bevins.

Shit, the Governor was crying again. Whoever was talking to him must be someone that he's scared of.

"Is that so?" the same man said, and then walked into Eddie's field of view as he watched the man put an arm around the Governor's shoulder. He now saw the visitor's face. "You know what? That's not what I wanted to hear. And I know Serge would be very disappointed in you right now." The man then landed two heavy punches to Bevins' stomach. Eddie's hand shot to his mouth immediately. He hoped to God they didn't hear a sound come from him as he flinched. Bevins fell onto his knees wheezing as though he were in a lot of pain. Eddie then nearly gasped as the visitor withdrew a gun from inside his jacket. He also took out a black cylinder that he twisted on the barrel. *Shit, it's a silencer!*

There were two loud thuds as the man fired shots into the back of the Governor's head.

Eddie tightened his grip over his mouth. *Holy shit, they killed him.* He backed away slowly, shaking, even being careful not to breathe too loud as he stared at the double doors, waiting for the assailants to burst through. *Oh my God. What did I get myself into?*

"Should I still lift the prints?" asked the first man's partner. This one spoke in non-accented English.

"Fait-ca vite." *Make it fast.* "Je vais verifier l'autre chambre." *I'm going to check the other room.*

Eddie saw the assailant walk towards him. Eddie dove for the floor without a second thought and quickly scrambled to crawl under the bed when he heard a ringing on the opposite side of the door. It sounded like a mobile phone. Suddenly he remembered that his phone was on top of the bed. Shit, he could've called 9-1-1. He probably should've chanced escaping through the room's entrance. Then again, they might hear him and shoot him in the back as he ran down the hall.

"Oui," Eddie heard the assailant say. There was a pause. "C'est qui ca?" *Who is this?* He didn't hear his partner answer him. The gunman must be answering a phone call.

The bottom of the box spring scraped against the back of his head as he slid backwards on his stomach. He clenched his teeth, hoping it would minimize his tremors, as he watched the shadow through the crack under the doorway.

"We have to get out of here, and quickly," Eddie heard the assailant say just as the shadow disappeared from the crack under the door.

"Why, what's wrong?" said the assailant's partner.

"Someone just called me telling me that a news crew is coming this way."

"What? Who was it? How did they know about this?"

"I don't know. Hurry up with the prints. We need to get out of here."

"I'm done."

Eddie pursed his lips as he remained still. In the other room he heard footsteps quickly walking away, followed by the sound of a door closing. He then breathed normally for a bit before he crawled out from under the bed. Eddie followed the light from the double doors and walked to them. A tightness grabbed his chest as he questioned whether or not he could open the door.

He yanked the door open, looking both sides before glancing at the body on the floor. There was a moment's glance where he saw red splatter around a gaping hole in the back of the man's head. He turned away so quickly that he stumbled to the floor back in the other room. His stomach turned, and he was on all fours, crawling quickly, trying to get back up on both legs. Eddie stood but lost his balance as he fell forward, catching himself on the wall. Once he straightened out he made it to the bathroom where he rushed over to the toilet, lifted the seat, held his head over it and heaved out his last meal.

Damn it, he knew that this was a stupid thing to do. Why'd he let Jordyn and Corey talk him into doing this?

Christ, why didn't I listen to my father and give up writing? It's brought me nothing but trouble. I lost my girl, my job, maybe my apartment, and now I saw a man get shot. Just because I had to be so damn overzealous over this stupid book that nobody wants to read.

He raised his head, still on his knees, and reached up to flush the toilet. He was still out of breath for several moments when he remembered the phone. He rushed to the bed to grab it. He dialed nine, then one. He was about to dial the other *one* when it dawned on him...the killers spoke of lifting prints. *His* prints. He was just framed for Bevins's murder. He stuffed the phone in his pocket and ran out the room.

He nearly stumbled as he got in the hallway. When Eddie caught his footing, it was then that he saw a man and a woman several feet away—both much older and lavishly dressed—staring back at him outside the door to their room.

What the hell were they staring at? Eddie looked down. *Shit, my jacket's still open.* He quickly zipped up the fly to his pants— which was still undone—and pulled his jacket across his chest as though it were a blanket, holding it as he rushed pass the gray-haired Caucasian man and his wife. He did his best not to let them see his face.

Fuck the elevators—he was taking the stairs, anything that didn't involve waiting.

***

The man, after seeing the leather-clad black youngster rush past him and his wife, watched him as he burst through the door to the emergency stairwell.

"Good heavens, you don't see that every day, do you?" said his wife as she unwrapped the mink scarf from around her neck.

"Honey," the husband said, as he turned towards the end of the hallway. "Go wait in our room." He then began to walk towards the end of the hall.

"Oh come on. The person in the other room's probably having an affair, what else is new? It's none of our business anyways."

The husband made a quick glance over his shoulder as he walked faster. "I told you to wait inside. Now do it." *Leather-clad punks in this hotel? And he looked unusually scared of something.* That's when the man noticed that the door to room 514 was slightly ajar.

"Hello?" he knocked as he pushed the door slowly open. "Is everything o—oh my God." He stumbled into the hallway until he backed into the wall.

His wife turned to her husband frantically. "Honey, what is it?"

"Call 9-1-1. Call security—just call someone. That kid just killed the man next door."

Chapter 7

Eddie skipped the last set of stairs in the grey-colored emergency stairwell, crashed into the exit door, and flew out into the opulent surroundings of the hotel lobby.

Don't look at anyone…you'll just look more guilty. But he couldn't help doing so. Everyone was staring at him. He didn't have to see them, he could sense it. It was as though his sensory perception had increased since he heard everyone whispering. It was then that he felt a draft. *Shit, my jacket's open again! I thought I zipped it up.* Phones were ringing around him, and the receptionists all seemed to be answering them at the same time. Even cell phones started ringing around him. *My gosh, everyone knows. They found the body—they think that I killed him.*

"Eddie, wait up," came a voice.

Who was it? He didn't say his name to anyone in the hotel, except for the Governor. How did anyone else know his name? The revolving door of the front entrance was directly in front of him, and it appeared to keep getting further away. Eddie broke out into a sprint, slamming into the revolving door and pushing against it to make it move faster, but the heavy door pushed back against him. He didn't look back, but he heard footsteps rushing behind him. Hotel security was after him.

Eddie didn't even wait for the revolving door to allow a decent space for him to pass through. He burned the side of his legs and arms forcing himself through the thin opening. That's when he was greeted by a mixture of exhaust fumes and cold air.

The coolness on his face and neck was not enough to distract him, he just took off to the right—it didn't matter which direction he took. It was all about getting away as fast as he could.

"Eddie," someone shouted again, seconds before a hand grabbed his arm, causing Eddie to cry out. He spun around swinging his arms out to strike the perpetrator.

"Damn it, Eddie! What's wrong with you?" It was Corey. Thank God. He must have passed through one of the ordinary doors beside the revolving one. "Didn't you hear me calling you back there?"

Eddie didn't answer him. He struggled to catch his breath as he held onto his best friend for support.

Corey grabbed Eddie by both shoulders. "What's wrong? What are you running from?"

Eddie panted as he held onto Corey's upper arm for support. Again, he saw the image of the blood spatter that shot out from the front of Governor Bevins' head, and bits of skull and his brain that bounced off of the carpet before he hit the floor.

"Yo, bro, you're starting to scare me," said Corey. "What the hell happened up there?"

It was then that Eddie saw past Corey and noticed some more activity in the lobby. There were two men that looked like pro-football running backs wearing blazers and ties, questioning the receptionist. Seconds later the receptionist pointed right at both him and Corey.

"Run!" Eddie tried to pull out of Corey's grip, just as he saw both men running towards them. One of them started shouting into his walkie-talkie loud enough that heads all over the lobby turned. It was only then that Corey turned and saw them. Eddie didn't waste any time hauling ass with Corey close behind. Corey caught up to him and was able to grab his shoulder in time before he crossed the intersection and redirected him around the corner towards the car.

Dodging a few pedestrians, they made it to Eddie's car which was parked about fifteen cars away, not too far away from the street corner. Corey already had the keys in his hands as he quickly let himself in. When Eddie checked behind, the security guards were at the street corner looking around. One of them then eyed Eddie and pointed him out to his colleague. Seconds later they charged him like two bulls.

Eddie pounded the passenger door window as he kept checking on the guards that closed in on him. "Come on, open up!"

Corey reached over and unlocked the passenger door. Eddie yanked it open and jumped in, slamming the door behind him as Corey fired up the car. Thank goodness the car didn't give them any trouble as the engine caught the first time. Eddie was startled as one of the security guards managed to grab hold of the door handle beside him. He wasn't able to get a proper grip as Corey pulled out of the spot without even checking for traffic. He then floored the gas pedal as the hatchback sped off.

Minutes later they were travelling westbound along the Ville Marie Expressway, leaving the downtown skyscrapers behind.

Corey turned to Eddie. "Are you going to tell me what the hell happened? Why were those men chasing us?"

"He's dead."

"What? Who's dead? What are you talking about?"

"They killed him. I hid in the other room. Two men...one of them pulled out a gun and shot him in the head three times."

"What are you saying? What two men? Who got shot?"

Both of Eddie's hands shot up to the sides of his head. "I don't know who the men were."

"First of all, slow down and chill for a bit." Corey glanced at him before turning back towards watching the road.

Eddie felt his heart pounding in his chest as he watched Corey steer the car over into the slow lane.

"Tell me what happened," said Corey. "Starting with what happened when you went up to the hotel suite."

Eddie swallowed once and held his head low, staring at the dash board. He then looked back up. "The client wasn't a woman. It was a guy."

Corey did a double take, as he tried to split his time looking at Eddie while keeping his eyes on the road. "What?"

Eddie shot an angry stare at Corey. "It was a man!"

Corey didn't say anything, as though he was trying to absorb what he was told. He then started stuttering. "I...what the...how the—"

"That's not the worst of it. He's the Governor of New Hampshire. He was confessing something to me when two men came into the room and shot him."

"Two men just walked into the room and shot him right in front of you?"

"I told you I was hiding in the other room."

Corey paused again as though he were in thought. He still didn't appear to fully accept what Eddie told him. "Did you get a look at them?"

"Yeah, I got a pretty good look."

"Did they see you?"

"I don't think so."

"You don't *think* so? This is serious, bro. Did they see you or not?"

"No, they didn't see me," Eddie yelled.

"You're sure about this."

"Yes, I'm sure." The conversation went on hold as Eddie saw red, blue, and white flashes reflect throughout the inside of the car. He looked behind him and saw a squad car closing in behind them. "Oh shit. It's the highway patrol."

"No shit, you don't think I noticed?" Corey slowed down as he pulled over to the shoulder with the patrol car on his tail.

Eddie looked behind and saw the squad car had practically attached itself to their bumper. He then looked at Corey. Why the hell was he stopping? "What are you doing?"

"What does it look like I'm doing?"

"You're trying to make it easy for them to catch us. We just fled a crime scene."

"Yo, man, just chill." Corey stopped the car and killed the engine. "It's probably nothing more than a speeding ticket. Just be quiet and let me do the talking."

At that moment, the Sureté de Quebec (SQ) highway patrolman emerged from his vehicle, closed his door, and walked up toward the car. They had everything in common with US State Troopers except SQ officers didn't wear those large brimmed hats.

Corey saw the officer approaching his side, and rolled down his window just as he got to his door. Eddie felt beads of perspiration rolling down his face as he looked away through his window. Fortunately, SQ officers did not usually travel in pairs as the Montreal Police officers often did.

"C'est bien ton auto, monsieur?" *Is this your car, sir?*

"No, it's my friend's car. He's not feeling too well, that's why I'm driving," Corey replied in English.

Eddie then noticed that a flashlight was beaming on him. *Play sick, put on a show.* He began to moan and put one hand to his stomach. Maybe that would fool him.

"Really? Let me see your license and registration," said the officer, and turned off his flashlight. "You realize dat you were speeding forty kilometers above dee speed limit?"

"Naw, sir. Like I said, my friend's not feeling too well. I was rushing to get him home. He's been moaning for the whole ride. I guess I didn't notice how fast I was going." Eddie watched Corey out of the corner of his eye as he reached into his pocket and took out his wallet. Damn, he was a natural, but Eddie still wouldn't take a chance at looking at the officer. He stayed as he was before. Suddenly the flashlight went back on again—but not on him.

"Eh, you look familiar. 'Ave we met before?"

"Naw, man, I don't think so," Corey answered.

Oh shit, they must have been caught on the hotel's security cameras. An APB must have been put out. The entire police force must be out combing the entire city for them.

"No, no, no. I know I've seen you before. And your accent too, I know you from someplace," said the officer.

Corey, for God's sake, stop looking at him. Eddie turned his face away even more.

"I'm telling you, it ain't me. Whatever it is or wherever it was. Trust me, it ain't me."

Surprisingly the officer began to chuckle. "Eh mon Dieu. Ca se peux-tu?" *Oh my God. Is this for real?* "You're that guy that tried to sing on TV, on that singing show. I can't believe this."

Jesus Christ! Eddie felt a huge weight disappear from the bottom of his stomach as he began to breathe normally. He then heard the officer chuckle.

"Oh that? Yeah, that was me," said Corey.

Eddie, who had a miraculous recovery, turned to the officer. "Yeah, it's him. He really sucked ass, didn't he? I can't take him anywhere anymore." Corey then shot him a stern look that evaporated Eddie's fake smile.

The patrolman handed Corey back his license and registration. "Listen, I'm going to let you off with a warning. It's only because you provided weeks of laughter to my colleagues at work. Just try to respect dee speed limit and slow down, eh?"

Corey nodded, still relaxed as before. "Thanks officer, I'll be more careful." A voice was heard through the officer's walkie-talkie.

"Just 'old on a second. Don't go anywhere," said the officer as he stepped away.

Eddie figured that he was going to get a pen and pad and ask for Corey's autograph. He couldn't believe it. Something good finally came out of Corey's failed audition. "Can we go now?"

"Hold on, the officer said to wait. Just keep cool, and we'll drive away from this without any problems."

Eddie wished he were as level-headed as Corey, who was relaxed, and tapped the steering wheel with his fingers. In contrast, he was trying to control his breathing as he kept his eye on the officer through the rear-view mirror above the dashboard. He guessed right. The officer was walking back with a notepad and also what appeared to be a digital camera. Suddenly he stopped, as he appeared to be checking the back of their car. He stood there for a few seconds, and then he leaned closer as though there was something he was trying to find. Shit, could he be looking at the license plate? The hotel security, they must have seen the car's plates before they sped off. "Corey?"

His friend turned to him. "What?"

"Start the car."

"I told you to relax, everything's cool."

"Oh yeah?" Eddie pointed to the rear-view mirror. "Then why's he checking the license plate?" They both stared and both saw that he stepped back and drew his gun.

"Both of you, out of dee car now," the officer barked. "Keep your 'ands where I can see dem,"

Eddie didn't know if it was panic or an adrenaline rush. But Corey's hand jumped to the key and started up the car.

That's when they heard the gunshot and Eddie felt a scream leave him as he ducked, both of his hands shot up. He glanced to the left to see that Corey had done the same. From what he saw, Corey was visibly scared. Everything was silent, except for the passing cars. Eddie waited for the officer to scream out more orders. To his astonishment, they didn't hear any. He raised his head and peered between the car seat and out the back window. He couldn't see the officer. "Where'd he go?"

Corey looked behind him and then glanced at Eddie. He then unbuckled his seatbelt, opened his door, and leaned out to look behind the car. "Oh shit."

"What is it? You see him?"

Corey stepped out and walked to the back of the car.

Eddie felt a drop of sweat roll off the tip of his nose. He wiped his face with a stroke of his arm and watched Corey, who was staring towards the ground. He unbuckled his seatbelt, opened his door, and approached the back of the car from his side. That's when he saw the officer lying on the ground right between both of their cars. His gun lay on the ground a few feet away from him.

Eddie looked up at Corey. "What the hell happened? He just fired his gun at us. Now *he's* lying on the ground?"

"I don't think he shot at us," said Corey. "Your car backfired when I started it."

"It did?"

"Yeah, I'm sure of that."

"Then why'd you duck?"

"I did it out of reflex when you screamed."

"This don't make any sense. My car couldn't have killed him."

"I don't think he's dead. There's no blood, so it's not like he accidentally shot himself either."

"Are you sure?" Eddie took a step closer, when suddenly he slipped. He saw the road spin, felt his head strike something hard, then felt the coldness of the ground on the side of his face.

"Yo, bro, you okay?" he felt small slaps on both of his cheeks.

Corey was holding him. "You alright?"

Eddie sat up and held the side of his head where he had bumped it. He then stared over to the officer, who was still lying on the ground. It was then that he noticed the shininess of the ground by his boots. Still holding his head, Eddie leaned forward and reached with the other hand towards his boots. He touched the ground and rubbed it. It was cold and very smooth—black ice.

"I think I know what happened," said Eddie as he looked at Corey, who nodded back at him.

The officer's walkie-talkie made a lot of noise. Eddie crawled over and removed it from the officer. It didn't take long before he realized what was being said on the police bandwidth.

"There's an APB out for both of us," said Eddie.

"Really. You think?" said Corey as he pointed to the officer. "He was just about to shoot us. He just happened to slip on the ice and bash his head, possibly against the bumper of his car, after being startled by the backfire."

"Well, we got lucky, twice. Get in the car. We have to get out of here before some rubbernecker spots us." Eddie headed to the driver's side with the walkie-talkie.

"Where are you going with that?"

Eddie got in and rested the walkie-talkie on the dash. "We can track all police activity with this." Simeon Wolf would've done the same thing. Once Corey got in, Eddie drove off.

"So, where do we go now?"

"We'll just keep heading west until we get out of the city. That's where we'll abandon the car."

"Okay, genius. I'm about to get frostbite. We won't have any transportation once we dump the car, and the police are looking for us. What do we do next?"

Corey was right. Who would've thought that they'd be in this deep? Why the hell was this happening to him? It's like he'd been cursed. Eddie pondered this as he sped up and emerged from the shoulder, as they listened to the dispatcher through the walkie-talkie. Corey was now officially identified as Eddie's partner-in-crime.

Chapter 8

The Lamont Residence, Laval-sur-le-Lac, Quebec

L amont downed the last bit of Bordeaux and held onto the empty wine glass. He looked down at his feet where Marc-Antoni had cuddled in a slumber. He wound up his arm, ready to pitch the empty glass into the bright embers that burned in the fireplace when it occurred to him that the sound might wake up his wife, Chantal. He rested the glass on the side table and stared out the large window that overlooked the back yard. The current snowfall would add an extra five centimeters to the ten centimeters that had accumulated.

He rested his elbow on the arm of the leather couch Chantal had recently purchased at some Italian furniture store he had never heard of. Why the hell did she go about replacing the old furniture anyways? The old set was fine. Without any warning, he just came home from work one day, entered the house, and *bam*. There was a new dining and living room set. When he had asked her what became of the old set, she told him that she donated it to charity. Then she lectured him on how she had already discussed this with him. Did she? Who knew? Everything's been going above his head lately, especially the shit his company was facing. At least Chantal didn't replace the entertainment unit. It took him about five weeks to figure out which of the four goddamned remote controls controlled the HDTV, the DVD player, the Blue-Ray disk player, the CD player, and any other player that was invented lately that he couldn't remember the name to.

Aside from the television, the only other noise that was barely audible came from the fireplace. It was the only other source of light in the room aside from the television.

The job was done. Governor Bevins was dead. That's the only subject that could be found on every channel he switched to. But where the hell did these two black punks come from? He picked up his mobile, looked across the room to make sure that the doors were closed. He then dialed a number.

"Oui," came a reply.

"What in God's name have you done?"

"I've done what you asked me to do, sir."

Lamont looked back at the television. "Then why is it that I'm watching the news right now, and seeing that someone else was there? Who are these two guys, Eddie and Corey?"

"I don't know much yet, but my sources will be able to inform me of where they live. They'll be taken care of."

"Did they see you?"

"I doubt."

Bullshit. "What were they doing there? Why didn't you see them?"

"It appears that the Governor's into male domination. We didn't see them when we were there."

"Male domination? Like those freaks in those...those tight leather or vinyl outfits with whips?"

"We believe so."

"And your instincts didn't tell you that he had company? You couldn't check to make sure that there weren't any witnesses?"

"We were about to check when you called to warn us about the news crew."

Lamont held out the phone in front of him, wondering if he heard right. He then put it back to his ear. "What? What news crew? I never called you this evening"

"You didn't?" There was a short pause, as though the man was in thought. "Then if it wasn't you, who was it?"

"I don't know," said Lamont.

"Then whoever it was, he was looking out for us. Because a

news crew *did* show up soon after we left. Did you tell anyone else about what was being planned?"

"Don't be dense. Of course not."

"May I suggest you be more careful when you contact me," said the man. "Whoever this *good Samaritan* is, we cannot trust him yet, since we don't know who he is."

Lamont cleared his throat. "That's your area of expertise. You should be the one to find out who it is."

"Anyhow, even if Eddie and Corey saw us, their testimony won't do much. Another set of fingerprints were on a few select items inside the hotel suite. We made sure that the same prints would be found on the murder weapon. As for the two witnesses, it won't be long before I find out where they live. Once the police find drugs in their house, they'll be known as drug addicts looking for a quick fix. No one will believe their story."

"See to it that you fix this problem. I want to be able to sit down in front of the TV tomorrow evening and learn that these kids were either arrested or killed." Lamont then pressed the off button.

The sound of the door opening startled Lamont as he turned to see Chantal. She wore a green velvet nightgown—her birthday present from him. He let out a sigh of relief. "I didn't know you were there. Why aren't you asleep?"

"I was going to ask you the same question," his wife answered with her arms crossed. She didn't appear to be upset, just concerned.

Lamont focused his attention back towards the television when he heard a loud sigh come from Chantal.

"Will you *please* turn off the television and come to bed?" She walked over to him, grabbed the remote, and switched the TV off. She then turned to Lamont. "I know that Tony was your friend. But what good does it do, to torture yourself by watching news of his assassination all night long?"

Poor woman, she didn't have a clue. Lamont got up from the couch, causing Marc-Antoni to shuffle to the side. He rubbed his eyes as though they itched and looked at his wife. "You're right, my dear."

Lamont then wiped away a tear that wasn't there. He landed in his wife's arms and he breathed in the lovely strawberry scent of her hair.

"I'm so sorry that this happened," she said.

"So am I," Lamont replied, hiding his grin in her hair.

Chapter 9

Twenty kilometers west of the island of Montreal

Eddie and Corey had driven for almost half an hour and were a fair distance off of the island of Montreal. In order to save the battery on Corey's phone, Eddie called Flick's restaurant from a phone booth along the way. When Robert answered, Eddie asked him to pass a message to Jordyn, asking her to call him from a phone booth. While researching his last novel, he learned that the police could track phone calls made from her cell and then use the connection to track his and Corey's current location. Since Corey's phone was 'pay-as-you-go', their location would be more difficult to trace. Eddie figured that it would've been too early for the police to know of his connection to Flick. Therefore, it wasn't likely that they'd be listening in on their conversation through Flick's phone.

Eddie and Corey now sat in the car with the engine turned off. Corey had turned on the speaker of his mobile and held it so that they could both listen to Jordyn.

"Guys, I'm calling you from a phone booth, freezing my ass off. Please tell me that it ain't true what they're saying on the news."

"It ain't," said Corey.

"I didn't kill anyone. You know I don't own a gun," said Eddie.

"Things just didn't go the way we expected," said Corey.

"No shit, you don't think I already figured that out? How the hell did the New Hampshire State Governor get involved?" asked

Jordyn.

Eddie, sucking his teeth, pulled the phone out of Corey's hand. "He's involved because the high-profile client Theo set me up with *was* the New Hampshire State Governor."

There was silence on the other end. She was definitely caught off guard.

"That son-of-a-bitch! I can't believe that Theo would be so fucking careless." There was a brief pause. "I'm sorry. I never thought that he would be this disorganized."

"Stop beating yourself up, Jordyn," said Corey. "It wasn't your fault. Eddie was right all along. This was a stupid idea."

"But how did this happen?" asked Jordyn. Eddie then told her everything that happened up until the shooting.

"Oh my God, you saw who did it?" she said. "You guys have to turn yourselves in and give a statement."

"I don't know about that. The killers figured out the Governor had company, I heard them talking—especially about lifting prints. That's how they framed me."

"Well, both of your faces are all over the news—Canadian and American stations, the internet, radio—you name it."

"Shit, man." said Corey.

"Yeah, they're displaying your driver's license photos," said Jordyn. "My cell phone won't stop ringing. I feel like throwing it down the sewer. You have to turn yourselves in. This is the only way you can hope to clear your names. Where are you guys now?"

Corey leaned closer to the phone. "Somewhere west—"

"You're better off not knowing." Eddie interjected. The police may catch up with Jordyn and interrogate her.

"I don't think you guys have a choice. By daybreak, most of the country would've heard the news and seen your faces. How long do you think you can go on running?"

Eddie sighed. She had a point. Both he and Corey were out in the country where there were fewer black people than there were nuns in a male strip joint. Who wouldn't recognize them out here? He could see them being chased by an angry mob in pick-up trucks, trying to run them off the road into a ditch—where they'd then be clubbed to death with baseball bats and hockey sticks. "All right, we'll head back to town and turn ourselves in. Maybe we won't look as guilty if we do so." He then looked at Corey.

"It couldn't get any worse for us," said Corey. He didn't appear to be too proud of the idea. Then again, neither was Eddie.

"All right then," said Jordyn. "Be careful and good luck. I think you'll be all right. Besides with what you know about this Serge Lamont guy, the proper authorities will have to investigate once you spill the beans. I don't think anyone will believe that you made this up."

Eddie smirked. She's right. He had a shitload of info that could be verified. The most that could happen to him and Corey was being detained in a holding cell overnight. That would be enough time for the police to verify his statement. Both he and Corey would be out of jail by lunchtime tomorrow and be cleared of all charges. "We're heading back now. We'll call you when we're at the police station."

"Okay, talk to you later. I love you."

"Love you too, babes," Corey replied.

Eddie then turned off the phone, handed it back to Corey, and started up the car. "I don't know why we didn't think of that earlier."

"That's because we both panicked," said Corey.

Beyond the access ramp that led to the highway, Eddie saw a gas station. The sign clearly said that it was open twenty-four hours. He looked down at the fuel gauge and noticed that the needle was covering the letter E. He drove past the access ramp and headed to the gas station. Eddie stopped in front of the pump and turned off the engine. He looked inside the convenience store that was attached to the station. There was only one attendant.

He remembered the days when gas stations were nothing more than places to fill up. The most that one could find was a mechanic in the adjoining garage. Now on-site convenience stores had become more common over the last ten years. Although it was a convenience, he saw it as another ploy for the gas companies to maximize profits. Especially whenever gas prices fell, the prices of their store items suddenly rose to compensate. Oddly no one was complaining about three-dollar candy. He took out a twenty-dollar bill and gave it to Corey.

"Here. Give this to the guy inside. I'll pump the gas." Corey took it and went into the store. Eddie got out, walked to the side of the car where he flipped open the filler lid and unscrewed the cap. He waited for Corey to hand the gas station attendant the money so that he would activate the pump.

Eddie watched as Corey handed the attendant the money. Seconds later the pump was activated and he started to fill up the car. He watched Corey as he disappeared to the back of the store. Eddie guessed that he went to the bathroom. Come to think of it, he had to go too.

It was quiet around here. He didn't know the area too well and figured that the nearest house was miles away. When he looked inside the store again, the attendant still had not moved. He was still hunched over the counter, reading a magazine or a book. Who could blame him? Although Eddie had never worked a graveyard shift, he clearly saw how boring a job it must have been. Business couldn't be booming at this hour. But at least the guy had a job, unlike himself.

It didn't take long before Eddie maxed out his twenty dollars. He'd be lucky if he got up to half tank. He replaced the nozzle, closed the lid and walked into the store. Inside, Eddie saw the two aisles filled with junk food, candy, and a few automobile accessories. Along the wall were refrigerators filled with beer, soft drinks, and other beverages.

At that moment Corey left the restroom. Eddie raised his hand and Corey passed him the keys as he passed. It didn't take long for him to relieve himself, wash his hands and leave the bathroom. On his way back to the counter, he saw Corey staring upwards at the flat screen television that hung from the ceiling near the corner. He handed the key to the attendant, who was too engrossed in his magazine to notice him.

"Hey, check this out. They're still talking about it on the news." Eddie stood beside him and watched. It was a press conference and on the bottom of the screen was displayed: Breaking News.

"What's happening now?" Eddie asked.

"They found the murder weapon," Corey answered. Eddie looked back at the television and saw the news anchorman speaking in a small square at the bottom corner of the screen, announcing the press conference. The anchorman disappeared as the press conference room came into full view.

Eddie nudged Corey. "Come on, let's go."

"Wait I want to see this."

"I think we should be going."

"It's not going to change anything," Corey answered.

Eddie turned and looked at him when he suddenly caught a glimpse of the detective in charge standing in front of the podium. His jaw dropped and the back of his throat tightened.

You got to be shitting me. He looked over at the attendant—that's when he saw him turn a page and caught a glimpse of two naked women engaged in a sexual position. It was enough to distract the attendant and it was also both his and Corey's saving grace at this moment.

He gently tugged on Corey's arm and whispered. "We can't turn ourselves in."

Corey turned to him. "Why? What's—"

"Shhh." Eddie's narrowing of his eyebrows was enough to hush Corey, whose mouth hung open as though he wanted to say something.

"What's the matter?" Corey whispered.

"We can't turn ourselves in because of him." Discreetly he nodded in the direction of the television, referring to the detective. "That's the man who shot the Governor."

Chapter 10

CCI told you to put down the phone," said Edward loudly. Monica dismissed his order with a single wave before she turned her back to him, which incensed him even more. *I ought to just go over there and yank the phone cord from the wall. That would show her.* It would also calm his blood pressure, which he swore kept rising from all the times the phone had been ringing in the past hour. First it was family and friends that called, followed by colleagues from work. Then there were those nosy acquaintances from church. As God was his witness he swore that those church people had nothing better to do. They only wanted to know their business just so that they could have something to gossip about. In a few days people will be pointing fingers at him and Monica, saying how *they* raised a killer. He knew of three people at church that would have already started spreading those stories.

An hour before, he'd made everyone close all of the blinds and pull the curtains shut in every window. A media circus was outside their home, filming and snapping photos, hoping to catch a glimpse of something that they could either print in tomorrow's paper or show on the news. Edward knew that he'd never hear the end of it from their neighbors, who'd blame them for not being able to get in or out of their homes—not to mention losing sleep.

"I said to put down the phone," yelled Edward. Monica obviously didn't listen to him, so Edward turned away from her and dropped into his favorite recliner. He snatched the remote from the small table beside him and turned on the television very loudly so that she wouldn't be able to carry on her telephone conversation. He'd lost count of all of the times that this chair was there for him during his most stressful times. He remembered the days when Eddie was an infant, he used to toss him in the air and catch him. And in this very chair, Edward would even rock him, pretending that they were pirates on a pirate ship, braving the stormy Caribbean Sea, avoiding cannon blasts from other pirates. He never imagined the day would come that he'd be in the same chair watching developments in a murder case that allegedly involved his son. Almost every station he flipped through— both Canadian and American—had Eddie's and Corey's pictures posted. How in God's name did this happen? *Uggh*, that stubborn boy never wanted to listen to him—now this.

Denise walked into the living room. "My phone won't stop ringing."

"Where is it?"

She showed it to him.

"Give it here." He snatched it from out of her hand, popped off the back, removed the SIM card, pocketed it, and handed the phone back to her. "Problem solved."

"Why'd you do that for? I know how to turn it off."

"Sure, just so you can turn it back on again and check your messages." He then spun the chair around towards Monica. "I said to put down the damn phone. And yank out the cord so that it stops ringing." *Where was Beverly? She better not be causing any trouble.* "Beverly, what are you up to?" There wasn't any answer. "Bev?" he called out louder. That's when he heard her walking down from upstairs.

"I heard you the first time," she yelled as she walked into the living room. "Why do you have the TV turned up so loud?" Beverly walked over to it and turned down the volume.

"What were you doing?" Edward growled.

"I was making sure the blinds in the rooms upstairs were shut. Them news people got the whole street blocked off."

Monica put down the phone and disconnected it from the jack. She then joined everyone.

Her husband turned to her. "Who were you talking to? I told

you to stop answering the damn phone."

"That was Father Petrie," Monica answered as she slumped down on the other couch. "He was wishing us well and that he would continue praying for us. Especially for Junior and Corey."

"He ought to pray that I don't get my hands on that boy before the police do," answered her husband.

Beverly turned to him. "Oh stop talking nonsense. We don't know what happened." She then pointed to the living room window, referring to the media circus outside. "*They* don't even know what happened."

Edward leaned forward in his chair towards Beverly. "They seem to know more than us. Junior was spotted fleeing a murder scene this evening. You want to tell me what he was doing at the Mont-Royal Hotel in the first place? He ain't got the money to spend there. Unless he was working there, he didn't have any business there with them rich people."

"Why are you looking at me?" asked Beverly. "I don't know why he was there. But I know he didn't go there to shoot someone, I'll tell you that."

Denise turned to her. "Then he should just turn himself in. He's just putting himself into more trouble by not doing so. It's so typical of him."

The doorbell then rang three times in rapid succession. Monica got up to answer it when Edward looked at her. "Where are you going? Sit down."

"I'm going to check and see who it is," Monica answered.

"If it's important, they'll come back in the morning."

At that point there was a loud banging at the door. "Mister and Madame Barrow? My name is Detective Daniel Mercier from the Montreal Police Department. I have some questions I need to ask you." The voice had a French-Canadian accent.

Monica looked back at Edward, who mumbled something under his breath. She stood there until he finally got up and joined her. They both then walked to the front door. Her hand went to the door handle when Edward shot his arm out and placed his palm on the door. "Whatever he asks, just remember *not* to volunteer any information." He then looked back and said loudly to both Denise and Beverly. "Both of you go upstairs. We're going to handle this." The last thing he needed was one of them having a slip of the tongue, especially Beverly.

When they were both upstairs, Edward let go of the door and stepped back. Monica opened the door. Before them stood a man who was close to Edward's height and who appeared to have lost a few days sleep. It must be the price to pay for being a detective. Mercier flashed his badge and walked in so quickly that both Edward and Monica were forced to step aside.

As Monica closed the door to the flashing camera lights and screaming reporters, Detective Mercier turned to them. "Normally I would've asked both of you to come down to the police station. But with what's going on outside, I thought it would be easier on you to come here instead."

"That's very considerate of you, detective," said Monica.

"I'm sorry that both of you have to go through this tonight. I promise to keep my questions brief. May we go to the kitchen?" Mercier gestured.

"Of course," Monica replied.

Edward, with both hands in his pockets, watched the detective as he observed his surroundings on his way to the kitchen. *I guess he expects to find my son hiding somewhere in here.*

"This is a nice house you have, Mister and Missus Barrow," said Mercier as he arrived at the kitchen table. "May I ask what both of you do for a living?"

"I'm a pharmacist and my wife's a nurse," Edward answered.

"A pharmacist? This is a nice neighborhood for a pharmacist. Who's your employer?"

Edward narrowed his eyes and pointed a finger to himself. "*I'm* the employer." *You call yourself a detective, you bastard. Coming into my house and thinking that I robbed it. Typical white police officer.*

"Detective, it's late," said Monica. "Please sit."

You're lucky my wife knows when I'm about to boil over. Edward took his usual chair at the head of the table, with arms crossed, while Monica sat adjacent to him.

Mercier sat down opposite Monica and adjacent from Edward,

and took out a notepad and a pen. He scribbled some notes on it while he glanced at both Edward and Monica. "I'm just going to ask you a few questions. All that I ask is that you be as brief and to-the-point as possible. I don't want to see any harm coming to your son. My hope is that even if we can't find him, then at least by some means we can convince your son to turn himself in. To begin, when's the last time you saw your son?"

"Thursday night," answered Monica.

"Where was this?" Mercier scribbled on his notepad.

"He came over here for dinner."

"And did he appear to behave normally?"

"Of course he was."

"Did you ever suspect that he was involved with the sex industry?"

Edward and Monica's eyes widened as they stared at each other. Edward then leaned forward towards Mercier. "No, we didn't. What makes you say that he was involved in anything like that?"

"Some bondage equipment was found at the crime scene. And an eye witness claims to have spotted your son fleeing the crime wearing a leather sex outfit."

Both Edward and Monica slumped back into their chairs and sighed. Edward's head fell into his hand. He then looked back at Mercier. "*My* son, involved in such...such filth? Come on."

"And while he was living here, did either of you ever find anything in his room that would've led you to believe that he was involved in this sort of lifestyle?"

"Eddie's a young man," said Monica. "We've never had any reason to search his room. He was always busy at his computer."

"Do you know what he was doing at his computer?" Mercier asked.

"Writing," said Monica. "He dreamed of becoming an author."

Mercier's left eyebrow rose, as though he was not expecting that answer. "An author?" Edward figured that Mercier was playing dumb in order to study their reaction. The police would've already confiscated Eddie's belongings from his apartment, including his computer. He should have already known of all of the contents on the hard drive.

"That's a surprise, considering his other hobby," said Mercier. "I know that this is a shock for you, but this is what was found at the crime scene. And we know that your son was there. May I ask how long he's been living on his own?"

"Why's that important?" asked Edward.

"From my experience, I believe we can trace his change of behavior back to when he moved out of your home—maybe even before. I mean, he leaves this beautiful house for—I'm sorry to say this—a dump, with his friend." He flipped back a page of his notepad. "Oh yeah, I almost forgot to mention this. But in his apartment, we found a small amount of cocaine in his roommate's bedroom. According to his landlord, they were often late paying the rent. This could possibly account for your son taking up his night job." He flipped the page forward and looked at Eddie's parents. "I can only suspect that the three of you didn't get along, am I right?"

"And how's that any of your business?" said Edward, but Monica put a hand on his arm.

"What my husband means to say, is that Eddie felt that he was old enough to live on his own, that's all," said Monica.

Mercier sighed as he flipped through his notepad. "Well sometimes when kids make quick decisions on impulse it's not usually the best. And he was obviously desperate enough for cash that it wasn't enough to service an American politician in his hotel room. But I'm sorry to say, all evidence points to the fact that he might have planned to rob the Governor. And as a result, the Governor was killed."

That son-of-a-bitch. Edward jumped up so fast that his chair flew over backwards to the floor, and slammed his fist on the table. "Where do you get the nerve calling my son a killer?"

Monica jumped up and grabbed her husband by the arm. "Edward, sit down."

"My son is *not* a killer, you hear me?" he yelled, waving a finger at the detective.

"Detective, I think it's about time you left. You know the way out," said Monica. The detective got up and made his way out of the kitchen.

"He's not a killer," Edward screamed again. Monica pulled on his arm as he tried to follow Mercier, but he yanked himself out of her grip. Monica then ran in front of him and stood between him and the detective while he continued yelling at Mercier.

"That's enough," Monica yelled at Edward.

He then backed off and retreated back to the kitchen with one huge wave of his arm towards Mercier. "Get out of my house." *First he thinks that I'm not my own boss and then that I'm robbing my own house. Now he's accusing me of raising a killer. These damn police are all the same.*

Mercier headed for the front door when he turned around. "I must advise you, if you talk to your son, tell him that it's best that he turn himself in, for his own safety."

Edward turned back around. "You better—"

"Thanks for telling us," said Monica. "Please leave."

Mercier left.

Edward marched to the corner of the dining room and grabbed a bottle of Barbadian rum from the liquor chariot. He snatched one of the glasses from the same tray, not caring that it clinked against the others. He removed the cap and poured himself a full one, not even bothering with the ice.

"Please don't tell me that you're going to start this nasty habit of yours again," said Monica from a few feet away, staring at him in disgust.

He put the bottle down on the tray and went back to his chair in the living room, ignoring her as he grabbed the remote and turned on the television.

"Fine. Since you're not listening to me, you can sleep on the couch. I don't want to be sharing my bed with a drunk."

It's my bed too. He heard her footsteps on the stairs as she stomped up. The *boom* of a slamming door followed a few seconds later. He didn't care. He planned to sit right here in this chair all night. He had done so in the past whenever he and Monica got into an argument. Several hours later, they'd be talking again. But now he couldn't think of that, since now, the anchorwoman spoke of the police following a lead from a gas station attendant, somewhere west of the city. He rested an elbow on the arm of the chair and let his head drop into his hand. "Please, Lord, don't let them kill my son."

Chapter 11

"**W**ill you pull over?" Corey said loudly. "I can't now, we're not far enough from the gas station," answered Eddie.

"Stop worrying about the gas station. You saw the cashier. He was too busy looking at his porn magazine to recognize us."

"Yeah, until he glimpses the TV."

"He didn't even look at you. Besides, he saw me. Did you hear him say, 'You're that Canadian Idol dude?' No. So relax."

Eddie glanced at the speedometer to make sure the needle didn't go beyond 100 kilometers per hour, the posted speed limit. "Did it occur to you, that the police would question all gas station attendants along this highway, showing each one our pictures? We ain't in Montreal. There ain't any black people around here. All the police got to do is ask them if they saw two black guys tonight—they won't even need our photos. The first one that says yes, they'll review the surveillance tapes, spot our car and they'll be on to us. They'll probably set up check-points between here and the Ontario border."

"Then, in that case, we have to get off of this highway," said Corey.

"Why? We're safer in the city?"

"Because the highway patrolman stopped us on this highway. This is the first place they'll be looking for us, if they haven't started already. Besides, you just said that the police will be setting up check points." Corey took out his cell and dialed a number.

Eddie turned to Corey, "How many minutes do you have on

your card?"

"Twenty, maybe thirty, minutes left," Corey answered. "I'm calling Robert to get him to call Jordyn for us. She's going to have to come and get us."

"You're sure she's going to do this?"

"I know my girl, she will. I might have to argue with her a bit, but she'll come and get us eventually."

"By the way, tell her to remove the cell phone battery from her phone before she comes."

Corey shrugged his shoulders. "Why?"

"Because the police could trace her phone's location. If she leaves the battery inside then she'll lead the police right to us. Your phone doesn't work the same way."

"Gotcha," Corey nodded.

Corey was right. Jordyn was their best chance at getting help. Aunt Bev came across his mind but he couldn't risk contacting her. Knowing his parents, they'd give him up in a second. Gosh, this was too much, and now his stomach grumbled loudly. "Tell Jordyn to bring us something to eat."

Several minutes later, they exited the highway and were on the side of a two-lane country road, surrounded by snow-covered trees on either side. It wasn't completely pitch-black. There was enough snow illuminating the area, that one didn't need a flashlight in the dark. Eddie heard the creaking of Corey's seat as he reclined it. In a matter of minutes, it was lights out for him.

Screw this! Eddie thought. He got out and shut the door. He turned the collar up on his jacket—covering his neck—and walked several feet away from the car. The frost bit into his fingers. He clamped them into fists and shoved them into his jacket pockets as the snow crunched under his boots. He played back the evening's events in his head.

All that came to mind was seeing Bevins' head blown open like an apple being struck with a hammer. He had read several books since he was a teenager—from John Grisham to the more recent, Barry Eisler. He couldn't shake Grisham's graphic description in *A Time to Kill* on how the two rapists suffered at the hands of Carl Lee Hailey—the father of the black girl whom the two white men had raped. He remembered the parts about blood, brains, and skull fragments being spread all over the courthouse stairs as Carl Lee Hailey blew them away with an automatic rifle. The last image of Bevins in his head was of a man lying on his stomach, his arms splayed out in no particular fashion, and his head...oh God...the hole in the back of his head. It was big enough for him to glance inside and see through to his brain. The blood that poured out, obviously from the exit wound—shit, he never saw so much blood in his life.

"Eddie, where are you?" came Corey's voice from behind, interrupting his thoughts. He heard a door slam and running steps coming towards him.

"You scared me for a minute when I saw that you weren't in the car. Aren't you cold, bro?" Eddie took his hands out of his pockets and rubbed them together quickly. He then cupped them over his mouth and breathed on them. He heard Corey's voice, but he wasn't listening. That's when he felt a hand on his shoulder.

"Come back in the car. You'll catch pneumonia," said Corey.

"I don't care." Eddie answered.

"What do you mean, you don't care?"

"I mean it. I don't care."

"Man, don't start this. Not now."

"You ever see a man get shot before?" There was silence, as though Corey searched for the right words to say.

"No, I haven't," he said. "You're obviously still freaking out. Hanging out here ain't going to help."

Eddie then turned to Corey and looked him in the eyes. "They were in the next room, not even ten feet away from me. They could've easily killed me too—"

"And they didn't. They were too much in a rush to come looking for you. And I'm glad they didn't either, 'cause I'm not ready to lose my best friend. Just count your blessings." He then patted Eddie on the shoulder and turned him to face the car. "Come on, let's go back inside the car. It's freezing out here." Corey put his arm around Eddie as they walked back to the car. When they got inside, Corey started the car and turned the radiator up to maximum. In this temperature, the inside of a car could get very cold in less than five minutes when the heat wasn't on.

A little over an hour later, Eddie spotted headlights through the rear-view mirror. As it approached it drove onto the shoulder and stopped behind his car.

Eddie shook Corey. "She's here, wake up." Corey grumbled, as though he was in the middle of a dream.

Eddie was first to get out while Corey followed. Eddie went to sit in the back of Jordyn's car while Corey got in beside Jordyn, where she attacked him with a long embrace and a set of kisses. Christ, it's not like he came back from Afghanistan.

"Oh my God, are you all right?" said Jordyn.

"We're fine," said Corey. "How are your folks doing?"

"Are you kidding? They'd kill me if they knew that I was here with you right now. They haven't stopped calling me."

"Did you remember to take out your cell phone battery?" asked Eddie.

She turned towards the back seat and handed Eddie a bag. "Yes, Robert told me when I stopped by Flick's. He prepared you guys some fish and some rice. I also picked up some hot coffee along the way."

Eddie looked beside him and saw the two grease-stained paper bags. He handed one to Corey. "He's still open?"

"Of course. You guys are top news. Flick's place was crowded when I got there—everyone's watching the TV. I don't think he's ever had this much business in one evening. Last I heard the FBI was heading up here to assist the RCMP."

"Oh shit, not them," said Eddie as he dug into his meal. Thank God for Flick.

"What did you expect?" Jordyn said as she turned to Eddie. "A state Governor was murdered and you're the prime suspect." She then did a U-Turn and drove back towards the highway. "I don't understand why you feel that you can't turn yourselves in to another police station and expose Detective Mercier as the killer and that he's working for Serge Lamont."

"Because we don't have any real proof—only what Eddie saw. Besides, who's going to believe two unemployed black guys? They've already framed him and tagged me as an accomplice." said

Corey.

"We don't even know how many more police officers are on Lamont's payroll," Eddie added. "We could be walking right into a trap. They'd probably shoot us on sight."

"Okay, I get it." Jordyn turned onto the ramp and entered the highway as she glanced at Eddie through the rear-view mirror. "Do you remember anything the killers said that we could use?"

Eddie finished eating one chicken leg and half of the rice in the aluminum-foil pan. "I don't know. I can't remember."

"Try and think of something. Our lives depend on it," said Corey.

"I said, I don't know," Eddie yelled. Damn, this was getting annoying.

"Don't yell at me," said Corey. "Damn it. Do you know the shit we're both in?"

"No, I don't. Why don't you refresh my memory?"

"Guys!" Jordyn screamed, silencing both of them. "I didn't drive all the way out here just to listen to you two bitch at each other."

Eddie let his head fall back into the seat. "Where are we going anyways?"

"My friend, Donalda," Jordyn answered.

"Who's she?" Eddie asked.

"She's a friend of mine who's out of town. She left me the keys to her apartment so that I could feed her cat and water the plants."

Eddie rubbed his stomach. That should be a safe place to hang out for the time being. He then saw Jordyn glance at him through the rear-view mirror.

"I know that this may be asking a lot from you, Eddie. But is there anything that the Governor mentioned that could implicate Lamont and Mercier, anything that would be difficult for you to make up? Why don't you recount the story from the point that you started teasing him with the whip?"

Eddie sighed as he closed his eyes. He took in a deep breath and exhaled. "I asked him how naughty he was. He told me that he was abusing tax dollars to pay for the hotel room, his wife didn't know about him being gay." Stop, breathe deeply, and think some more.

"Okay, now what else?" Jordyn asked.

"I came clean to him, told him who I was, and why I was really there. He jumped on top of me. Like, I mean, I thought that he was going to rape me, but he didn't."

"Go on."

"That's when we started drinking. He got drunk real quick and told me that he wanted to confess stuff to me."

Corey sighed. "Shit, that don't tell us much."

"Will you shut up?" said Jordyn without changing her tone of voice. "You're not helping him."

Corey turned to Eddie. "You thought that you were going to be raped tonight? Think about what's waiting for us in prison."

"Goddammit," Jordyn screamed. Now, she lost her cool.

Corey sighed. "We ain't going to last long. I guess the police are going to catch up with us soon. Survival of the fittest. That's what they always say."

Eddie looked up at Corey and then two fingers went to his lips. *Survival of the fittest? Wait a minute, yes, of course.* "He *did* say something else. He told me that I could find it all in Darwin's grave."

"Darwin's grave?" Corey looked back at him. "Who's Darwin?"

"I don't know. But that's what he said."

Jordyn switched lanes to overtake a salt dispensing truck. "I mean, it's a start. It would help us to know who Darwin is."

"But who else would know about Darwin? Does he have a last name?" asked Corey.

"Not that Bevins mentioned," Eddie answered.

"That narrows it down to either a place or a person," said Corey.

It wasn't much, but it was a clue.

Chapter 12

They drove for another forty minutes before they arrived in the south-western borough of LaSalle, which was twenty minutes from downtown Montreal. Eddie looked up and down the street before stepping out the car. There was no wind, but even with his hands in his pockets, he opened and closed them quickly to prevent the frost from getting to them.

The last time he'd checked the digital clock in the ca, it was after two in the morning. Practically all the lights were out in the surrounding houses. Yup, it should be safe to walk outside. He followed Corey and Jordyn as their shoes crunched through the thin layer of snow up an outdoor staircase to the top floor of the duplex where she took out a set of keys and let them in.

Eddie closed the door behind him, undid his jacket, and turned to Jordyn. "Does Donalda have a boyfriend?"

"No, she doesn't, and I'll tell you right away that she's not into guys, if you catch my drift," Jordyn answered.

"That's great," said Eddie. "Maybe she has some men's clothes that I could borrow." Anything to get out of this leather outfit. He was sure that he had a rash up his butt crack by now.

"Her clothes are too small for you."

"Corey and I can't be seen wearing *these* clothes. We'll be picked out of a crowd," Eddie snapped his fingers. "Just like that." The news reports detailed everything that they were both last seen wearing when they were spotted at the hotel.

"Shh," said Jordyn. "We don't need to wake up the people downstairs."

She was right. It was best to keep the footsteps to a minimum also. But the Darwin enigma still bothered him. He sat down on the couch beside Corey and seconds later, a grey, furry creature jumped up onto his lap. It sniffed at his belt and moved upwards. It must be the leather. Eddie stroked the cat a few times before he looked for Jordyn, but she was already in the kitchen. Don't tell me that she was looking for something to eat again.

Corey reached for the remote and turned on the television, lowering the volume once it was on. To no surprise, they were still in the news. He turned to Eddie. "There's your moment of fame."

Eddie sighed. "Yours too."

He stroked the cat, which then kicked back and relaxed on his lap. He listened to what was being said on the news. Same ol' same ol' for a few minutes until, unexpectedly, the scene switched to the view of a house in the country, and the media circus that surrounded it. There was also a large crowd that gathered in front of the house, and most appeared to be holding candles.

He turned to Corey. "Turn it up a bit." Corey pressed the volume button. It turned out that townspeople had gathered in front of the Governor's country cottage in the Eastern Townships, which was east of Montreal. Obviously, it was a replay from events that took place earlier in the evening. His wife was inside and refusing to come out and make a statement. So far, the big question that everyone was asking was, what was Tony Bevins doing in a five star hotel suite in the first place?

As expected, theories had already inundated the airwaves. All of these so-called experts were being interviewed. Shit, there they go, taking advantage of Eddie's spotlight. The next thing he'd be hearing in the near future would be about these guys signing six-figure book deals. It never ends. The tabloids would have their fun with this story too, no doubt. Poor Missus Bevins would have to suffer through this. Imagine learning this way that her husband was cheating on her, if she hadn't already known. Suddenly the cat jumped off his lap and ran down the hall towards the kitchen.

Eddie looked at Corey and nodded to the television. "Do you think she knows who Darwin is?"

Corey shrugged his shoulders without answering. A moment

went by and he looked at Eddie suspiciously. "Why do you ask?"

Eddie knew what had to be done. And it would take some major cajoling to get these two to go along with him. When he looked at his best friend, he saw by Corey's facial expression that he'd guessed what he was thinking.

"No," Corey shook his head. "No, don't even think of it."

"And you have a better idea?"

"I know that we ain't going to do what you're thinking of doing."

"We're being hunted by the same men who killed her husband."

"And you think that you can just go to his cottage, knock on the door, and that his wife's going to help us?" said Corey.

"It's worth a shot," answered Eddie.

"You think she's going to want to talk to you?"

"I think that there's a chance that she'll listen to us. If she does, then she'd be able to help us clear our names."

"Will you listen to yourself?" Corey stood and looked down at Eddie. "You're wanted for killing her husband."

"And what do you suggest that we do?" said Eddie. "Keep running and hiding?"

"We just need to keep low until we think of something else."

Eddie gestured with an index finger pointed to his temple. "Did you stop to think that her husband's killers may go after her too?"

"They're already after us," Corey answered. "We have to keep low."

"Okay, we can keep low. How long are we going to do that?"

"As long as it takes."

"So you're saying that we should just keep moving from one place to the next? Who do you think you are, Bin Laden?"

There was the flush of the toilet down the hall and a crimson-faced Jordyn stormed into the living room, stopping short of, what appeared like, striking them. "For God's sake. How many times do I have to tell you guys to keep it down? You're going to wake up the people downstairs. Do you want them coming up here?"

"Tell that to him," said Corey as he pointed his thumb to Eddie. "He wants to meet the Governor's wife."

The shock was visible all over Jodyn's face. "Now, I know you're crazy?"

"You're right. I was crazy enough to attempt this publicity stunt. Look at us now. We're in deeper shit than we could ever be our whole lives. If we're going to come out in the open and expose a killer among the police, we're going to need proof. If you guys don't want to go with me, fine. I'll go and see her on my own." Eddie turned away from them and watched the television.

Corey disappeared around the corner and walked down towards the kitchen. Jordyn walked quickly after him. There was an exchange of words. Although it was all whispers, Eddie knew that they were arguing. Obviously, it was about him. He grabbed the remote and flipped through the channels, only to see the same damn thing on all of the major stations. He hit the power button and the images shrank to a small white square in the center of the screen.

Screw this.

He got up and went to the bathroom, closing the door behind him. He didn't have to relieve himself. He lowered the toilet seat and sat down. Eddie looked around the bathroom and noticed the perfume-scented soap in the tray by the sink, the walls and countertop painted the same color. There were even two small framed pictures on the wall—the ones with babies sitting among toilet paper that have become popular in the last few years. And to think that he and Corey never thought of decorating their bathroom at home, if only they could both afford to. Everyone else was living better than he was.

Resting his elbows on his knees, he let his head drop down into his hands. It was an odd place to reflect on things, but some of the best ideas for his book—as well as solutions to plot holes—came while he was using the john. It reminded him of the movie *Back to the Future* that he saw a few weeks before, for about the fifth time. Doc Brown discovered the Flux Capacitor after he slipped off the toilet seat while attempting to hang a clock. What kind of genius hangs a clock in the bathroom anyways? And wasn't it some Greek philosopher...what's his name...Achilles...naw...Archie something...that discovered buoyancy while taking a bath? Then again, who the hell was he kidding? Eddie was no genius.

What was it that he read once in another author's online blog?

It had something to do with assassins surviving by thinking like the opposition...okay...

The Governor's killers framed him. They suspected that someone else was in the room with Bevins, but they were interrupted at the last second. Someone had alerted them—that's why they left in a hurry.

It also kept bugging him that Theo would tell him that he was meeting a woman and not a guy. How could he have been so stupid? He was in his early thirties with over ten-year's experience. Hell no, he couldn't have made such a careless mistake. That, he was sure of. Theo had to have known more than what he was letting on. Sure, they didn't get along...but to put him in a position where he could've been killed? Even Theo couldn't have been that wicked. Or...was there someone else pulling his strings? The lipstick smudge on the wine glass that Eddie and Jordyn had noticed while they were over there. A client? No way. Theo wouldn't be entertaining someone while his leg was in a cast. And from what Eddie knew, Theo wasn't currently involved with anyone. Maybe it was just a fuck friend of his.

He stood up from the toilet and left the bathroom just as Jordyn and Corey were walking back towards the living room. Eddie sat back down facing the television. Jordyn and Corey stopped a few feet away.

"We'll go along with your idea," Jordyn said. "We don't like it, but we figured that we don't have any other options left."

"That's cool. But first we're going to go talk to Theo."

Corey sighed, dropping his arms to his side. "You just keep on getting brighter ideas, don't you?"

"Trust me, I'm sure he was playing us when Jordyn and I met him the other night."

"Even if he was playing us," asked Jordyn, "do you think that he'll just come out and admit it to us?"

"He'll talk, *that* I can guarantee. 'Cause I'll go Uma Thurman on his bitch-ass if I have to."

Chapter 13

Edward left the bedroom and walked down the stairs from the second floor, dressed in his McGill University jogging clothes. The cold shower helped to wake him up after having overslept, and the atmosphere was calmer since some of the media vultures had dispersed. The smell of fried bacon and plantain circulated through the stairway, and he suddenly felt the rumbling of his growling stomach. Normally at this time, the family would have already been sitting in church. Both he and Monica would be warming up with the choir in the choir room. And he would've held back at least three cusses against those who were tone deaf. But he wouldn't be leaving the house this morning, and he forbade anyone else to do so unless the house was on fire.

When he walked into the kitchen, Monica was pouring an omelet mixture onto a scalding frying pan while Beverly and Denise set the table.

Beverly glanced up at Edward. "You're finally up?"

Edward ignored her, rubbed his right eye instead, and looked around. "Where's the paper?"

"Good morning to you too," said Monica. "We're not reading anything at the table. The same thing goes for the TV. We're just going to enjoy a nice breakfast."

We'll see about that.

Denise left the table and brought back a plate that was piled high with toast. "Here, Daddy, sit down and relax."

All of this pampering for me? What were these women up to? He walked out of the kitchen into the living room. He found the remote where he'd left it on the center table. He picked it up, aimed it to the television, and pressed the power button. Nothing happened. He pressed it again a few more times, and still the television wouldn't turn on. And why did the remote feel so light? He flipped it over and opened up the battery cover—it was empty. *Lord have mercy! Monica gone trouble the remote.* He sighed as he slammed it back onto the table—almost hard enough to put a crack in it—and turned towards the kitchen. The three women ignored him.

He walked to the television and pressed the power button to turn it on. The first thing that he heard was the sound of static. A few seconds later, all that he saw on the screen was snow. *They gone trouble the TV.*

He went to the front door to check for the newspaper. It would be a quick snatch, fast enough to grab the paper and too quickly for the vultures outside to snap his picture. He unlocked the door, psyched himself up a bit, then yanked it open and looked down on the porch.

Nothing there.

He slammed the door just as he heard one of the vultures screaming, "There he is." He took a deep breath and let it out loudly as he gritted his teeth, doing his best not to scream out the obscenities that had piled up behind them. That's when he saw Monica in front of him. She appeared to be forcing a smile.

"If you're thinking of turning on the radio or going online to check the news, you'll be wasting your time."

"You think that—"

Monica raised a hand, while keeping the smile. "We're going to sit down at the table as a family. And there won't be any more discussion. We'll talk some more about this once we're done. Do you understand me?"

It was pointless. How was he going to overpower these women? His family was already divided enough as it was. His son—Lord knew where he was at this moment—was already a case on his own. So why make the situation worse? He balled up a fist and slammed it sideways on the wall. There, that felt better. He then walked towards Monica, who put an arm around his waist as she walked with him to the kitchen. He knew that Monica was keeping something from him. Maybe it was something new on the news that would upset him. For now, he'll play along with her little scheme. He'll find out what it was soon. He always did.

Chapter 14

Dorval, Quebec.

I t was close to nine o'clock in the morning when they arrived at Theo's house in Dorval, thirty kilometers west of downtown. The other evening when Jordyn brought Eddie over, he could hardly see the house from the street since it was tucked behind the backyard of another house. It was only accessible by the long driveway that could've been mistaken for an alley. Some strange idea for a developer—having all of the other houses built close to the road while stashing one away out of sight.

Eddie figured that since it was early Sunday morning, most people would still be in bed sleeping. With the bone-chilling frost that kept his hands deep in his pockets and his collar turned up, no one would be crazy enough to be outside. Besides, most of the residents in this part of town didn't even shovel their own driveways. They hired contractors to do the job for them. So far he hasn't seen any.

Eddie closed his door, just as he looked up, at the sounds of the roaring turbines of a commercial jet that flew overhead. The residents must be used to planes taking off and landing at Trudeau International Airport, that was less than two kilometers away. Eddie spotted Theo's black BMW at the back of the driveway under a thin layer of snow, parked with the front facing the road. After having walked the twenty-five meter stretch of the driveway, Jordyn, followed by Corey and Eddie, walked up the ice-covered wooden steps to the front patio and rang the doorbell twice in rapid succession. The pockets weren't enough to keep his hands warm so Eddie crossed his arms tightly, covering his hands as he shook his arms and shoulders. When he looked at Corey, he saw that he did the same. *Dammit, could Theo take any longer to answer the damn door?*

Jordyn rang the doorbell again—three times—as she put her mitten-covered hands to her mouth to breathe warm air on them. Contrary to popular belief, wearing either mittens or gloves in the winter did nothing when the temperature dipped below ten degrees Celsius. Exposure to temperatures that dipped below that, especially if there was a wind-chill, was an excellent way of losing your fingers to frostbite unless you kept moving them to keep up the blood flow.

Eddie moved past Corey. *This is ridiculous.* "Move aside. I'm going to break this door down."

Jordyn shoved a palm into his chest. "Hold on. He's in a cast, remember. He's not going to be rushing to answer the door."

"I don't care, now move."

Corey grabbed Eddie from behind as Jordyn was pushed back slightly. She unintentionally grabbed the door handle and the door gave way, causing all three of them to tumble inside on top of each other in a flurry of white dust—Jordyn being underneath Eddie, who was under Corey.

"Uggh, you see what you did?" said Jordyn.

"How was I supposed to know the door was unlocked?" said Eddie. "And I swear to God, Corey that better be your cell phone I'm feeling on my ass."

"Man, shut up. And get your face out of my girl's breasts," said Corey as he slapped Eddie on the back of his head.

Ouch! Eddie's hand went to the back of his head.

"You guys better not start now." Jordyn stood up. "Will one of you get the door?"

Corey shut the door as he turned to Eddie and Jordyn. "Why's his door unlocked?"

"I was just thinking the same thing," said Eddie as he looked around. They were in the living room. There wasn't any carpet, just hardwood floors. The flat screen wall-mounted television was on, showing one of those boring infomercials about some kitchen gadget that always appeared to work well on television until you bought it and actually used it.

Jordyn walked past the living room into another hall and looked both ways. "Theo, you up? You left your door unlocked."

No answer.

Eddie joined her, followed by Corey. "Do you think he stepped out?"

"I doubt it. He's always careful of locking the door before leaving the house," Jordyn answered. "Theo!"

This wasn't that big a house. There was only the main floor and a basement. You'd only expect two, maybe three people at most to live here. And what was that noise? It sounded like running water. Eddie followed the sound to the kitchen. He walked up to the sink and saw water splashing off a grease-stained plate with a few bones beside it. On the counter was a three-quarter-filled glass of orange juice. From what Eddie observed, after the last time he came here with Jordyn, Theo kept his home a lot tidier than this. Who'd leave the house after having left the tap on and an unfinished glass of juice? He grabbed the faucet and twisted it, shutting off the water when he heard Corey yell.

"Oh my God!"

"What is it?" Jordyn's voice came seconds before Eddie heard her scream.

He ran out of the kitchen, lost his traction on the ground and rebounded off the wall, just as he saw Corey holding Jordyn. Her head was buried in his chest as they stood in front of the door that led to the basement stairs. Eddie suddenly felt a pain in the middle of his chest and his throat tightened. Seeing how Corey refused to look down the stairs as he moved Jordyn away from the doorway, Eddie felt his legs get heavy underneath him. Somehow he managed to drag them forward.

"You don't want to look down there," said Corey. But Eddie ignored him. It only made him want to see what was down there, no matter how bad. The five steps that it took him to get to the doorway felt like ten. It took a moment for him to see Theo's limp body at the bottom of the staircase, and only a fraction of a second for Eddie to notice that Theo's head was twisted around more than humanly possible. He shrieked as he spun around into the wall.

He fell to the floor, landing on his ass. Furiously he pushed hard with his hands and legs against the floor to move away from the doorway as fast as he could. He stopped when he made it back to the living room. He turned around, breathing hard, as he got on his knees in front of one of the couches, and buried his head into it.

It was like the whole world was collapsing in on itself—one huge black hole growing in size as everything around it was sucked right into it. Although Eddie tried to hang on to whatever solid object that he could grab, he felt himself slipping away. He hit a hard surface, his hands covering his face, as he felt the air around him getting thinner. He could no longer breathe normally.

It was then that he heard the crying. The louder it got the more it appeared to pull Eddie out of his quagmire. A white ceiling was all that was in his field of view. He then heard Corey trying to hush Jordyn the best that he could as she kept repeating the words, "Oh my God."

But who could blame her. Theo—although he was an asshole—still had a history with her. And coincidentally he happened to accidentally fall down the stairs, what could've been several hours after some crooked detective popped two rounds into the head of a sex-crazed Governor he was originally supposed to meet.

Wait a minute. *Accidentally* falling down the stairs?

First, there was the running water. Theo was washing the dishes, what could be so important that he had to hop on one leg and get something from the basement. Wouldn't Theo have turned the tap off first?

Holy shit, they were in the middle of a crime scene!

"We have to get out of here," said Eddie as he sprung to his feet.

Corey looked up at him as he cradled Jordyn. "Bro, please."

"I ain't horsing around. We have to get out of here. I know this is hard, but just trust me on this one." He reached over to grab Jordyn's arm. "Come on, let me help you."

Corey helped Eddie lift Jordyn onto her feet, and they walked to the front door. She was still sobbing.

"Try not to touch anything," said Eddie. "When we're outside, we're going to walk—not run—and keep our heads down."

They made it back to the car, and helped Jordyn into the backseat. As Corey got in behind the wheel, he fired up the engine. Eddie held his door open and he spotted a neighbor's curb-side mailbox. There was a bag that hung below it, one specially designed to hold newspapers. He ran to it and removed a Montreal Gazette from the newspaper bag, then ran back to the car. When Eddie got in he removed the elastic band, and flipped open the front page. "Oh, Lord."

"Let me guess," said Corey as he drove off. "Both of our pictures are on the front page, right?"

"Jordyn's too," Eddie answered.

"What?" Jordyn's sobbing was interrupted. She leaned forward between the front car seats and popped her head around Eddie's shoulder. She wiped the tears from her face. "What do they want me for?"

Eddie read the first few lines of the article until he came to Jordyn's name. "They don't want you, they want me and Corey. They're saying that we've kidnapped you."

Jordyn snatched the paper from Eddie's hands. "What the fuck? Can they do that?"

Corey glanced at them. "Of course. It's more sensational."

"Not to mention a police tactic," said Eddie. "They've identified you as being Italian. They didn't mention anything about your Jamaican background." Eddie raised a hand and let it drop on his leg with a slap. "Two black guys kidnapping an Italian girl. That should grab more people's attention."

"What are you thinking now?" Corey turned to Eddie.

"I think that someone killed Theo. Whoever did it, wanted to shut him up. So they pushed him down the stairs, making it look like he had an accident."

"Why can't you believe that it was just an accident?" Corey asked.

"Come on. Who leaves the front door unlocked and running water in the kitchen? Trust me, someone killed him."

Corey got to the end of the road where he stopped for a woman and her husky. The woman didn't look at them, as the husky appeared to be pulling her. Once they crossed, Corey turned onto the intersecting road. "What about MO? You know, they're always talking about that on those TV crime shows."

"What about it?" said Eddie.

"You said that the police shot the Governor. Why would they make this one look like an accident?"

"I don't know. I don't even care right now."

"So what do we do now?" asked Corey.

Eddie checked the fuel gauge. They were down to half tank. It might just be enough to get them out to the Eastern Townships. "We have to go see Missus Bevins." He looked over his shoulder at Jordyn. "How much cash do you have left on you?"

Jordyn looked inside her purse. "About two-hundred-and-ten."

That's more than enough. They wouldn't have to stop at any ATM machines. The police would have alerted all of the banks to be on the lookout for Jordyn's bank or credit card if it were used, and to call them immediately. Eddie took back the paper from Jordyn, glanced at it one more time, then rolled it back up, putting the elastic back around it. First it was murder. Now he and Corey were also wanted for kidnapping.

Corey glanced over at Eddie. "Do you know what we'll do next if Missus Bevins doesn't help us?"

"Yeah, try and survive long enough not to wind up like Theo."

Chapter 15

Monica couldn't do much to calm down her daughter or her sister. The three of them squabbled as to how they would break the news to Edward—who was in the bathroom. She knew that the moment that he heard about the kidnapping accusation, he'd go ballistic—which wouldn't do him any good considering his high blood pressure. And once that happened, God help them all.

"I told you that you should've spiked his coffee," said Beverly.

Monica turned to her. "Are you crazy? He has high blood pressure. You trying to kill him?"

"He's handled it pretty well so far," said Denise. "You realize that he slept with the bottle last night."

Beverly shook her head. "You should've let me handle mixing a cocktail and putting it in his coffee. That would've put he down *real* good."

Monica shook her fists. "We're not going to get my husband drunk, so stop bringing that up. It'll probably just make things worse."

Beverly pointed a finger at her sister. "I'll like to see how you handle him when he finds out that Eddie kidnapped some girl."

"Kidnapping? Who kidnapped who?"

Oh, Lord have mercy!

They all turned to see Edward nearing the bottom of the stairs. While the others fell silent and cowered behind her, Monica felt that she was the best person to speak to him. After all, she was the one that got up from a sleepless night to find Edward sleeping on the sofa that morning. It was a spur of the moment thing, but when she collected the newspaper at her doorstep and saw the front page headline along with the photographs of her son and his friends, she knew she had to act quickly to make sure Edward didn't see it. That's when she removed the batteries from the television remote as well as the cables from the satellite television terminal. She then woke up Beverly and Denise to help her remove all other forms of communication. The internet, the radio, the telephone—they all had to go. She even hid the car keys, in the event that Edward was brave enough to go out to listen to the radio in the car.

Maybe she should've listened to Bev about spiking the coffee— just a little. Had she done so, her husband might have been easier to talk to. "We were just talking about what we're going to do next."

"I have an idea. Give me back my newspaper and plug the TV back in, so that I can see where my son is at."

"He's *my* son too," Monica yelled pointing a finger at her chest. Edward was startled as he froze in his tracks. He appeared to be surprised at hearing her raise her voice like that, something that she normally didn't do. Keep it calm, this was no time for an argument. She turned to Denise. "Will you go get the cables and hook the satellite back up?"

Denise nodded and headed towards the basement stairs.

"I'll go get the paper," said Beverly.

She didn't think that that would be necessary, but at least it gave her a chance to be alone with her husband. "Come."

Edward then followed her to the dining room where they sat beside each other at the table. A lot of great moments happened around this table. It served as a buffet table for all of the get-togethers that they hosted. Then there were the birthday parties that they held for their children. Easter, Thanksgiving, and Christmas dinners were always held here as well. Those were the most festive times—until last week when Eddie came by. Lord, she didn't want to even think about it. But since then, there hasn't been a cheerful moment in this house.

She placed her hand on her husband's arm, and tried to make him uncross them. He finally gave in. "Before you blame Bev and Denise, I want you to know that it was my idea to disconnect the

TV and the internet, and hide everything else from you."

Denise came back upstairs with the cables and went to the television set in the living room. Edward did not say anything, as though he was forcing himself to remain as calm as he could.

"I'm not going to wait for Denise to hook back up the TV or Bev to show you the paper, so I'm just going to tell you myself what's been going on. Can you promise me not to fly off the handle?"

Edward nodded, but did so with a suspicious look on his face— as though he was bracing for an impact.

"I'm sure that the press has it wrong. But according to them, the police are now accusing Junior and Corey of kidnapping Jordyn." She continued to stare into his face. Monica failed to see a reaction. She waited a few seconds, yet still, there wasn't any change in his facial expression. Did he even hear her? "Are you okay?"

That's when she heard a chuckle. It then grew slowly into a laugh. His protruding stomach jiggled as it vibrated the table. His head then fell back as he stared up at the ceiling. "Oh Lord Jesus!" He then looked back at her. "Kidnapped? As in he helped Corey forcefully coerce his girlfriend into joining them? *This* is what you, Bev, and Denise went out of your way this morning to keep from me? I cannot believe what I'm hearing."

Monica couldn't break a smile. "I know how outrageous this may sound to you. But with these kind of accusations—whether they are true or not—they make Eddie look more guilty than he did before."

Edward pulled his hand from underneath hers, rested his elbows on the table, and let his head fall into his hands. He let out a huge sigh as he rubbed his forehead. Monica put her hand on Edward's back and rubbed it to keep him calm. As big a man as he was, he could've never gotten through this alone. Every tragedy that ever happened—she was the one that took care of everything that he was in no shape to handle. When Edward's father passed away three years before, she was the one that went to the travel agency and booked their plane tickets—putting everything on her credit card. She was the one who then packed their bags and saw to it that they had a taxi to take them to the airport. This was the exact same spot where they sat after they got the news. He needed her now, and she had to give him the assistance that he needed.

Beverly appeared, but stopped when she saw them. Monica looked up at her elder sister. She too had been there for both of them through their worse times. There was the time when Monica gave birth to Denise. Around the same time Edward had purchased a building for his pharmacy. Things went well at first, until the other businesses that he had leased office space to, started having financial problems and went bankrupt. It was a huge financial strain on both of them since it took weeks to find other business tenants.

Then Junior came along—unexpectedly—and their debts skyrocketed. That's when Beverly stepped in and offered to take both children off of their hands until they were able to get back onto their feet. The children spent an entire year with her in Barbados and she never asked for anything in return. Maybe it wasn't a coincidence that she was in town at this time. As in the saying, *everything happens for a reason.*

Beverly sat down on the opposite side of the table and put the newspaper to the side. "I don't like to cut in. But it's high time that I spoke to both of you. What you choose to do afterwards is up to you."

"We're listening," said Monica. Edward looked up.

"You cannot go back and change the past—what's done is done," said Beverly. "But I'd like both of you to think about what you could've done differently, if you had a chance to go back in time."

"In terms of what?" asked Edward.

"About what you could've done differently last year, before Junior moved out?"

"What do you mean, different?" Edward glared at Beverly. "I can't control what that boy wants to do with his life. He wanted to move out, so I didn't stop him."

"But why do you think he moved out, whereas Denise stayed?"

"Because he's stubborn."

"Is that all? It's because he's stubborn? Why do you think that he's stubborn?"

"I don't know where he gets it from?" Edward sat back in the chair and crossed his arms. "He just wants to have things his way.

I was tired of arguing with him. He'll just have to learn the hard way, and when he does, he'll grow up and he'll see that I was right the whole time."

Beverly put one hand on the table and tapped a finger on it a few times. "Listen to yourself. Is this really about Junior having what he wants, or is this more about both of you having what you both want?"

Monica raised an eyebrow. "What *we* both want?"

"Yes," said Beverly. "You heard right."

Monica's mouth dropped open slightly as she tried to recover from her sister's comments.

"When I visited last year, just before Junior moved out, I remember seeing that boy at the computer. I couldn't imagine him having to do so much homework while he was on break. It turned out that he was writing his book. Sometimes I'd get up in the middle of the night to get a glass of water, and I'd still see him on the computer."

At that moment, Denise walked by and headed for the stairs when Beverly looked in her direction. "Come sit with us. This involves you too."

Denise walked in and took a seat next to her aunt.

"Did any of you ever ask Junior if you could read his manuscript, at least the first chapter?" Beverly looked at Denise, who quietly shook her head. She then looked to the opposite side of the table to her sister and brother-in-law. Monica looked down at the table while Edward looked to the side. She took that to mean that they didn't.

"I asked him if I could take a look at what he wrote. He was happy to let me read the first chapter, but nothing else. 'Cause Junior's very secretive about his work. I'll admit that I thought that it wasn't too bad for a first draft."

"So are you telling us that our mistake was not asking Junior to read his book?" asked Monica.

"You could've all started out by showing some interest in what he was doing."

"But we were," said Monica. "We didn't stop him from choosing his hobbies anymore than with Denise. But Junior's grades were sliding constantly and we felt that the best thing for him was to keep pushing him with his school work."

"And do you think that he was happy with his major? Do you think he took that major because *he* wanted to or was it because you put a lot of pressure on him to it?" Beverly waited for an answer, but she didn't get one. "That's what you need to know. I can tell you from my experience as a teacher, after seeing the way parents are constantly after their children to become *this* or to become *that* when they grow up, it makes me sick. It's no surprise that those are the children that I end up giving the most attention to...because if I didn't, they all would've dropped out of school."

She turned to Edward. "Up until last Thursday when Junior was over here, you were *still* getting on his case about how he was wasting his life trying to become a writer. How do you know that he won't succeed as one?"

"Has he ever had anything published the real way?" Edward asked, nodding his head. "Has he ever tried writing essays or research papers that could be published in newspapers, periodicals, or journals?"

"No, he hasn't."

"Then I rest my case," Edward concluded.

"One question," asked Beverly, "have you ever suggested that he do so?"

"What for?" Edward asked.

"You've just said something that *I* never thought of. You must be convinced that if Junior took his first steps, by writing articles or essays, then maybe he would've been off to a better start. Am I right?"

Edward smirked and shook his head.

"Don't you laugh at me," said Beverly as she stared him down with a pointed finger. "Because that's exactly what you did to Junior the other night that got him so upset. Don't you realize that by not showing any interest in what *he* likes, while pushing what *you* want him to do, that you were only pushing him away from you?"

"Listen," Edward said with a finger pointed upwards in front of him. "I see so many youngsters putting all of their eggs in one basket, like all of those athletes. And they don't even know their basic times-tables in math. Where are the parents? They don't seem to care about whether their children are passing or failing in their grades, because they're too busy watching TV all day long while they wait for their welfare checks to arrive."

"You're over-generalizing and you know it," said Beverly, "because many of my students got accepted to some of the best universities in England, the US, and even up here. And they were able to excel in both in academics and in athletics. In fact, some of them got athletic scholarships to American universities and still graduated with top honors. And what's even more interesting to know is that their parents encouraged them to do what they enjoyed as long as they kept up with their school work."

Edward didn't seem to care for what she was saying as he refused to look at her. Beverly looked at her sister, who appeared to be paying more attention. "Your husband was wondering where Junior gets his stubbornness from. I can tell you that it mostly comes from him."

That got Edward's attention, he finally looked at her, as though to say, *How dare you?*

"Yes, I'm talking to you." Beverly continued. "You ought to know by now, because I'm sure you were just like Junior when you were growing up."

That's when Monica chuckled. Beverly turned to her without saying anything. She wanted to see if Edward would say something first. He looked at his wife with a surprised look, as though he were caught unawares.

"No he wasn't," said Monica.

"You got that right," asked Edward.

Monica shook her head. "You probably wished that you were like Junior, but you weren't."

Edward turned to her. "What are you talking about?"

"You don't remember that day in Mister Abbot's class, back in high school. That was the day when we had to write short stories for English class?"

"What does that have to do with anything?"

"I think it has quite a bit. It was the day when we had to each read our short stories in front of the class." Monica then looked at her husband. "Do you remember what Mister Abbot told you when you finished reading yours?"

"Jesus Christ. What does that have to do with Junior?"

"Answer the question," said Beverly. "I want to hear this."

"Go ahead and say it, or else I'm going to tell them," said Monica.

Beverly watched Edward as he rolled his eyes to the ceiling and breathed loudly. Edward had held onto an embarrassing secret for decades that he thought would never be known. He remained silent, but she knew with all of them staring at him, he would eventually give in.

"That bastard of a teacher humiliated me in front of the whole class," said Edward. "I was glad to not have him ever again as a teacher."

Denise joined the conversation after being on the sidelines. "But what did he say to you?"

Edward sighed and closed his eyes. He then opened them and put both hands on the table. "I spent a whole week writing that story. I stayed inside after school and on the weekend while my friends were outside playing or went to the beach. The day that I read it in front the class, he didn't even give me a chance to read to the end. He rudely cut me off and said that even in fiction, there's a certain level of realism. And he said that my story was far too ridiculous to even earn an F, and that I would be better off *not* majoring in journalism or any writing field. There, are you happy?"

Silence.

Beverly crossed her arms with a hand over her mouth as she looked down at the table. She then broke the silence as she looked up at Edward. "I think that both you and your son share a lot more in common than you were willing to accept."

"I can't believe that I didn't spot this earlier," said Monica as she shook her head.

Beverly then leaned towards Edward. "I'm not going to ask how you felt after what that teacher did to you. But you didn't continue writing, did you? No, you moved on to something else. You were lucky to discover an area of study that you enjoy. Well guess what. Junior's become you, and you've become Mister Abbot. The only difference is that Junior defied you and kept on writing, whereas you quit."

Denise shook her head. "My God, no wonder he's always defending Corey."

Beverly stood up and pushed her chair back into the table. "This brings us to now. I don't know what Junior's gotten himself involved with, but now I have a very good idea how it started." She tapped Denise on the shoulder. "Come, your parents have a lot to talk about, on what they need to do next in order to encourage your brother to come home. Hopefully before he gets himself hurt."

Denise got up and joined her aunt. She picked up the other cables that she had left by the top of the stairs, so that both she and Beverly could reconnect the other televisions and the internet around the house.

Denise ran upstairs first, while Beverly stopped at the foot of the staircase and looked back. She saw Monica and Edward talking quietly to each other. At least she got things started for them. She walked up the stairs.

Chapter 16

There was little conversation between Eddie, Corey, and Jordyn as the trio travelled on Highway 10 through the flat terrain of the Eastern Townships which slowly transformed into the mountainous Appalachian region. Eddie looked at the car's clock and saw that it was almost midday. Lord, he was hungry. Donalda didn't leave much of anything to eat. Then again, why would she? They had practically eaten all of the granola bars and crackers that they were able to salvage from Donalda's kitchen.

It wasn't like either Eddie or Corey could simply pull up to a drive-thru or go to any restaurant. And up to this morning, Jordyn would've been able to do so. She still could...but not without attracting the kind of attention they all wished to avoid.

Corey suggested that since it was less than three hours since Jordyn's picture was published in the papers—and no doubt, shown on television—there was less of a chance that a large number of people would recognize her in public. They were now somewhere near Sherbrooke, having just left a pharmacy where Jordyn bought a few items for herself. They had also stopped at another store where she bought an inexpensive, but decent pair of gloves for both Eddie and Corey.

At the present time, both he and Corey sat in the car as they waited for Jordyn, who had gone to the restroom at a gas station. For both Eddie and Corey, it was a relief to be in a car that had better heating than the one Eddie drove. They would've been freezing by now in Eddie's old car, considering its lack of proper insulation.

"Do you still think about Vanessa?" Corey asked.

What the hell was this about? Why talk about my ex-girlfriend right now? "Why are you bringing she up for?"

"I was just wondering."

"She's the last person I want to be thinking of right now. For all I know she's doing everything she can to remove any proof that she ever knew me."

"Naw, don't say that."

"You don't think so? Of all of the people that called your phone or Jordyn's, was she one of them? No."

"Okay, I'm sorry."

"Forget about it," said Eddie as he watched a snowplough roar by on the two-lane road a few feet away. "You're lucky to have Jordyn. She could've abandoned us, yet she chose to stick around to help."

"She's deep in this as much as we are. She might as well help us."

"I don't mean that."

Corey looked at Eddie. "Then what?"

"She's always been there for you. More than you probably realize. She's put up with you more than anyone else would've."

Corey sighed as he turned away from Eddie. "Man, I don't need to hear this from you."

"You ain't got a choice. You've been fired from two jobs since last summer, and you've borrowed money from Jordyn that I doubt you've paid back yet. And, you've been drinking a lot lately. Yet she's still taking care of you."

"She's taking care of you too."

"I know she is. And if we get out of this, I plan to pay her back any way that I can. You should consider doing the same thing by getting your life together and stop being so down on yourself. She's the best thing that's happened to you. Don't screw it up."

Corey didn't answer. But when Eddie glanced past him, his jaw dropped. He knew that Corey saw him, since he too, was quick to look out his window, curious to know what Eddie was looking at. It was Jordyn. Her locks were gone and her hair was cut short to her ears. As the sun shone off it, traces of reddish highlights reflected.

She got in the backseat with some sandwiches and a few juice cartons. She shut the door and looked at them as they gawked. "What's the matter?"

Eddie looked at Corey, who, lost for words, returned the same look. He then turned back to Jordyn. "Nothing. We were...I mean...I was just wondering what kind of sandwich you brought me...I mean us."

Jordyn gestured to her wig. "Look, I know that it was a rush job, but come on."

"It ain't that," said Corey. "You just look...more...masculine."

"I was going to say, you look like a Romulan from Star Trek," Eddie added.

Eddie dodged Jordyn's hand, which wound up slapping Corey on the forehead. "Here, take your damn sandwiches." She tossed the two plastic-wrapped sandwiches up front, and they bounced off the dashboard. Both he and Corey tried to hold back a laugh, but were unsuccessful. Gosh, how long has it been since he laughed. Come to think of it, this was why he loved being around these two. But he felt that there was something else that was different about Jordyn. Not in the way that she expressed herself that time, but more as though she was not telling them something.

As Corey started up the car and took back to the road, Eddie turned to her. "You okay, Jordyn? I mean, putting aside the fact that both Corey and I are kidnapping you."

"I'm cool," she said while she stared out the window.

Bullshit! Who do think you're talking to? You can't look at me with a straight face and say so. It reminded him of the time that he came home from work just after he and Corey moved into their place. He'd said, "Hello, how are you?" to her while she was on the couch, watching TV. She hadn't even looked at him when she answered him, telling him that she was alright...she behaved the exact same way just now. Later on that day he had found out from Corey that her parent's house had been robbed and they were blaming her, for not turning on the alarm system—being that she had been the last one to leave. Two computers—one of them had her father's client list—were among the missing valuables. The animosity blew over eventually.

Come to think of it, it was sort of what he was going through right now with his parents. He didn't know whether he could forgive them for the way they treated him. God, they must be going through hell right now. All of the nosy people from church, and some of their neighbors, must be talking and pointing fingers at them, saying things like, "Those are the people that raised the murderer."

But hey, they brought it on themselves. He would've never thought of taking up Jordyn and Corey's idea had his parents chosen to support his dreams of being a writer. If they were going through the hell that he was going through right now, then too bad for them. His hell was worse. So they couldn't blame anyone but themselves for what they were going through.

They travelled east on Highway 10 for another twenty minutes through the Appalachian Mountains before they headed south on Highway 55 towards the town of Hatley. They already knew in advance that the Governor's country house was on the lake, which narrowed it down to Lake Massawippi—the only lake that was close to Hatley.

When they arrived in the town, they stopped at the first florist that they saw. Jordyn went inside to buy some flowers and asked for directions to the Governor's house, telling the owner that she lived a few minutes south of the Quebec-New Hampshire border, and wanted to pay her respects. Five minutes later she was back in the car with a floral variety, wrapped in see-through plastic, and tied with a red, white and blue ribbon. She gave the directions to Corey and they found the house in little time.

Eddie stared at the massive two-storey house. Its off-white exterior contrasted with the color of the snow that separated the house from the road by at least forty meters. There were two floors, but the house stretched wide. Eddie imagined there must have been at least five, if not six bedrooms inside. A gray SUV was parked on the side just where the driveway ended.

When he had looked at the Governor's website earlier that morning with Corey and Jordyn, there wasn't any mention of the Governor and Missus Bevins having any children. This house was almost three times the size of his parents' house. As to why they would need so much space when there were only two of them was beyond him. He could hear Aunt Beverly saying something like, "Them two people need so much house for what? Just so that they could keep scaring each other every minute?"

Corey stopped the car and Jordyn got out with the flowers. She walked up to Corey just as he lowered the window. "I'll try and do this as quickly as possible. Just stay put."

"I hope she warms up to you," said Corey. She smiled and then walked away.

Eddie wiped away the condensation on the window and stared out into a vacant snow-covered field that had nothing for miles. He bent forward to crack his lower back. Sitting in the car all this time took a toll on him. Sleeping on some cushions at Donalda's house the previous night didn't help either. Jordyn got to sleep on the bed while he and Corey flipped a coin for the living room couch. Eddie lost. He couldn't even convince Jordyn to let Corey share the bed with her. They've already done so several times, why would last night be any different. At least there were enough cushions to help him get through four uninterrupted hours of sleep.

Eddie turned to Corey. "What was up with her last night, making you sleep in the living room with me?"

"I don't know," Corey answered. "She's been a bit moody lately."

No shit. "You're on Canada's most wanted list, along with me... why wouldn't she be moody?"

"Naw, man. I'm talking about before this. Just a few days ago she's been...holding out on me."

"Holding out? You mean, like not letting you jump her bones."

"Yeah, you can say so."

"Welcome to the club."

"What club is that?"

"The *Masturbators* club."

"Shut up, I don't masturbate. I got a girl."

"Yeah, whatever." Eddie sighed.

Corey then looked out his window but it was all fogged up. He wiped it and leaned closer to it, as though he was searching for something. "Where's she going?"

Eddie leaned closer and saw Jordyn walking around the front of the house to the side and then disappearing around the back. There weren't any fences that surrounded the property and the nearest house was not even visible. "I don't know. It looks like Missus Bevins ain't answering the door."

"Or maybe she ain't home."

Oh hell no, this ain't going to happen. Eddie unbuckled his seatbelt and got out.

"Where are you going?" he heard Corey say to him from the car. But Eddie ignored him as he zipped his jacket and walked up the driveway. He heard a car door slam behind him, followed by running footsteps crunching through the snow.

"Hey, what are you doing? We're supposed to stay in the car."

"I'm tired of waiting," said Eddie.

"It's been barely like...two minutes." Eddie then felt Corey's hand grab his shoulder, making him stop. "Come back to the car, we can't risk screwing this up."

"Like hell. She's got to be home." Eddie then pointed at the vehicle. "Her SUV's here."

Corey let go of Eddie's shoulder. "Maybe she went for a walk."

"Or she's hiding inside." Eddie walked around the SUV and went to the back. "Yo, Missus Bevins. Are you home? We need to talk to you."

Corey ran up to him, nearly slipping on the icy asphalt. "Are you crazy? Keep it down. You want her to call the cops on us."

"I didn't travel all of this way for nothing."

Jordyn came running from around the back. "Jesus fucking Christ, Eddie! What the hell are you doing out here?"

"I want to get things moving. I've lost my patience."

"And you think this is the way to do it? Get your ass back in the car," said Jordyn through clenched teeth.

"Is there something that I can do for you?" A loud voice came from several feet away.

They didn't even hear the galloping of the horse as it approached with the woman on its back. She was dressed in full cowboy gear, complete with calf-length boots and Stetson. The white suede jacket gave her outfit the extra touch.

Jordyn immediately smiled as she walked up to her, holding up the flowers. "Missus Bevins?"

"Hello," she answered.

"We came here to personally give you our sympathies."

She stopped the horse and dismounted, a few feet from where Jordyn stood. She was slightly taller than Eddie—maybe because of the boots. She appeared to be in her early to mid-fifties, like his parents. She pulled the strap and brought the horse with her as she approached Jordyn, and she took the flowers with a smile. "Thank you, I appreciate it." She then stared at Corey and Eddie as though she were examining them. She stopped when she looked at Eddie.

Eddie felt his heart pounding. *Please don't let her recognize us. Not now.*

"That's an interesting choice of an outfit to be wearing in this weather," she said.

Okay, she didn't recognize us yet. "Oh, these aren't my clothes. We—"

"We came to pay our respects," said Jordyn.

"Thank you. That's very kind," Missus Bevins answered. She then walked off with her horse to a wooden fenced enclosure. "Is... is there anything else?"

Was that a hesitation in her voice? Shit, she's made us. Eddie was about to follow her, when Jordyn stepped ahead of him and turned, an outstretched palm indicating for him and Corey to stay put.

"There's...there's maybe something you can help us out with," said Jordyn. "I'm Shannon by the way."

"Nice to meet you, Shannon. What is it you need?"

Eddie watched Missus Bevins as she undid the strap from around the horse's neck. As the horse roamed free inside the enclosure, she closed the gate. There was also a small stable, not too far off, where Eddie assumed the horse slept.

"We had to see you before you went back to New Hampshire," said Jordyn.

"I wish that I could go. But the police want me to stay here for a few days, at least until they get further in their investigation."

Eddie found it odd that her husband's death didn't affect her as he had expected—unless she was good at hiding her emotions. Eddie watched, as Jordyn followed Missus Bevins to a neat stack of firewood that lined a section of the wall of the house. Above them were icicles—some as long as two feet—that hung from the shingles that made up the roof.

Eddie turned to Corey. "Do you think that she's made us yet?"

"Just keep still," Corey whispered back. "We don't want to startle her."

Something was wrong—Eddie sensed it. He'd blown it. He should've stayed in the car where there was less of a chance of her recognizing both him and Corey.

"We really need your help," said Jordyn. "We wouldn't have come all of this way, if we weren't certain that you can help us solve the misunderstanding that my friends and I have gotten involved with."

Missus Bevins stopped at the edge of the firewood and turned to face her. She appeared to be frustrated. "Go on. Just get it out in the open."

Holy shit, she's placed us. She's just holding back. He glanced at Corey, who responded with an expression that said, *what the hell are we supposed to do?*

"My name isn't Shannon," said Jordyn.

"I know," Missus Bevins said as she pulled an axe from behind the firewood. Jordyn quickly backed off, towards Eddie and Corey.

Shit, that's why she went there. Eddie raised his hands in surrender. "Whoa, we just came here to talk."

"Really," she said, letting the axe swing beside her like a pendulum as she approached them.

The three of them walked backwards, maintaining a buffer zone between them.

"Look, I know what you saw on TV and in the papers," said Eddie. "I didn't kill your husband."

"He's telling the truth," Corey said. "My friend was set up. He didn't do it."

"Is that so?" She kept walking towards them. The axe swung even more. "It wasn't enough for you to take advantage of my husband? You had to come and attack his widow?"

"It's not what you think," said Jordyn. "Whatever you read in the papers, don't believe it. They didn't kidnap me. I came with them on my own free will. We just want to be able to explain ourselves, if you just give us a chance."

Missus Bevins breathed heavily as she grabbed the handle with both hands. Eddie knew that she was ready to use it. The anger in her eyes illustrated enough of that fact.

"Get off of my property," she said.

Jordyn held both hands out in front of her, pleadingly. "Please, hear us out."

"Now!"

"Who's Darwin?" yelled Eddie. But it didn't appear that she heard him. Instead she let out a scream that resembled a war cry. as she rushed them, holding the axe the same way a baseball player would hold a bat.

Eddie didn't know whether her scream or the axe scared him more, but he hauled ass along with Corey and Jordyn. Shit, she could call the police on them at any time. In minutes they'd be swarming the town, if not the entire region.

They managed to outrun Missus Bevins as they made it back to the car. Corey quickly fired up the engine and they were gone. Eddie punched the dashboard as he watched the house fade off in the distance. "Fuck! We drove all the way here for nothing. Now what the fuck are we supposed to do?"

***

Missus Bevins rushed into the house through the front door, her Rottweiler waited anxiously for her behind a second door, and jumped up on her as she entered.

"Not now, Darwin," she said as she shooed him away. The nerve of those three coming to her house. Did they actually think that she wouldn't recognize them? And where was the phone? Suddenly it started ringing. It was on the coffee table in the living room, right where she had left it after having learned of her husband's murder. It rang a second time just as she grabbed it.

"Whoever it is I'll have to call you back," she said.

"No, no, no. It's me, Chantal."

Chantal Lamont? Serge's wife. Why is she calling me now? "I really can't talk right now, Chantal. I have to call the police."

"Why? What happened?"

"The young man who killed Tony—he was just here—and he came with two of his friends. I managed to scare them off."

"Oh my God!"

Missus Bevins sniffed and wiped away a tear with her free hand. "I'm fine, thank God. They said that they came to talk...I don't know. I have to let you go and call the police before they get away."

"No, you mustn't do that. Don't call the police, whatever you do," Chantal said in a whisper.

"What? Why not? And why are you whispering?"

"I can't talk to you here, I'm afraid that my husband will catch me. I'll call you back from a safer location."

"A safer location? My God, what's going on?"

"You have to find that young man and bring him back. He's *not* your husband's killer."

Chapter 17

Dorval, Quebec.

Detective Mercier slowed down as the media vultures swarmed around his car. He had an inner desire for his car to accidentally slide across the ice and hit a few of them. That way, he could escape a charge of criminal negligence. Instead, he ignored them as they flocked on both sides of the vehicle, shoving their mikes and cameras at him as he drove by. Through the thickness of the flock, he spotted five news vans—all parked along the side of the road with their unsightly fifteen-meter-high antennas.

He arrived at the yellow tape and held his badge up to the window. A young officer—who didn't appear to have many years behind his badge—lifted the tape and allowed Mercier to pass. He spotted an ambulance among the many police cars. And crawling around the driveway leading up to the house, were the crime scene regulars.

Mercier parked his car at the side of the road, finished the coffee that was in his thermos, and got out. He suddenly realized that he forgot his hat at home when he felt the cold nip his ears. But this wasn't the time to appear wimpy. Not with the neighbors staring out their windows from the inside their homes. So he braved it, as though it were fall weather.

Twenty-three years in the force and he'd never screwed up like he did last night. Not checking the adjoining suite, that was just dumb. Then again, there wasn't enough time after he received that anonymous phone call warning him that journalists were heading towards the hotel. With all of his resources, Mercier still couldn't find out who had tipped him off. Although he wanted to pursue it further, doing so could arouse suspicion that he was at the crime scene at the time of the murder. But whoever it was, the mystery caller saved his ass a shitload of trouble.

Why did this have to happen? Everything else was taken care of, including the hotel video surveillance. Once he had obtained the footage, he immediately passed it on to Fischer—Lamont's computer expert—to edit it so that both he and Nuttal couldn't be seen walking down the halls. He was supposed to be the best— that's why Fischer was on Lamont's payroll to falsify the investment statements of every client.

Now he gets thrown this curveball. If he'd had the time, Mercier would've killed the male whore on the spot. If not, at least make it look as though he and Bevins had struggled over the gun. Bevins shoots the prostitute out of self-defense. And rather than face being exposed as a deviant, he kills himself. It should've been an open and shut case, resulting in him getting a good night's sleep.

Instead, he'd been up all night, fuelling up on coffee, and travelling west, out of town, to see some fat-ass gas station attendant that let the two sons-of-bitches slip right past him. How stupid could the kid have been, to miss two black guys whose faces were plastered on every television screen across the country? And he claims that he was too busy studying to notice when they came in. Bullshit. He was most likely reading some video game magazine, porn—or both. He certainly looked like the nerdy type that wasn't getting any.

Now if things couldn't have gotten any weirder, his partner, Nuttal, calls him telling him about some dead body that he'd be interested in. Apparently, a friend of the victim stopped by the house to borrow some DVDs and they found the body.

"Mercier." A voice came from the driveway leading up to the victim's house. It was his partner, Detective Nuttal, who walked quickly to him.

"You better have a good reason for getting me to come out

here." Mercier scowled.

"Let's talk in the car."

Fine with me, Mercier thought, just as he was about to rub his ears to warm them up. "You said that you didn't want to say too much over the phone."

"Damn right I didn't," Nuttal answered as both he and Mercier closed their doors. "Not with so many people around."

"So?"

"It's odd. The victim's name is Theodore Warren. He also goes by the alias, Master Tiger. He's into the same kinky BDSM shit as the Barrow guy we're looking for."

"Woopty-do. Why should I care?"

"Out of curiosity, I had Warren's fingerprints taken. Get this. They match the prints that were found all over the suitcase that Barrow had left behind in Bevins's hotel room."

Mercier rubbed his eyes. God was he itching to get some shut-eye. "So, these two knew each other."

"Couldn't it be more obvious?"

"So how did Warren die?"

"At first it appeared that he fell down the stairs by accident. But the crime scene guys believe that he was pushed. The killer wanted to make it look like an accident."

"Really? Any suspects"

"We're still working on it. But there's more. The crime scene guys found *three* other, different sets of footprints on the driveway. And they're fresh—meaning that Warren had visitors early this morning."

Fortunately no snow fell today, Mercier thought.

So Warren had company this morning. Mercier wished he knew the time they came, but the crime scene specialists would probably be able to figure that out—as well as the shoe sizes. Possibly even estimate the weight of the visitors. But his first guess was that Warren was visited by Barrow, Stephenson, and the girlfriend—he couldn't remember her name at the moment. Why would they come here?

Mercier turned to Nuttal. "Are you sure that our three suspects don't have any criminal records?"

"If you're referring to the ones that we're after, no. Barrow was laid off from his job, Stephenson's unemployed, and Rinaldi's a barmaid. That's all we have on them."

Rinaldi—Jordyn Rinaldi—that's the name. Mercier rested his elbow on the windowsill as he stared up the driveway leading to Warren's house. "Why would they come here?"

"Do you think Lamont isn't telling us something?"

"I don't know. But for now, we don't mention any of this to him, you understand? We'll just have to keep—"

Just then, Mercier's mobile phone rang. He removed it from its belt clip and hit the *on* button. "Detective Mercier."

"Detective, this is the dispatcher," came a female voice in French. "I've received a phone call from an André Chevalier, who's currently in the town of Eastman. He's a store owner who believes that the kidnap victim, Jordyn Rinaldi, came into his shop. Here's his contact number."

"Hold on," Mercier said, as he reached into the inside pocket of his coat and took out his notepad and pen. He then wrote down the phone number as the dispatcher called it out to him. Without thanking her, he hung up and dialed the number he was given. The phone rang once and was answered.

"Allo," came the voice.

"This is Detective Daniel Mercier of the Montreal Police Department. Am I speaking with Monsieur André Chevalier," he asked, speaking in French.

"C'est moi-même." *It's me.*

"I've just received word that you believe you saw the kidnap victim, Jordyn Rinaldi?"

"Oh yes, without a doubt. I opened up the store. As I brought in the stack of newspapers, I noticed her picture on the front page with two guys. A young woman fitting her description walked into my store a few hours later, wanting to use the bathroom. I didn't think anything of it at first, but I found it very odd that she took so long in the bathroom—almost half an hour. I thought that something was wrong with her. When she left, she had changed her hair. That's when I became suspicious."

"How do you know for sure that it was her?"

"I watched her leave and get into a red car with two guys inside."

Mercier grabbed his partner's hand a bit too tightly. "Was it a red hatchback?"

"Uh, as a matter of fact, yes it was."

"Did you get a good look at the men inside the car with her?"

"No, they were too far away. But I know that there were two of them."

Finally, some news Mercier wanted to hear. "And where are you exactly?"

"I'm just off of Highway 10, at a gas station near Eastman."

Gas station? Shit, they always had video surveillance.

"Did you see the direction that they headed?" *East, please let it be east.*

"I saw them head east towards Sherbrooke."

Tabarnak! He couldn't believe it.

"Thank you, Mister Chevalier, you've been very helpful. I'll be in touch with you soon." Mercier then hit the *off* button.

"Tell me you got something," said Nuttal.

"Oh, yes, we've got them. And I also know where the three bastards are going."

Chapter 18

Eddie rubbed his knuckles to soothe the pain. He could've broken them with the force that he used when he'd hit the dashboard. Although the Bevins country cottage was out of sight, Eddie saw that Corey had not let up on the gas pedal. The car felt very light on the road's surface—he swore that they even skated at times. Corey could lose control of the car at any moment.

"Slow down. You're trying to kill us?" said Eddie.

"Shut up," Corey yelled.

"What?"

"I said, shut the fuck up. Your mouth has gotten us into more than enough trouble already."

"You should talk. You could've said something back there before she attacked us."

"Oh sure, what difference would it have made?"

"You would've shown that you're not such a pussy."

"Guys," Jordyn intervened, "knock it off."

Corey pointed a finger at Eddie. "Don't start with me."

Eddie puffed out a loud sigh as he shook his head. "I can't believe that you just left us hanging back there."

Jordyn turned to Eddie. "Don't blame Corey. You had no business getting out of the car and exposing yourself. That's what we agreed on."

"We had to improvise. I thought that she was ignoring you," said Eddie.

"So what?" said Corey. "You know that you can't be seen in public."

"Who's around to recognize us?" asked Eddie. "We're in the middle of this frozen wasteland for God's sake."

"She could've been inside the whole time and called the police the second that she saw you," said Corey.

"Oh, so now it's my fault. Go ahead and blame it all on me. You guys came up with this stupid idea of me getting freaky with some bastard who gets himself killed."

"I swear to God, I'm warning you," Corey said.

Eddie slammed the dashboard with his hand. "I never should've listened to you two."

"Stop hitting my dashboard," Jordyn yelled.

"I'm through listening to you two. All you're good for is taking the easy way out of everything. I was dumb thinking that you guys could ever give me intelligent advice on anything."

Eddie felt himself thrown forward, the seatbelt biting into his chest. Something else crashed into the back of his car seat, he realized that it was Jordyn who wasn't wearing her seatbelt.

"Jesus Christ! What's wrong with you?" Jordyn screamed.

When his head snapped back in his seat, he noticed that Corey was furiously unbuckling his seatbelt. *Oh, that's it. Now he wants to fight me.* Eddie felt the adrenaline coarse through his veins as he rushed to undo his seatbelt. He shoved the car door open and got out just as Corey was midway past the hood.

"You want to take your best shot? Come on." Eddie puffed as he engaged Corey, who managed to get his longer arm around Eddie's neck and force him head-first into the hood of the car. He heard Jordyn screaming for them to stop. Eddie managed to free one hand and swung it, striking Corey in the jaw. Corey released him, giving Eddie enough time to get up off of the hood and charge him. He plunged his head into Corey's stomach and went to grab his legs. The force of the impact combined with the slippery surface caused Corey to lose his footing, and they both skidded to the ground. They rolled over the icy surface a few times until Corey managed to put Eddie between himself and the road. Before Eddie could look Corey in the eyes, he saw a fist flying at him a split second before he was hooked in the jaw. The pain of the blow didn't sink in before he received another on the opposite side.

Somewhere in between consciousness and semi-consciousness, he heard Jordyn screaming. Irrationally, his arms shot up to cover his face, blocking Corey's punches as he caught two more to the wrist and to his elbow.

A weight suddenly lifted off him, or more or less, was pulled off him. Eddie didn't open his eyes yet, but he still heard Jordyn screaming at Corey, telling him to stop. That's when Eddie lowered his arms, opened his eyes, and saw Jordyn on the ground with Corey. His heart pounded, big clouds of vapor puffed in front of him as he eyed Corey, who returned the stare. All three of them remained on the road until Jordyn got up a few moments later, followed by Corey. But Eddie didn't get up. It was as though reality caught up with him...he'd just told off and picked a fight with his best friend. As for the words that expressed how he felt at the moment, they just didn't come.

Corey scowled at him. "You're lucky she pulled me off you. I would've killed you."

Eddie then saw Corey storm over to the driver's side door.

Corey turned to Jordyn. "Come on. We've got to go. He doesn't need us, and we don't need him."

Eddie then heard the engine start, but Jordyn stayed awhile longer and looked at him. He watched her as the tears streamed from her eyes. It didn't matter how many times she wiped them away—it wasn't enough.

"I'm sorry this happened," she sniffed. "You've really fucked this up for all of us. You're such an asshole." Jordyn ran back to the car, got in, and the tires spun against the surface before it got traction. It wasn't too long before the red hatchback became a small dot in the distance.

Okay, he deserved that. He was an asshole, he could live with that. After all, that's the level that he'd finally dropped to. He was an outcast from his own family and he lost his only real friends... oh yeah, and the entire country's hunting him for a murder that he didn't commit.

Some accomplishment.

The leather jacket and pants provided him with enough

insulation from the frozen surface of the road. God knew how long he could've sat there without feeling anything. But if he stayed where he was for too long, especially in this temperature, he'd wind up the same way Jack Nicholson's character did at the end of *The Shining*. Unless a speeding vehicle ran him over first.

He rubbed a hand on his jaws, which began to hurt as he opened his mouth, and thought about the idea of freezing to death—covered in ice. Who'd miss him?

He got up and walked to the center of the two-lane highway and stood where the yellow line would be. He looked both to the left and to the right. There was nothing but an empty white road with tire tracks. Then he looked forward and saw the frozen lake and the foot of a mountain in the distance, speckled white over dark brown. A spot of yellow light peaked out behind it. *How about that, the sun just had to make its final appearance before it set.* There must be an hour of sunlight left at least. For Eddie that was the most depressing thing about Canadian winters. There just wasn't enough daylight. But not this time, he would try to catch that last bit of daylight and make it last.

He walked towards the lake. As he cleared the shoulder and walked onto the field, he sunk knee deep into the snow and fell forward. His chin went below the surface slightly. He got up, wiping off his face. A little stumble wouldn't stop him. He lifted his knees higher as he continued onwards. He still sank, and the freezing snow shooting up the inside of his pant legs made him raise his knees higher, like a galloping horse. There was only about another thirty meters to go and he'd be at the lakefront. Progressively, the snow level decreased until it was up to his ankles.

Without hesitation, he took his first step onto the ice. There, that was easy. He took a second step. Then a third, and then walked normally. This would be his final journey.

He grew up close to the river, remembering that even though winter temperatures got as low as minus forty with a wind chill—making it feel like minus fifty at some times—the river never froze. There'd be a few to several ice chunks floating downstream, but that was all. He'd often hear about people falling through the ice. He didn't know what made other people want to risk their lives for the sake of some cheap fun. As for Eddie, he knew what he was doing and why.

He kept his eye on the foot of the mountain as he walked. There was still quite a distance to go. He peeked over his shoulder and saw that he'd covered a lot of ground. He even saw the Bevins' house in the distance. Oh well, he was sure half the country wouldn't miss him if he died. Soon enough they'll all have their wish granted. The surface couldn't stay this solid for much longer. He was bound to fall through at any moment.

About three more minutes went by when Eddie felt the frost bite through his face and then he couldn't even move his mouth. Why the hell hadn't he fallen through the ice yet? Eddie stomped the surface as hard as he could. All he heard was an echo. The ice was way too thick. And as he watched the clouds obscure the sun one more time, he wondered if that would be its final appearance. Maybe it was, so why bother continuing? There was nowhere left to go. No one would think of looking for him out here. And even if they did, they'd be too late. Eddie thought of this as he unzipped his jacket, letting the frost permeate through to his thin leather vest. Now he felt the real coldness. As though he were a wounded soldier, he dropped to his knees, and then onto his side.

This was how he pictured Simeon Wolf would die on his last mission. He'd be all alone—on a beach or a frozen wasteland— hungry, penniless, and without any friends or family to give a rat's ass about him. Just as Eddie felt at the moment.

He curled up into a fetal position. His lips trembled as he felt the numbness start to creep up on him, starting with his fingers and toes. Forget about the numbness, they were just so goddamned cold, he couldn't even wiggle them. The rest of his body would soon follow. The hypothermia would get him soon. He'd fall asleep without feeling a thing.

He felt himself in a loving pair of arms, wrapped with a thick, fuzzy blanket, as his mother carried him to his bedroom. He knew that he could walk, but he preferred it when his mother carried him. Maybe it's because she loved to carry him, since she wouldn't have much time left to do so before he got too big. His fingers and toes were frozen. He knew better than to stay out when it was too cold outside. After a snowball fight, he'd always be soaking wet. Come to think of it, he deliberately got himself covered with snow from head to toe because he knew that his mother would always greet him with his favorite blanket. She'd then snuggle with him in front of the fireplace. He never wanted her to stop, but she'd get up to make some hot cocoa—or hot chocolate—whichever one was available. Denise would be elsewhere, most likely at her friend's house—which was good. He would have mom all to himself for the afternoon. Sometimes he'd doze off soon afterwards and would wake up just before dinner. Yes, sleep. That's all he needed now. And his eyes began to get heavy.

The hands were on him and they moved him. He heard his mother's voice, *I'm here with you. Please stay with me.*

"I don't want you to leave. Please don't leave me," Eddie mumbled to himself. He felt himself being pulled up, as though he was sitting. His mother was right behind him and rocked with him as she zipped his jacket back up, grabbed his hands and made him rub his chest vigorously.

"Stay with me, you're going to be all right. Just hang in there."

That's when he felt something sticky streak across his face, followed by puffs of warm air. In fact, they were puffs of warm breath, followed by more wet streaks across his face...he was being licked. Eddie opened his eyes and saw a Rottweiler.

"Are you with me? Come on, please answer me."

That voice, he recognized it. Eddie turned his head slowly to one side and then to the other. He still couldn't see who it was.

"It's okay, I'm here. I'm so sorry for what I did. I shouldn't have doubted you."

"Missus Bevins?" mumbled Eddie.

"You can call me Nancy." Eddie lost count of how long she held onto him, but it felt like it had been a while. He slowly felt some heat return to his body. "Come on, up you get now."

Eddie felt a pair of hands grab him under the armpits and help him to get up.

"Keep moving your hands and feet. The rest of your body will warm up on its own."

And there she was, wearing a wool hat, coat, and a large scarf covering most of her face. The Rottweiler ran ahead, stopping every few feet to look back at them. She came to get him. It was too good to be true.

"Where are your friends?" she asked.

"I...I don't know," Eddie answered, still mumbling.

"You left with them, didn't you?" It was then that she put a hand to his shoulder to stop him. She came closer to him and turned his head as though she were examining it.

"Oh my God. Were you fighting?"

Eddie shook his head lose from her hands. "Yeah, but I'm good." He then rubbed his glove-covered hands over his mouth a few times. He still felt the pain on the side of his jaw that was struck.

Nancy hooked her arm around Eddie's, staying very close to him as they cleared the lake, retraced Eddie's earlier steps back across the field to the road where Nancy's SUV was parked on the shoulder.

She unlocked the back seat passenger door with the remote and opened it. The Rottweiler jumped inside first, and then Nancy helped Eddie inside. She walked quickly to the trunk and came back with a blanket, wrapping it around Eddie. "Here. This should help."

Eddie thanked her, able to move his lips a lot easier than before.

"My God, what were you thinking trying to cross that lake? Were you trying to catch hypothermia?"

Eddie thought about what to say for a bit. A few seconds later he looked up and saw that she was still staring at him, as though she were waiting for a reply. "That was the whole idea." Eddie then looked away, too embarrassed to look her in the eye.

Nancy didn't answer. Instead, she stood there and continued to stare at him. A few moments went by and Eddie saw through his peripheral vision that she still hadn't moved. That's when he looked back at her. She stood there—expressionless—as puffs of vapor came from her mouth.

"I'd smack you so hard, if I didn't feel sorry for you." She closed the door and got in up front. She strapped on her seatbelt and fired up the engine. "In the meantime, we have to find your friends before it's too late. You're all in very big trouble. A lot more than you probably know."

"How'd you find me? I mean, how'd you know where to look?" Eddie asked.

"I got lucky," Nancy answered. "I was speeding along the road hoping to catch up to you when I noticed a set of tire tracks on the shoulder, as though a vehicle was out of control." She then slowed down as she went around a curve and drove down a small incline. "There isn't too much traffic that passes through here, so I figured that it must've been your car. That's when I noticed several footprints. I take it that's where the fight took place, right?"

Eddie nodded. He watched her eyes stare back at him through the rearview mirror.

"It was just blind luck that I happened to look in the direction where the footprints went and that's when I saw you walking on the ice, just seconds before you collapsed."

The Rottweiler leaned over and started licking Eddie on the side his face. He put his hand up and gently turned the dog's head away. "Is he always like this with strangers?"

"Who, Darwin the Second?"

Darwin the Second?

"He's only like this since I'm being friendly with you. Had he been outside earlier when I had the axe, he would have ripped your arm off. You wouldn't have time to raise a hand at me before he took you out."

Eddie took one look at Darwin and slid a few inches away from him. "Why'd you come looking for us? What made you change your mind?"

"A friend of mine called me and told me that they knew who killed my husband. This is someone that I trust dearly, and they insisted that I find you. That's why we have to find your friends, and quickly. Their lives are in danger too. If someone recognizes them and calls the police, it'll just be a matter of time before my husband's killers find them. And they'll come after you next." Nancy then made a sharp left, following the road around a curve. "I was such a fool. To think that you'd actually risk coming all of this way to find me, just to rob me. You could've been hiding elsewhere. For you guys to do what you did, you'd either have to be brave, or incredibly dumb."

Eddie felt that Nancy drove way too fast. There must have been sheets of ice that were hidden underneath the snow-covered surface. But somehow Nancy managed to keep the SUV from sliding out of control. He didn't measure the distance they had travelled, but Eddie leaned forward when he saw a red hatchback on the shoulder. He pointed towards the vehicle. "There they are."

"Are you sure?" Nancy asked.

"I'm positive."

Nancy slowed down as she drove onto the shoulder, coming to a stop behind the hatchback. Eddie was a bit slow getting out, but he joined Nancy beside the car as she leaned towards the window and placed her hand horizontally against the surface to block out her reflection as she peered inside. When Eddie got there, Nancy made room for him. The fogged up glass impaired his view, but he saw two figures in the back seat. Eddie lifted the handle and pulled the door open. When he looked inside, his heart sank. Jordyn sat on Corey's lap, her head buried sideways in his chest. Corey held onto her as he sat sideways with his legs stretched out over the car seat. The soles of his shoes were inches away from where Eddie stood. She appeared as though she squeezed his arms to make him hold her tighter.

Jordyn then turned her head without moving the rest of her body, and looked at Eddie. Corey did the same. And it was then that Eddie saw the tears on both of their faces.

"What do *you* want?" asked Corey.

Their tears were contagious, as Eddie struggled to keep his composure. He couldn't believe that he had caused all of this. Whether they were out of gas or the car broke down, he didn't know. But either one would explain why they were both sitting here in the middle of nowhere.

As for the words that he couldn't say before, when they left him behind, they finally came. "Can't an asshole apologize for being an asshole?"

A few moments of silence went by. Jordyn then made a sound that bordered on crying and laughing. Corey did the same thing too. Eddie felt the first tear roll down his cheek as he chuckled, climbed over Corey's legs and closed his eyes, feeling a set of arms and hands squeeze him. Half of him was on the floor and the other half was on top of them. The longer that he held onto them, the more he felt so stupid for what he had said to them earlier. He wouldn't have gotten this far had it not been for them. For all he knew, he'd either be in a jail cell or sitting at the bottom of the Saint Lawrence River wearing cement shoes. "I'm so sorry. I shouldn't have yelled at you."

"I'm sorry too, bro," said Corey, muffled by their tight embrace.

"Me too," said Jordyn. "I'm the one that got us in this mess in the first place."

The group hug lasted for a few more moments and then Eddie stuck his head up. When he looked behind, he saw that Nancy wore the warmest smile.

Jordyn held onto Eddie's head and used her thumbs to wipe the tears from his cheeks. She then kissed him on the forehead. "Forgive us."

"Of course I do," said Eddie. "You forgive me too, right."

"Of course we do," said Corey. "We're always going to be a happy family—all *four* of us."

Eddie knew that he must have heard wrong. He looked up at Corey and stared at him. He didn't have to ask Corey as to why he said *four* instead of *three*. The answer was written all over his face.

"That's right, bro." Corey then formed a teary-eyed half smile. "I just found out that I'm going to be a daddy."

Chapter 19

About an hour and a half had passed since Eddie was asked to be the godfather of Corey and Jordyn's future child. It was touching, considering that people were out to kill them. Eddie had ridden back with Nancy while Jordyn and Corey followed them. It turned out that nothing was wrong with their car. The two of them had had an argument after they left Eddie behind. It was at that time that Jordyn told Corey about her being pregnant. Eddie imagined how horrified Corey must have been considering that their chances of survival were next to none. They must have lost hope and given up.

Fortunately for them, Nancy knew the owner of a clothing boutique in town and convinced her to open up just for her. While the others remained in their vehicles, Nancy bought all three of them regular outfits. She even suggested making a few phone calls in order to get a security team to come up. However, Eddie convinced her that they couldn't trust anyone since they didn't know how far Lamont's reach was.

Finally, the relief Eddie needed to get out of those leather clothes. Back at Nancy's house, Eddie took one of the best baths he'd had in years. With five bathrooms to choose from, he managed to get the one with the whirlpool. To top it all off, Nancy prepared the best Quiche Lorraine that he ever ate outside of his mother's kitchen. Nancy said that she didn't believe in having any housekeepers, chefs, or any other domestic employees whenever they were away—although she could clearly afford them. If given a choice between cooking for herself and having someone do it for her, she chose the former.

Eddie, Corey, and Jordyn had moved from the dining room into the living room while Nancy was in the kitchen preparing some coffee. Since they arrived, she insisted that they don't speak about the events that led up to the present moment until they were having coffee. Eddie was so hungry, he was glad to hold off on any conversation until after he ate.

It was then that Eddie learned that while they had stopped at the gas station in Eastman, Jordyn had purchased a home pregnancy test. It had been last week when she noticed that she was late in her cycle, but she didn't know how to break the news to Corey. Who could blame her? He'd just lost another job and was constantly borrowing money from her. Her parents couldn't stand Corey. Jordyn's father even threatened to use his golf clubs on him if he ever got too close to their house. His recent drinking only complicated matters. Then again, Corey couldn't have felt much better, learning that he'd be a father within a year. The timing couldn't have been worse.

This made Eddie wonder what he would've told his ex, had she called him right now telling him that she was pregnant with his child. He'd probably hang up on her...naw, he wouldn't be so obtuse. But it wouldn't be the kind of thing he'd want to hear at this moment. When he looked across the table and saw how Corey had his arm around Jordyn, comforted by the roaring fire in the woodstove beside them, he appeared to be taking it very well. In fact, Corey had taken this whole experience better than Eddie did. From the moment that both he and Corey had hightailed from the hotel last night, up to now, Corey had always been the more level-headed of the two.

Eddie turned to the sound of Darwin II's jingling dog collar. He was slightly ahead of Nancy as she walked into the living room with a tray with coffee mugs and a pot, sugar, cream, and milk.

"You won't believe how nice it is to finally have some company. All it's been since last night were non-stop telephone calls from friends, the media, your Prime Minister, my husband's counterparts down south, the President and the First Lady. It just wouldn't stop." She rested the tray on the coffee table and poured a cup for everyone. Darwin II walked over to the woodstove and lay down in front of it.

"What about the rest of your family?" asked Eddie.

"They've called. I told them not to come up, because I'd be back home before the end of the week. It's fortunate that I had some pull to get the press from camping out in front of this house."

"Fortunately for us, too," said Jordyn.

"They all think that everything was rosy between Tony and me," said Nancy. "The truth is that our marriage practically ended almost five years ago. I never forgot the time that he left to go to Washington, DC, one Monday morning six years ago—I couldn't go with him. In full view of our employees, he walked out the door and *kissed* the dog. He then *shook* my hand."

"Was it the political pressure that kept you both together?" asked Jordyn.

"That was part of it. As you know, the First Lady is always expected to stand beside her husband, no matter what he does." She finished pouring the cups, added some cream and sugar to her own and took a seat. "I've just been unhappy these past few years. The former First Lady was a licensed physician. That never stopped her from practicing."

Eddie added some cream and three teaspoons of sugar to his coffee. "Whatever stopped you from doing what you liked?"

Nancy gave a slight chuckle as she shook her head slowly. "You know what? I honestly cannot say."

Corey left his coffee black and only added sugar. "No offence, Missus Bevins—"

"Call me Nancy."

"Sorry, Nancy. With a five-bedroom house like this, and these nice clothes you bought for us—thanks again, by the way—you should be the happiest person in town with all the money that you have."

"I understand what you're saying. But the truth is I grew up looking after my two younger brothers and three younger sisters. I wanted to have children, but Tony didn't. This country house and all the perks that come with it are nice, but it's not the same as when you're used to having people around. The only people

Tony would have over are his so-called friends, who were just interested in him because he's the Governor. He didn't want me doing anything else that didn't fit into his schedule. That's when I realized that our marriage was going downhill." She took a sip of her coffee. "Now, getting to the heart of the matter. How did you three get to know my husband?"

Eddie put down his coffee, rested his forearms on his legs, as he thought of the best way to break the news to her. After a moment's pause he said the first thing that came to mind. "I lost my job and I needed a way to make quick money. But I wound up being at the wrong place at the wrong time." He then continued on with everything else that happened up until the point that her husband was shot.

Throughout his narration, he watched Nancy to see what her reaction would be. He expected her to be shocked, or disgusted. Yet she remained taciturn. In fact, she was so calm she just continued to sip her coffee as though she had known about her husband all along. This was contrary to both Corey and Jordyn's reactions, they were clearly surprised that he had left out the parts about his novel. Of course he could've mentioned that to her. But the more he thought of it, the more he was embarrassed to talk about it. Why mention something that no one wanted to read or know about anyways? Well, Jordyn, Corey, and Aunt Bev showed interest. But they were too close to him and were just being nice. It seemed that every time that subject came up, it just seemed to cause more trouble for him.

"So, you're sure that Detective Mercier was the man that shot my husband?" Nancy asked.

Eddie nodded. "I'm positive. I couldn't see the other man that he was with, but I'd recognize his voice if I heard it again."

"And they're connected to Serge Lamont," said Corey.

"That's right," said Eddie. "We think that Lamont had them kill your husband to shut him up about the whole Borealest situation before it became a scandal."

Nancy smiled as she shook her head. She put down her coffee mug and went over to the fireplace, telling Darwin II to move aside. "I believe you. Had I not been so upset earlier, I would've realized that you weren't whom the police were making you out to be." She then opened the doors to the woodstove, and they all felt a blast of heat and the scent of burning wood. She grabbed a poker and shifted the log. Nancy picked up another one from the tray and put it in. "As I mentioned earlier, I should've known then that either you three were very dumb to come to see me, or very brave." She closed the doors to the woodstove, got up, and faced them. "I appreciate your bravery."

"Was that the reason why you came after us?" asked Eddie.

"Not at first. I got a call from Chantal Lamont—Serge Lamont's wife."

Eddie leaned forward. *No way.* "She called asking you about us?"

Nancy sat down and took back her mug. "Not necessarily, but it was a good thing that she did. I mean, it was perfect timing. I was just about to call the police."

Eddie leaned forward in his chair. "What did she say?"

"She practically corroborated what you guys told me, but she couldn't stay on the phone. I think that she was afraid that her husband would overhear her."

"Do you think that he knows?" asked Jordyn.

"I don't know, I hope not. I can't even do anything since she specifically told me not to call the police. Imagine, I could make one phone call and a security team would be up here very quickly. But if Lamont has as much pull as Chantal believes he does, then we'd just be setting ourselves up." She put her mug back onto the tray. "In fact, she called not too long ago while I was in the kitchen, wanting to know if I found you guys. She said she'd call back later. My God, I hope she's all right."

"Your husband told me that all of the evidence is found in Darwin's grave," said Eddie.

Nancy's eyes widened. "Darwin was our first Rottweiler. Those were Tony's favorite breeds, despite him being a dog himself."

Eddie scratched the back of his neck. *Yup, I saw that one coming sooner or later.* "What did you do with him when he passed away?"

"We buried him at the local pet cemetery." Nancy answered.

"Do you think that Tony buried incriminating evidence against

Borealest with Darwin?"

"It's possible."

"How far away is this cemetery?" Corey asked.

"A few miles," replied Nancy. "Tony was very influential in establishing a small pet cemetery in a section of the North Hatley Cemetery about five years ago, after Darwin passed on."

Jordyn finished her coffee and turned to Nancy. "I know that we're asking a lot, and we don't mean any disrespect, but it would mean so much to us if you could help us retrieve that evidence."

"Say no more," Nancy replied with a palm up. "I'll help you get it. I'm not proud about what Tony's done. He had a lot to answer for, but he didn't deserve to be murdered in cold blood."

By then, everyone had finished with their coffee and the mugs were back on the tray. Nancy went to pick it up, when Eddie stepped in. "Let me help you with that."

"Thanks, but I'll manage. You relax and make yourself at home. You're my guests." She then picked up the tray and left towards the kitchen. Darwin II lifted his head at seeing Nancy walking away— got up and ran behind her, his little stub of a tail flitting behind him.

When she was gone, Jordyn turned to Eddie. "Why didn't you tell her about your book?"

"What for? She don't need to know about it. It's not even important," Eddie answered.

"Like hell it isn't," said Corey. "That's the real reason why you agreed to our plan, isn't it?"

Eddie scratched in between his braids, which began to itch a bit. "What difference will it make whether she knows about it or not?"

"It might not make much of a difference to you," said Jordyn. "But Nancy's the first person to believe us and not turn us in. I think you owe it to her to be completely honest about yourself."

"Besides, you told her husband what you did," said Corey. "Why can't you do the same with her?"

"Alright," said Eddie raising his palms, signaling them to stop. "I'll tell her." Again, they managed to cajole him. But they were right. What *did* he have to lose by telling her the whole truth? Come to think of it, Tony showed his better side when Eddie opened up to him. Sure, Tony was unfaithful. He was a dog for cheating on such a nice lady such as Nancy. But at least Eddie had a chance to see his good side. And it was the soft, teary-eyed crybaby that was asking for forgiveness—a far cry from the oppressor that Nancy described him as, and how she said she'd lived under his shadow for all of these years.

Eddie got up and turned to Corey and Jordyn. "I'm going to go help her in the kitchen."

They nodded in reply and Eddie left. He walked down the hall. He thought about where he would begin. The flash drive that hung from his neck came to mind, when he heard the sound of breaking glass around the corner. That's when he ran, sliding to a stop across the hardwood floor. He turned the corner and ran into the kitchen—fearing the worst—only to find Nancy on hands and knees, picking up pieces of coffee mugs and the glassware that held the cream and the sugar.

She glanced up at him and threw a stop signal with the palm of her hand as Eddie stood in the doorway. "Stay back, there's broken glass everywhere."

Come on, who do you think you're fooling? Eddie looked at the floor and made a quick visual sweep. He then walked around her, minding the broken glass, and went to the kitchen island where the sink was. He opened the doors below for something to use. He first saw bottles of cleaning supplies, a few cleaning sponges. Ah, there it was. That's when he grabbed a small plastic hand broom with the dustpan clipped onto its handle. He closed the doors and came around to Nancy, who was picking up each broken piece, one at a time, and putting them in the tray.

"I *told* you to stay back. I can do this myself," she said with a shaky voice. She was angry, but Eddie knew that her anger wasn't directed towards him. That's when he put down the hand broom and dustpan, grabbed Nancy's shoulder and turned her around and pulled her up gently to make her stand with him. He looked into her eyes. He easily saw that below that plain, solid, and artificial exterior shell, was a widow in pain.

"You should know that your husband was planning to come

clean to you on everything. Tony wanted to change, he just didn't know how. I think he would've wanted me to tell you this."

She stared back at him for a few seconds and then she finally broke. She threw the shards onto the floor and threw her arms around Eddie. All he heard from her was crying as she hugged him tightly. He returned the embrace, conscious to the fact that she must have held her deepest feelings in since yesterday. Now the reality finally set in that Tony was gone. She must have known his good qualities, as well as his troubled inner demons. This could very well be why she stayed with him all these years.

Just then, Eddie saw Jordyn and Corey standing in the doorway. He didn't have to say anything to them, since what they saw was self-explanatory. They walked inside, minding the glass, and joined them in a group hug. Darwin—who had followed Nancy earlier—found his way to the entrance to the kitchen where he sat staring at them.

God, he didn't want to cry anymore, and he wasn't going to. But it was so goddamn contagious, especially since he was the last person in this room to see her husband alive. This was by far the most trying week of his life.

Chapter 20

D etective Mercier forced down on the gas pedal as he overtook one vehicle after another, speeding along Highway 10, as they approached the junction to Highway 55 that would take them south to the town of Hatley. Damn these road conditions. He didn't dare drive any faster at the risk of flying off the road and becoming another Quebec road statistic. Time was way too precious for him and Detective Nuttal to have that sort of delay. He counted the seconds that it took him to overtake another minivan. *Tabarnak,* both he and Nuttal would've been at Bevins' house by now had the roads been dry.

He was less than a year from retiring to a spectacular beachside condo in the Florida Keys. No more snow to shovel, no more winter tires to replace, and no more underpaid detective work. All he saw himself doing at that point was sailing off into the Atlantic on the old classic yawl rig sailboat he'd been eyeing for months. At a $60,000 price tag, he'd be able to go fishing every day, host parties, and commute to the Bahamas where he could screw around with every girl that money and booze could buy whenever his wife wasn't around. Instead, he was rushing halfway across the Eastern Townships, constantly hearing Nuttal complaining that the heat was turned up too high. The windshield wiper fluid had almost run out too. All for what? Because they screwed up their job the other night.

His cell phone vibrated loudly in the coin tray between him and Nuttal. He picked it up, glanced at it, and saw Lamont's name flash on the display screen.

"Callisse, qu'est ce qu'il veut maintenant?" *What the hell does he want now?* Mercier put the mobile down and pressed the button on his Bluetooth. "Oui."

"What the hell's wrong with you two?" Lamont barked through the phone.

Oh, Christ. What the fuck's he complaining about now? "Excuse me, sir?"

"I don't know what I'm paying you guys for. I expect both of you to keep me up to date on everything. You understand me?"

Mercier noticed that Nuttal looked in his direction. Obviously he heard everything clearly from where he sat. "I'm not sure what you're getting at, sir?"

"Don't you dare bullshit me! What's this I hear about some black guy breaking his neck this morning? You thought that I wouldn't find out about that? You don't think that I watch the news? I've got five goddamn TVs in my house for Christ sake."

"Yes, sir, I apologize for that." Mercier switched lanes to overtake another car. "Both Nuttal and myself didn't see the possible connection at first. All we know is that the victim, Barrow, Stephenson, and Rinaldi all knew each other. As to how he died, all I can say is that it happened under mysterious circumstances."

"Yeah, yeah, whatever. And I guess you weren't going to tell me about Fisher either, right?"

Fisher was the computer expert that Lamont hired to falsify all of Borealest's documents. Up until now, neither their clients nor the government authorities were aware of anything foul. But what was the deal with Lamont anyway? "I'm sorry, sir. What about Fisher?"

"I'll give you five clues, and then maybe you can figure it out for yourself. Rope. Neck. Garage. Noose. Screaming wife. Do I need to give you more, or can you solve the puzzle yourself?"

Tabarnak, Fisher hung himself. "Fisher committed suicide?"

"Very good, Sherlock Holmes," Lamont answered. "How many more dead bodies am I going to find out about on my own?"

"Sir, you must believe me. This is the first time we've heard about Fisher."

"Go figure. I was about to question him today as to why there's another five million dollars missing from Borealest's accounts that wasn't calculated before. Now the dipshit goes and dies on me before I could find out where *my* money went."

Mercier knew that his eardrums would be ringing after this conversation was over. *Five million dollars missing, just like that?* That wasn't his problem. Just as long as his share wasn't compromised. And where did he get the audacity to refer to it as *his* money. If you're going to steal the money, fine. Just don't be so goddamn incompetent on choosing the places to invest it. Now because of that, Bevins threatens to come clean, putting us all in deep shit. "Nuttal and I didn't know about Fisher because we're following a lead on Barrow and Stephenson."

"Humor me."

"They were spotted heading east on Highway 10."

"East on Highway 10?" Lamont then paused, as though he were in thought. "You think they're going to see Tony's wife?"

No shit, you dumbass. God, I wish I could say it to your face. "That's what Nuttal and I suspect. We're less than half hour's drive away from Tony's country house right now. God willing, we can end this all tonight."

"You better end this all right," said Lamont. "And you can forget about arresting them. I want them dead. You hear me? D-E-A-D. Dead. And I don't want to take any more chances. So when you see Tony's wife, kill her too."

Chapter 21

Although he would've preferred to have gone to the cemetery earlier in the evening, Nancy suggested that it would be better to go later at night when the entire town was asleep. Sure, Nancy would've had some pull in getting her dog exhumed but it would've raised too many red flags—and no doubt would have alerted Detective Mercier. Corey and Jordyn had offered to clean up the mess in the kitchen while Eddie walked with Nancy back to the living room. Darwin II walked ahead of them, as usual. A chunk of wood fell off of another and bumped the wall of the woodstove as they both sat on the couch. Darwin II took his usual resting place in front of the woodstove.

"Thank you," said Nancy. "It's funny how this can happen to you when you've dreamed of one thing at one point in time. Then when it happens, you regret the thoughts that you once had."

Holy shit, you wished your husband was dead?

"Don't get me wrong, I've only dreamed of *separating* from Tony."

Okay. Eddie rubbed his eye and looked back at her. "I separated from my girl just last week."

"Really? I could write a book about why it's better to get to know your spouse before marrying them. Then again it would be a bit morbid for me to do so now. You know, it would look like I'm trying to profit off of Tony's passing."

Eddie looked away from her and leaned forward, resting his forearms on his legs. He still hadn't told her the real reason as to why he was with her husband. But he couldn't tell her now. She was devastated—finally accepting what happened to her husband. She'd calmed down now, why should he ruin that?

"There's something I've been wanting to ask you," said Nancy.

Eddie looked over his shoulder. "Sure, go ahead."

"I've been around several people...in the government, business people, and regular citizens. Somehow you don't strike me as the type of person that would be...let's say...involved in the sex industry."

Jesus, now she gone start it. I might as well tell her. "Listen, I haven't been completely honest with you. I'm not a dominator, or male dominatrix, or whatever I'm supposed to be called." He got up and walked to the stone portion of the wall that surrounded the woodstove, put an elbow against it and leaned. "Money wasn't the only reason I was so desperate to do this." He then fell silent as he felt a blockage in his throat. He felt his breathing increase as his throat hurt. *Come on, you've come this far. Just tell her.*

"It's all right, dear. You can tell me."

Dammit! Now she was pushing him to talk. Oh what the hell. He turned around so that he faced her. "I'm a wannabe novelist. I can't get my book picked up by agents or sold to a publisher to save my life. I've only sold forty ebook copies in the last six months that I couldn't publish traditionally. I've tried everything. I was even scammed twice by fraudulent agencies and almost once by a vanity publisher. The job at the bookstore was my only means of connecting to the book world and the only way to pay the bills. I...it was stupid what I did." He didn't know what to expect from Nancy. But when he saw her face light up in a smile, it caught him off guard.

"Well I'll be damned. You're a writer." She put a hand to her mouth to cover a chuckle. "Isn't this a coincidence? I have a confession myself. I used to be an editor at Windmill Press in New York City, until I left to become a literary agent. I soon quit when I married Tony and moved with him to Concord. Wow, what a change—"

"There's more. I'm sorry." Eddie walked away from the woodstove and sat down beside Nancy. "I lost my girl to another guy and I got into a fight with my family because they thought that I was going nowhere in life writing this book. So to prove them wrong, Corey, Jordyn, and I had the stupid idea of doing a publicity stunt, you're husband—to our surprise—turned out to be the one that we were going to set-up."

Eddie paused when he heard Corey and Jordyn arrive. They both sat down adjacent from Nancy.

"But nothing happened," Eddie continued. "I mean there wasn't any sex...you have to believe me. Your husband wasn't even the person we intended to set-up."

Jordyn then leaned towards Nancy. "The guy that arranged Eddie's appointment with him was my ex-boyfriend, Theo. He told us that Eddie's client was a woman. We only recently learned that he might have deliberately misled us."

"As for this morning," said Eddie. "Corey, Jordyn, and I went to confront him and we found him dead in his house."

Nancy's hands shot up to her mouth. "Oh my God. How did it happen? You'll have to pardon my ignorance, but I haven't turned on the TV in over twenty-four hours."

"We think that he was killed," said Corey.

"And the ones who killed him made it look like an accident," said Eddie.

"We got our fingerprints all over the place," said Jordyn.

Nancy then waved a hand in a dismissive manner. "Don't worry about that. You all knew him. It's normal that your fingerprints as well as others would be all over his house."

"That's true," said Eddie.

"Besides it won't change anything," said Nancy. "The two detectives who murdered my husband would've found a way to connect you to Theo's death."

Eddie stood and paced up and down. "Maybe I'm being paranoid, but I think that I was set up. And Theo was in on it. Maybe he was working with Serge Lamont who also had him killed off because he knew too much."

Nancy stood as Eddie was pacing back towards her. "We'll get through this. We'll head over to the pet cemetery later on and dig up the evidence that Tony told you about. Then we'll go to the proper authorities. Hopefully by tomorrow afternoon, your names will all be cleared."

Her words were comforting. But Eddie still felt agitated, and he knew that Nancy sensed this as she held onto both his shoulders.

"I'm not angry with you. We've all done stupid things in our lives. And believe me when I tell you that it's extremely difficult to get published when you're a first-time novelist. Many celebrities get it easier just because of their celebrity status, and some of their books aren't worth shit. It wasn't the smartest thing that you all did but I understand why you did it. As for those that didn't support you and discouraged you, you shouldn't let that stop you."

Eddie and Nancy sat back down. She then held her chin as though she had something on her mind. "There's an old African parable that I used to tell my younger siblings. It's about a group of migrating elephants. They find a short cut, but the only problem is that it involves climbing a steep hill. The first elephant attempts to climb it. He's having a lot of difficulty, soon afterwards the other elephants yell at him, telling him to give up and that he'll never make it. As a result, that elephant tumbles once and he gives up.

"A second elephant makes an attempt at climbing the hill. Again the others shout out and discourage him. Like the previous elephant, he also falls down and gives up.

"Then there's a baby elephant who's very motivated to try. So he climbs. The other elephants laugh at him, thinking that he won't do any better. He falls once, but gets up and keeps going. The others keep laughing at him and yell at him to give up, that he won't make it. Although he falls a second time, he gets back up and keeps going. Until, to everyone's surprise—except for his mother—he makes it to the top. The other elephants turn to the mother and ask her, 'How did your son do that? Why didn't he listen to us? He could've hurt himself.' The mother laughed and replied. 'My child couldn't listen to your discouraging remarks even if he wanted to. Because my son is deaf.'"

Eddie chuckled to himself as he understood what Nancy was getting at. It was all about being the baby elephant. Hopefully Corey would take something away from this too. He saw Jordyn snuggle up next to him.

Nancy then patted Eddie's hand. "I have a lot of experience

and many connections in the publishing industry. When this is over, I'd be glad to read your manuscript and tell you what your strengths and weaknesses are to make your novel more saleable."

Eddie smiled. "I'd appreciate that. Thanks."

"No problem." Nancy then got up, walked over to the fireplace, looked on the ledge above it and saw the television remote next to the box of matches. She took it, stepped back, and pointed it to the wall-mounted 32-inch high definition television above the ledge. When the television was on, the first thing they saw was the news.

Eddie wanted to leave the living room. He was fed up with the accusations of murder and kidnapping. To make it even more sensational, the TV stations made him appear to be a professional hit man—with his leather outfit and all—as though he had walked straight out of a Hollywood movie. He swore that the TV stations that aired this shit must be making a fortune in advertising sales from this sensation. But when he saw both his parents with mikes and digital voice recording devices held up to their faces, he couldn't remain seated.

They were outside in front of the driveway to their house. They were bundled up and had camera lights flashing on them every few seconds. His mother was the one doing the talking.

"So, if you're watching, Junior, we do not condone the things that we said to you last Thursday. Your father and I are not proud of the pressure that we put on you that's alienated you. But to everyone else who's watching I will not accept these ridiculous allegations that my son's been accused of."

Eddie's father then cut in. "I don't know how you all police conduct your investigations. But I'm going to tell you all this. We didn't raise our son to be a criminal. He's not a murderer and he's not a kidnapper, do you all understand me? He is not a murderer and he's not a kidnapper."

Monica then stepped back in front of him just as she normally did when her husband was agitated. "The girl on the front of this morning's paper, who was labeled as a kidnap victim, is the girlfriend of my son's best friend. They've all been friends for a long time, and it's silly to think that my son and his friend would resort to kidnapping her. I would also like to add that if my son—

Junior, if you're watching this, I'm begging you to please come home and we'll go see the police together. I know that we've had our differences, but you must know that we love you, and always have, even though it doesn't appear to be that way all the time. And I accept the fact that your sister, your father, and I were completely out of line with our behavior last Thursday night. I'm hoping that you'll find it in your heart to forgive us." A tear rolled down her cheek and she turned away from the mike and into Edward's embrace.

Edward then leaned slightly towards the audience as he hid Monica's face from the cameras. "Thank you, everyone. We have nothing more to say." He then walked away with Monica amidst a foray of questions.

Nancy lowered the volume on the television as she stood and joined Eddie. "You haven't spoken to your parents lately, have you?"

Eddie shook his head. "Naw. Now you know why."

"We thought it best not to contact our parents," said Jordyn.

"I certainly don't blame you," said Nancy as she faced everyone. "Get dressed. We've got some evidence to dig up."

Chapter 22

Afew dripping, foot-long icicles hung from the arched wrought-iron gates to the cemetery that was surrounded by a seven-foot high brick wall. Nancy parked the SUV close to the wall, a few feet away from the entrance—leaving enough room for Eddie to open his door. Corey, who rode in the backseat with Jordyn, got out and held the door open for her, but she shook her head.

Corey leaned his head inside. "Aren't you coming?"

Jordyn was leaning against the window and she looked at Corey. "You guys go ahead, I'm not up to it."

Nancy walked up and stood beside Corey and peaked inside. "Are you sure you're okay staying here by yourself?"

"I'm fine, just a little tired," said Jordyn. "Don't worry about me."

Corey gave her a nod. "Alright, babes. We'll try not to take too long."

Nancy was about to walk away when she turned back to Jordyn. "How's your phone?"

Jordyn took out her mobile and looked at it. "I took out the battery."

"We've been using mine, sparingly," said Corey as he looked at Nancy. "Don't worry. No one knows my number yet."

"Right," said Nancy. She then reached into her pocket, took out her cell phone, and handed it to Jordyn. "You call Corey if there's anything. And there's a blanket in the back in case it gets too cold" She then looked at him. "How's your phone?"

"It still has a bit of juice left in it."

Eddie came around and lifted the trunk. Inside were three shovels and some flashlights. "You hang tight," he said to Jordyn. She turned around and gave him a short wave. Corey closed the passenger door and joined Nancy behind him. Eddie handed them each a shovel and a flashlight.

Scaling the wall wasn't much of a challenge. Eddie led the way as he climbed up onto the hood of the vehicle, then to the roof where he was close to the same height as the brick wall. He threw his shovel and his flashlight over the wall, and then made the leap from the roof of the car onto the foot-wide surface. He landed comfortably, mindful of any ice accumulation, which thankfully, was nothing major. He then dropped down to the other side. The height of the snow, which just came a few inches above Eddie's ankles, helped to soften his landing. Nancy followed—throwing her shovel and flashlight over the wall. A few moments later she landed beside Eddie, proving to be quite adept for a woman her age. Corey was with them a few moments later.

They each picked up a shovel and flashlight. Nancy then led the way. They walked on the driveway that led from the entrance, which had been cleared of the snow.

Either he was very nervous or the temperature had risen slightly, because Eddie didn't feel as cold as he did earlier. Maybe it was both. He knew that once he started shoveling, his body temperature would rise even more.

Similar to the other night, the snow reflected enough light for him to see very well in front of him without having to use his flashlight. Had it been any other night of the week, there's no way his ass would be out here in this weather. Corey was the only person that could get him out here.

Nancy appeared to know the cemetery well. He would've already gotten lost. He knew that they reached the pet cemetery when the tombstones changed. The ones ahead of him had dogs and cats carved on top of them.

"It's right over here," Nancy pointed as they were off the path and back into the snow. "Tony wanted a very lavish tombstone with all sorts of perks. But I insisted that we avoid doing so, as to not outshine and possibly offend the other pet owners."

It was moments later that they came to the marble tombstone. The surface was shaped like a dog. Nancy shone her flashlight on it. "Here it is. I hope we're not doing this for nothing." She was the first to scoop some snow and throw it behind her. Eddie and Corey dropped their flashlights and joined her.

Eddie hadn't shoveled like this in years. Just clearing the snow made him work up a sweat. With the amount that they had to shovel, they had no choice but to take breaks in between. The frozen earth did not make it easy to dig. Corey was the only one that went non-stop. Lord knew where he got his endurance from. Fortunately for him, they probably shaved off another half hour. Forty minutes went by as Eddie and Corey stood deeper in the ground as a mound of earth and snow rose to close to eight feet. Nancy gave up digging, and chose to move the mound away from the pit so that none of it fell in.

Corey lost his grip on his shovel after appearing to have struck a hard surface. "I got something?" Corey got down on his knees and began to clear away the dirt.

Eddie picked up the pace to dig some more around the casket.

Nancy peered down at them. "I'd dig to see if there was another container sitting beside the casket. I don't think Tony would've put anything inside with Darwin."

That made sense, and Eddie focused his attention digging around one end of the casket while Corey focused on the next. It wasn't too long before Eddie's shovel hit another solid object. His heart raced as he tossed the shovel to the side and got down onto his hands and knees. "I found it." He heard Corey approach as they both cleared the earth off the top of what appeared to be a metal box.

"We'll need to dig some more to get this out," Corey said as he picked up his shovel. Eddie backed away, panting as though he had run a marathon. He knew that his arms would be sore in the morning. No bother, that was the least of his worries, as he watched Corey dig away non-stop. A few minutes later, they lifted the box on top of the casket. This wasn't the ordinary safe that Eddie was used to seeing at office supply stores where he'd shop—

it more resembled the high-end safes that could only be opened with the use of explosives if one didn't remember the combination code. It was very heavy, as both he and Corey struggled to lift it out to Nancy, who then helped to pull it across the surface. She then helped him and Corey out of the grave, and they surrounded the portable safe.

Nancy then pointed to what appeared to be a combination lock. "Ouch, do you have any clues as to what the code is?"

Eddie cleared away the bit of dirt that was on it. There were six spaces. "What's Darwin's birthday?" It was obvious, but it was worth a shot.

"It's July 16, 2002."

Eddie punched in the numbers, 071602, and then pulled. The door didn't open. He tried again, switching the places of the numbers. Still nothing.

"Try Tony's birthday," Nancy suggested, and she gave him the date. That didn't work either.

They tried numerous combinations, the obvious and the least obvious that Nancy thought of. Eddie got up, turned around and kicked the snow.

Corey turned to Eddie. "Hey, cool it, buddy. No one said this would be easy. Besides, wasn't Darwin some kind of explorer?"

"No he wasn't," said Eddie as he turned to face him. "He was a shipmate and travelled to the Galapagos Islands where he studied birds. He gathered enough evidence to formulate his hypothesis about the theory of evolution through natural selection. He even wrote a book about it, called the Origin of Species."

"Hold on a sec," said Corey as he took out his cell phone. "Oh damn, the battery's gone dead."

"Don't worry, we'll be back with Jordyn soon," said Nancy.

Corey then spoke as he read his phone. "Try these numbers, 674446."

Eddie didn't know where Corey got the numbers from. With nothing to lose, he got back down on his knees in front of the safe. He entered the numbers, and pulled the handle. There was a click and the door opened.

Eddie's eyes dilated as he shot a glance to Corey. "Damn, how'd you figure that one out?"

"I guessed that since Tony was obsessed with Darwin and all, I figured that the combination numbers might be connected. Then you mentioned the title of his book. On the phone, guess what this numerical sequence spells?"

Nancy chuckled. "They spell the word *Origin*. Tony also had the word engraved on the back of Darwin II's amulet."

Eddie looked at the stack of papers that took up most of the space inside the safe. He took out the top sheet and read it. "It's ironic because these papers document the origin of this scandal."

"We'll have plenty of time to look through them back at the house," said Nancy as Eddie closed the safe.

"Sure thing," said Corey as he turned to Eddie. "Let's fill back this hole in the ground."

"Don't be silly," said Nancy. "I've had my workout for the evening. Don't worry about that. Once this mess is settled and you guys are off the hook, it'll be easier for me to talk things over with the church."

Eddie was about to pick up the shovels when he was startled by Nancy's loud shriek. He lost his balance and fell back onto his hands when he saw the two dark figures approach—both armed.

"Salut, Eddie," said the one that Eddie recognized as Detective Mercier. He appeared to be more than pissed off. It was the same expression he had after he shot Bevins. "You're a real pain in the ass to find." Eddie stood up slowly, keeping his hands visible. Corey and Nancy held their hands up as well. Eddie was beyond trembling...his body quaked at the sight of the guns pointed at him.

"You're probably wondering how we found you," said Mercier. "Well, let's just say that the girl was identified when you made one of your pit stops. I thought that you'd be back at the house. Only when we got there, you had just left. We saw some tail lights in the distance and we lost you. We drove around a bit and then we saw the SUV parked outside. By the way, where's the girl?"

"She wasn't feeling too well, so she stayed behind," said Nancy.

"Then we'll go pick her up after," said Mercier.

They didn't see Jordyn in the SUV. Hopefully she ran off to get help. Eddie then looked at Mercier's partner. Surely he was the one that assisted in killing the Governor.

Mercier then pointed his gun at Nancy. "I've always wanted to ask you how on earth could you stay married to the same man for all these years, even sleep in the same bed with him, and not know that he's gay." He then chuckled and Eddie watched him eye him briefly. "Now you're helping the little fucker who's probably had more intercourse with your husband than you probably had your entire lives together."

Eddie watched Nancy's face go cold. It was as though any moment she would rush up to Mercier and smack him. He had no doubt she was thinking that.

"You're such a bastard, you know that?" said Nancy.

Eddie cringed as he heard her say that. *Shit, Nancy, don't antagonize him while he's pointing a gun at you.*

"Shut up, if you know what's good for you," said Mercier. "Your damn husband's the only reason why I have to do this. He should've kept his mouth shut." He then glanced at the portable vault. "What's that you got there?"

"They're old family heirlooms. They're of no monetary value," said Nancy.

"Digging for family heirlooms? At this hour? Come on lady, who do you take us for," said Mercier who then pointed his gun at Eddie. "Open it."

"We don't know the combination," Eddie answered. *That was lame.* He then watched as Mercier's silent partner holstered his weapon and approached him. The man was at least six feet tall, and had broad shoulders, just like Mercier. Eddie knew that he had fear written all over his face as he slowly backed away, but the man already had one hand on his shoulder while the other one shot straight into his stomach. Eddie swore that he'd cough up an internal organ, as he was lifted off the ground slightly and landed on his knees. He rolled onto his side in the snow—clenching his teeth as hard as he could to avoid crying out as he held onto his stomach. The pain swelled deep.

"Yo, leave my friend alone," he heard Corey yell. He didn't see what happened since he had his eyes closed tightly. But Eddie heard Nancy scream, followed by a scuffle, he felt some snow land on his face. He then heard his best friend crying out before he heard him hit the ground.

"Stop," Eddie cried out as he paused to take a deep breath. "I'll open it, just don't hurt us. Please, I swear. We don't want any trouble." He opened his eyes and was looking directly at Corey. There was red snow next to his face. Corey was bleeding from his mouth and one eye was shut tightly. He still breathed, and stared back at him with one eye. Although Corey struggled, he managed to slowly extend a hand out towards him. It made it in the air halfway until it fell into the snow.

"Corey," Eddie whispered. Corey breathed loudly as though he tried to say something.

"Did you say something?" Mercier asked.

Eddie coughed and strained to roll over onto his hands and knees as he looked up at Mercier. "I said that I'd open it. Please don't hurt us."

Mercier waved the gun in the direction of the safe. "Then open it."

Eddie crawled over to the safe and rubbed his hands on his pants to brush off the snow. He punched in the numbers into the same sequence as they were before and opened the door.

"Now move aside," Mercier said.

Eddie obeyed him and crawled to the side.

Nancy came over to help him stand. "Are you okay? Don't try to resist. It's pointless."

Her words didn't mean much to him. He watched as the other officer went down on one knee and reached inside and pulled out a stack that was about an inch thick.

"I'll need a flashlight," the man said.

Mercier turned to Nancy. "Give him your flashlight."

Nancy handed it to him. He shone it on the sheets that he flipped through.

The man then looked up at Mercier. "They're records," He then looked back at the papers. "They look like Borealest's transactions and I see a bunch of names...I see yours and mine on here. Even Fisher's name is there. Holy shit, this is evidence they were going to use against us. Tony's been spying on us."

"That son-of-a-bitch, we were all going to be filthy rich. Too bad for him that he's going to lose his cut." Mercier then looked at Nancy. "Yeah, if you were wondering, I'm the one that shot your husband. I can't say that he died a happy man. I interrupted his little fantasy session with your new friend."

"I got a light, should I just burn the documents?" asked Mercier's partner.

"Do it."

Eddie watched the man take a cigarette lighter out of his pocket. He heard two clicks while the man cupped his hand over the flame, and then brought the lighter to the paper. An inner momentum propelled him to move forward. He had to stop him from destroying the evidence.

"Hey," said Mercier, catching Eddie's attention. "You make one budge and I'll shoot you in the leg. That's if you're lucky. So stay put."

A few seconds went by and Eddie didn't see anything close to a flame. He then saw the detective cupping the lighter and saw him attempting to start a flame a second time. All Eddie needed to do was to kick some snow into the vault and the papers would be too damp to light. The snow might damage some of the sheets, but not as bad as what a well-lit flame could do. He watched as the man took out a few papers, about three to five, roll them up, and put the flame to the tip—it caught. He then lowered the small torch to the papers inside the safe.

Eddie saw a bright light illuminate inside the safe, and flames shot out from the inside. *Fuck, that was our only hope.* And there wasn't a thing that they could do about it. He looked over at Corey and saw him moving about slowly. Screw Mercier's threats, he was going to help his friend, even if it was last time that he'd be with him. He kept his hands visible, slowly knelt down beside Corey and helped him sit up. "You alright, buddy?"

Corey coughed and spat out some blood. "What happened?"

"It doesn't matter. They've just destroyed what we came for." Eddie looked over at the safe. The flames were too high for anything inside to have not been consumed.

"Excuse me, detective," said Nancy. "How do you plan to explain this when an investigative team shows up?"

"It's not too difficult," said Mercier as he approached her. "Your friends, Corey, Eddie, and Jordyn, are drug addicts. The cocaine that we found in Corey and Eddie's apartment confirms it. Eddie prostituted himself to your husband for the money. However, Tony's cheap and didn't tip enough. So Eddie shot him."

"No one's going to believe that," said Eddie.

"Don't be so sure about that. Because since you couldn't get enough money from Tony, you and your friends drove out here in order to extort some more from his wife. She then brings you out here under the pretence that some valuables were buried. But you didn't like what you found. So you shot her. Bang."

Eddie looked up at Nancy, who returned the glance.

Mercier then chuckled. "How's that for a motive? Not bad, eh. Oh, and get this part. Eddie, Corey, and Jordyn got into a fight because there's no money. Eddie, who has the experience of using a handgun, ends up shooting both his friends. But then, Eddie realizes what he did. He's all alone, no family, no friends, and no money. So he puts the gun into his mouth, pulls the trigger, and blows out the back of his head." He chuckled some more as he took a step closer to Nancy. "How do you like that, eh?"

Eddie didn't answer. But there was a question he'd been wanting to ask him. Now would probably be the only chance that he'd get to ask it. "Why'd you kill Theo? What did he have to do with all of this?"

Mercier's eyes narrowed slightly as he shrugged his shoulders. "Theo? Who's he?"

"You broke his neck and pushed him down the stairs of his house, or the other way around, and tried to make it look like an accident."

About three seconds went by before his eyes dilated and his mouth opened, followed with him nodding. "Ah, him. I was hoping you could tell me since he's one of your friends. I didn't kill him. Did you, Nuttal?"

Nuttal shook his head with a chuckle. "It wasn't me."

"So he wasn't working with you?"

"Tabarnak, tu poses bien des questions, toi-la." *Fuck, you ask a lot of questions.*

"I just want to know," Eddie insisted.

Mercier rolled his eyes and sighed. "No, he wasn't working with us. We don't even know the guy. There, are you satisfied?"

"Drop it."

Eddie couldn't see her, but he recognized Jordyn's voice. When he looked at Mercier, even he looked perplexed.

"I said drop it. I have a gun pointed to the back of your head. I found it in the glove compartment of your car," yelled Jordyn.

"Miss Rinaldi, am I correct?" There was silence. "Have you ever fired a gun before?" asked Mercier calmly as though he were trying to figure out a way to get out of Jordyn's line of fire. Eddie seized the opportunity to help Corey stand and move away with Nancy. The only problem was that Mercier still had his gun on her.

"No, I haven't. But I'm too close to you *not* to miss. So put your gun down. You should know that the *real* police are on their way."

Come on, Jordyn, take the damn shot. He ain't going to drop his gun. He mouthed the words to her hoping that she'd read them from wherever she hid, but it didn't appear that she noticed.

"And you think that they'll believe you? I'm a well decorated detective for the city of Montreal. I've been in the force for over thirty years." He then spun around and fired.

What happened next was way too fast for Eddie to assimilate. He never knew the real power of adrenaline, but he saw it first hand when Corey launched from where he was and lunged at Mercier as his back was turned—tackling him. That was when he noticed Mercier's partner as he reached for his gun. Eddie didn't even think, he just reacted. He threw himself at Nuttal's legs, knocking him forward. Eddie felt him strike something solid, and that's when he heard him screaming. With a single jerk, Eddie got a kick to the chest, knocking him away. He rolled over twice in the snow before he managed to look up. The man bawled with his hands covering his face as he ran around erratically. It was then that he realized that he must have fallen face first into the flaming safe.

Eddie's hand touched something solid—it was the shovel. He

picked it up while Nuttal was still disoriented. Eddie knew that he'd come for him, a chance that he couldn't give him. Eddie raised the shovel and charged him, mindful that this was the mother-fucker that punched him and beat up Corey. Eddie hollered as loud as he could, channeling the energy into his arms. He swung and landed a blow to the side of Nuttal's head. The officer stumbled sideways, twisted towards the open grave, and fell in.

Eddie turned just as Mercier threw Corey off of him and was about to get up. But Nancy was already rushing him with her shovel, and with one swing she struck him on the back of the head—dropping him face first into the snow. She struck him two more times.

But where was Jordyn? Eddie looked around. "Jordyn, where are you?"

"Over here, I'm okay," she answered as she emerged from behind a tombstone.

Eddie dropped the shovel and put a hand to his chest with a sigh of relief. Thank God Mercier missed.

Corey got up, walked over to the gun that Mercier dropped, and picked it up. "Are you guys okay?"

They all nodded.

Jordyn ran up to Corey and hugged him. "I was trying to reach you but all I got was the *not available* message. I was trying to warn you guys that these two were cutting through the chained gate with bolt cutters."

"My cell phone died," Corey replied. "How did you manage to avoid being seen?"

"I hid under the blanket way in the back of the SUV. They just missed me."

"After they left, I called 9-1-1, searched inside their car, and found a gun in the glove compartment. I was lucky that they didn't lock their doors."

"You could've shot him, you know."

"I know, but I didn't want to risk shooting Nancy. She was too close to him."

Just then, sirens were heard in the distance. Eddie then looked over at the safe, which sat with its lid flipped open as black smoke emerged from inside. He walked over to it and looked inside—there was nothing left but ashes.

Shit. What were they going to do now?

It wasn't long after, that a large number a lights flashed and the sirens boomed about them, as the first set of police cruisers charged through the entrance. Moments later over a dozen provincial police officers surrounded them.

"Lâchez vos pistoles," *drop your guns,* yelled one of them as they rushed towards Corey and Jordyn. They tossed their guns to the side and threw up their hands. Eddie and Nancy did the same.

"Officers," said Mercier who got up holding the back of his head. "Thank God you showed up. I was about to arrest these hoodlums when they attacked me and my partner."

"That's enough, Detective." said another officer with a Caribbean accent.

Eddie looked and saw a black man with slightly different clothing walk past the others. The closer he came, the more that Eddie could tell that the broad-shouldered, six-foot tall man who was probably in his early fifties, was from the Royal Canadian Mounted Police or RCMP. He must be the officer in charge.

He walked up to the safe. Smoke still emanated from it. He looked inside, and then he turned to Eddie for a moment before he turned to everyone. "My name is Inspector Conrad Smith. Will someone tell me what was in here?"

"It was evidence that my husband, Tony Bevins, left behind that proves that Serge Lamont—through the company, Borealest—was swindling his clients," said Nancy. "It also listed the names of all of the co-conspirators. Unfortunately, my husband was among them."

"Detective Mercier and his partner were among them too," Eddie jumped in. "That's why Lamont hired them to kill the Governor. They wound up framing me for it because I was there."

"Oh come on," laughed Mercier as he pointed to Eddie. "He's lying. They're all lying. I've never met Serge Lamont, there's not even any evidence that he's involved. Missus Bevins clearly paid these three to lure her husband to the hotel so they can kill him, because she found out that he was cheating on her. I came here and caught them burning something. I don't know what it was and we'll never know because they destroyed it."

"Like hell we did," yelled Corey.

"That's enough, all of you," Smith yelled as he looked at his officers. "Take them away."

What the fuck? Eddie saw the officers close in on Corey and Jordyn—even they appeared to be surprised. Unexpectedly, the officers rushed past them and went straight for Mercier and threw him to the ground.

"What the fuck are you doing?" Mercier protested. "Why are you arresting me?"

"I assume you know of your right to be silent, Detective, or should I just simply call you, *ex-detective* from now on? So I suggest you shut up," said Smith. He then walked up to Jordyn. "Miss Rinaldi, I presume?"

Jordyn shook her head. "Yeah."

Smith smiled. "You and your boyfriend can put your hands down now."

Both Jordyn and Corey simultaneously lowered their hands and sighed with relief.

Smith then placed his hand on her shoulder. "I should also thank you for recording Mercier's confession with your cell phone's camera and sending it to 9-1-1." He then turned to Mercier. "The RCMP has a copy and one was forwarded to my cell phone while I was on my way here."

"What confession? I never confessed to anything," yelled Mercier.

Smith then turned to Mercier. "Really?" He then reached inside his jacket and took out a small spiral notepad and flipped a few pages over. "Wasn't it Nuttal who said, and I quote, 'They're records. They seem to be all about all of Borealest's transactions and I see a bunch of names. I see yours and mine on there. Even Fisher's name is there. Blah, blah, blah. Tony's been spying on us.' To which you responded, 'That son-of-a-bitch, we were all going to be filthy rich. Too bad for him that he's going to lose his cut. Yeah, if you were wondering, I'm the one that shot your husband. I can't say that he died a happy man. I interrupted his little fantasy session with your new friend.' End quote."

If there was more light, Eddie knew that he would've seen how red Mercier's face became as he saw him grinding his teeth before he shot a glance at Jordyn.

"You little bitch," Mercier snarled.

"Who me?" Jordyn answered, pointing to herself. "With the way things are right now, you're going to wind up as someone's bitch when your ass is thrown in jail," Jordyn answered with a smirk.

"I'm a decorated detective for the city of Montreal," yelled Mercier as his arms were pulled behind him, cuffed, and he was made to stand. "Thirty-eight years in the force putting punks like these behind bars. How dare you treat me like a common criminal."

"You'd better watch what you say from now on," said Smith.

Another officer was at Darwin's gravesite when he called out to Smith. "L'autre est ici." *The other one's down there.*

"Va le chercher," *Go get him out*, answered Smith.

"Nancy," came a woman's voice with a French-Canadian accent. Eddie looked and saw she wore a leather jacket and had shoulder-length brown hair bouncing off of her shoulders as she hopped through the snow.

"Chantal," said Nancy. "Thank God you're all right. You had me worried."

Chantal stopped and hugged Nancy. "I'm fine, I managed to slip out of the house while Serge was on the phone. He doesn't know where I am, but the police should've picked him up by now. I came here as soon as I could."

Corey and Jordyn approached while Eddie walked up to join them.

Chantal then extended a hand to all three of them. "Hello, my name is Chantal Lamont. I'm so sorry for what my husband put you guys through."

Eddie returned the handshake. "It's okay. At least...now."

Nancy turned to Chantal. "But the evidence is destroyed. Names were listed on it, and now we'll never know exactly how many people were involved in this scandal. Come to think of it, it'll be harder to convict these officers and, sorry to say, your husband."

"Not necessarily," said Inspector Smith who approached them. "You must be glad that I'm not here to arrest you." He then offered his hand to Eddie, Corey, Jordyn, and Nancy. "The video recording that Miss Rinaldi made with her camera phone should be damaging enough to them. It'll take one hell of a lawyer to get all three of them off. With that recording, the provincial financial securities watchdog—L'Autorité des Marché Financiers, otherwise known as the AMF—will have no choice but to investigate Borealest. This time, with a fine-tooth comb. A fraud charge against Mister Lamont shouldn't come too long after."

"In addition to your testimony," said Chantal as she looked at Eddie. "He'll be sent to jail for life, along with Mercier and Nuttal."

They all watched as four officers lifted Nuttal from inside the grave and dragged him away. He appeared to be semi-conscious, but seemed to be in a lot of pain. He moaned while covering his face. Two ambulance technicians rushed up and met them half way.

Eddie then turned to the sounds of Mercier screaming. He just managed to catch him as he was being forced into the backseat of a police cruiser.

Smith then turned to them. "There's still a few things that I want to ask you just to help me write my report."

"Inspector Smith," said Chantal. "Can't you see that these people have been through a lot? We don't have to do it here, do we?"

"I don't mind us going back to my place," said Nancy. "What do you say?"

Smith nodded. "That should be fine. Lead the way."

***

The vultures swarmed around Serge Lamont's mansion as they fired off questions repeatedly. From what Eddie saw on the television in Nancy's living room, along with Nancy, Chantal, and Inspector Smith, Lamont appeared to be resisting arrest. It took more than three police officers to push him through the front door, as Lamont resisted by kicking up his legs up and forcing them against the threshold to prevent him from being pulled outside. The police didn't take too long to get him out, as he kept on screaming to everyone. "Why am I being arrested?

I'm the victim. I have rights." He screamed this repeatedly as he was dragged close to the cameraman. From what Eddie saw, the three officers appeared to enjoy displaying Lamont in front of the camera crews, especially when they struggled to shove him into the backseat of a cruiser.

But Eddie had seen enough for the time being. Nancy came out of the kitchen with a tray. She placed it on the coffee table and turned to Chantal and Inspector Smith. "The two coffee mugs are yours and I brought tea for the rest of us." Chantal and Smith thanked her as they took their mugs. Also on the tray was a plate of tea biscuits.

Eddie watched Jordyn and Corey as they walked down together from upstairs. By their pleasant facial expressions, he figured that in addition to telling Jordyn's parents and Corey's aunt that they were safe, they must have announced Jordyn's pregnancy. Nancy sat down next to Eddie on the couch when she nudged his arm. When he looked at her, she handed him her cell phone.

"Why don't you call your family? I'm sure they're anxious to hear from you."

She was right. But he didn't know if he was ready to face them yet.

"What's the matter, dear?" asked Nancy.

Eddie stared at the phone as he tried to come up with an answer. "I'm just...well...it's just..."

Nancy placed a hand on his arm. "I know how you feel. But you saw them on TV earlier. I'm sure whatever you're thinking, they were thinking the same thing before they worked up the courage to apologize to you on live television. You have the chance to do so privately." She opened up his hand, placed the phone in it, and closed his fingers around it. "Go ahead—you can use one of the bedrooms upstairs."

Eddie nodded, stood up, and walked up the steps. Instead of going to one of the five lavishly-decorated bedrooms, he found his way into the same bathroom that he used earlier. He closed the door and went to his favorite thinking spot. This time, he wouldn't think—he would just act. He sat down on the toilet bowl and dialed his parents' house phone. The phone rang twice before it was answered.

"Hello." The voice was the familiar deep baritone voice that he had grown up listening to.

Eddie paused and swallowed hard. He then took one deep breath and then exhaled. "Hello, Dad."

Chapter 23

Whd Eddie pressed the *off* button, the display read 56:34. He wasn't surprised at how much time had passed while he spoke to his parents, Aunt Beverly, and Denise. It was half past midnight. He then rested his elbows on his knees and let his head hang, staring at his feet and the bathroom tiles. It would be a two-hour drive back to Montreal. Eddie doubted that Nancy would let them leave her house at this hour, after everything they've been through. But he had also grown fond of her, and he felt guilty about the idea of leaving her all alone in this big house. Furthermore, his parents had mentioned that the media vultures were camped out in front of the house again. As for Nancy Bevins, the official story was that she had returned to Concord, New Hampshire. Of course, the press fell for it, and were all currently camped outside her residence down there—giving Eddie and his friends a break. He didn't entertain that thought because he didn't want to have anything to do with the media. They already destroyed his life from a botched plan that could've potentially worked.

A knock at the door startled him out of his deep thought.

"Yo, bro, you all right?" It was Corey.

"You gone nearly give me a heart attack."

"For real?" Corey opened the door. "I just had to be sure that you weren't playing with yourself, I know how you like your privacy."

"Man, shut up and come on in."

Corey giggled and closed the door behind him. "So how did it go with your folks?"

"Things are cool. It's kind of like we're starting over from scratch. I told them everything."

"Everything?"

"Every last detail. From Jordyn and I meeting with Theo—to what went on in the hotel room with Tony Bevins—to our escape."

"What did they say?"

"Nothing much. They mostly listened, which is a huge change from what I'm used to. Of course there was the occasional interruption when my father and Aunt Bev started bickering."

Corey leaned his back on the wall as he faced Eddie. "Sounds like you got them hooked."

"Boy, were they ever." Eddie yawned for a bit. Lord, would he love to be in bed right now. "I thought I'd never be able to get off the phone."

"Why shouldn't they. After all, you're the expert storyteller. I'm sure everyone's dying to hear about everything...as in, let's say... another novel."

"No man! I'm giving that up. That's caused me nothing but trouble. We almost got killed because of me wanting to get my book published—"

"We almost got killed because of your desire to succeed as a writer. There's nothing wrong with that. I mean...the part about writing. Didn't you learn anything from what Nancy told us earlier—the story about the elephants? Just stick to what you're aiming for. Whatever anyone else says, fuck them. You ain't doing anything illegal. So stop beating yourself up."

He's right.

"Don't you think I envied you these past several months?" said Corey, to Eddie's surprise. "You were always focused on your goals. And that's something I've been lacking for a long time." Corey then sighed as he sat down on the floor against the wall, his knees bent at a forty-five degree angle. He shook his head and then looked up at Eddie. "I don't know why it took Jordyn's pregnancy for me to realize that I need to get my ass in gear, when you've been telling me this for months. Now I know that I got to. 'Cause you know me, I ain't going to have my kid growing up and telling his or her friends that their daddy's more broke than MC Hammer."

Eddie cracked a smile. "Naw, I don't think you got to worry about them comparing you to MC Hammer. You can't dance like him."

"But I'm serious about what I said," said Corey. "I'm sure if you wrote about what we went through, people would be rushing to buy it. You'd probably be among the few celebrities who actually wrote their own book. This time you won't need to dress up in sexy leather with a whip."

Eddie chuckled. Leave it to Corey to always make him laugh when he was down. Corey then stretched out his arm towards him and formed a fist. Eddie responded with his own fist and they bumped them together. But Eddie grabbed his fist, pulled Corey forward onto his feet as he stood and hugged him. "Thanks."

"Back at you, bro," Corey replied. They then left the bathroom and walked back downstairs.

As Corey and Eddie walked into the living room, Smith was already questioning Jordyn as Nancy and Chantal sat adjacent from her. He had a pen and a notepad in which he jotted notes.

Smith looked up at Eddie as he entered the living room with Corey. "I was just coming around to you. I'll just ask you a few questions and then I'll be on my way."

"Yo, Inspector," said Corey as he and Eddie sat down on the couch. "You ever been on TV?"

Smith raised an eyebrow as though he were trying to remember if he ever had been. "No. I'm not regularly on TV. I gave a press conference once, but that was a year ago. I'd say that you have a pretty good memory if you remember that far back."

"Naw, it ain't that far back. I could've sworn that I saw you sometime recently."

"I hope I don't have a twin that was arrested or something," Smith answered with a smile and then turned to Eddie. "Miss Rinaldi told me that you met with Theo Warren, or Master Tiger, last Friday. Is that correct?"

"Yes," Eddie replied.

"And according to her statement, he's the one that set you up for a meeting at l'Hôtel Mont-Royal with one of his clients. Do you agree?"

"Yeah, but I expected it to be with a woman. Had I known that it was a guy, I wouldn't have done it."

"Okay," Smith scribbled some more on his notepad. "But if you weren't comfortable being with a man, why did you go through with it? You could've just stopped and walked away."

"I know. But Jordyn went through a lot to help me get this going, so I didn't want to back out. I thought I could hold him off long enough until the news crews busted us."

"Oh yeah, your publicity stunt. Miss Rinaldi told me all about that. I strongly suggest that you three don't ever try something like that again."

"Trust us," said Corey. "We ain't doing anything like that again."

"For sure," said Eddie, as he and the others shook their heads. He felt uneasy describing what he did with Bevins, but tried to keep it as brief as possible—leaving out the graphic details. He expected Nancy to walk out but she stayed, and she didn't appear to be bothered. He described everything up to the point that Bevins offered him a drink. Smith then questioned him on the rest of the events that took place after he saw Mercier and Nuttal show up.

Smith flipped a page of his notepad. "Why'd you go visit Mister Warren yesterday morning?"

"I had the feeling that I was set up," answered Eddie.

"Really, how so?"

"I didn't buy the idea that he'd mix up his clients, not with the amount of experience that he had."

"But people make mistakes. I know colleagues who've been on the force for more than thirty years and they make mistakes. Everyone does. Human errors happen all the time."

"Yeah, but when's the last time you've heard about a homicide being linked to human error?"

Smith thought for a moment and then nodded. "You've got a point. The three of you were brave going out in public, taking a chance at being recognized by someone who would've seen your faces on the news."

"We didn't have a choice," said Eddie.

"True. But how would you have gotten Mister Warren to admit that he deliberately set you up with the wrong person?"

Eddie looked at Corey who looked back at him. He knew what they would've done, although right now, it sounded a bit ridiculous. But he was so goddamned pissed off at Theo at the time. "We don't know. We would've figured out something at the moment, I guess."

"Except he was already dead when we got there," added Corey.

Eddie nodded. "That's when we decided that it was time to come see Missus Bevins. We were hoping that she could tell us about Darwin's grave."

"Yes, I remember, Darwin's grave."

"Except that his secret's gone now," said Nancy. "Mercier and his partner destroyed everything."

"It's not a total loss," said Chantal. "In light of everything, the AMF cannot ignore investigating Borealest."

"And neither will the RCMP," Smith added as he looked at Eddie, Corey, Jordyn, and Nancy. "Mercier's recorded testimony that Miss Rinaldi sent us should be enough. In the hands of a good prosecutor it should be able to put Lamont, Mercier, and Nuttal away for a long time."

Eddie then turned to Chantal. "But you're a witness too. How did you know we were innocent?"

Chantal sipped from her mug and put it back onto the tray. "Serge has been acting strange lately, and he's been a lot more secretive than usual. That jerk, Mercier, kept showing up at our house more often. I never liked the man, he always gave me the creeps, and I told my husband that I didn't ever want to see him in our house. But he never listened. Then, last Saturday I overheard a phone conversation he had earlier in which he had mentioned both your names. When I got up early this morning to use the bathroom, I noticed that his cell phone was recharging, but he'd forgotten to take it with him when he took the dog out for a walk. I decided to look at his call list. I also contacted Inspector Smith about my suspicions and forwarded him the list so that he could check it out."

"I verified the phone numbers and found out that he'd been

talking to Mercier," said Smith. "He's also been in contact with a computer programmer named Nick Fisher, whose body was found earlier today."

"Found?" asked Nancy. "You mean, he—"

"He hung himself," said Chantal.

"We're investigating him right now," said Smith. "My only guess as to why Mister Lamont knew him was because he was hired to falsify Borealests books. That way, investors and external auditors would never know about the company's actual financial status. Fisher must have caved to the pressure and committed suicide."

Eddie shook his head. Shit, another body. That's the third one in two days. Now he, Corey, Jordyn, and Nancy will be expected to testify against Lamont and his gang. What if Lamont's lawyers found a way to get him off the hook? He always read about court cases where the prosecution had solid evidence against a suspect, only for the case to be thrown out and the suspect was set free due to inadmissible evidence. Why didn't he think of that before? If that ever happened, then he and his friends would be placed in some witness protection program. By next year, he'd have a new name and would be picking up people's trash in some far away country like Australia or New Zealand to be out of Lamont's reach. The guy's already got two police officers on his payroll...Lord knew who else he had.

Eddie turned to Smith. "Tell me the truth. How sure are you about getting Lamont and those two policemen behind bars?"

Smith smiled and shook his head. "I wouldn't worry. I'm confident the RCMP's investigation will turn up enough evidence against Lamont, Mercier, and Nuttal—as long as you all cooperate."

Although it was a false sense of security, he'd have to live with it for the time being. "Sure, I guess." *So long as I don't have to be worried about being a sniper's target.* He had to get out of this room. He needed something cold to drink. "If everyone's done, I'll take away the teacups."

Nancy waved him off. "Don't be silly, I'll take care of that."

Eddie already had the filled tray in his hand and stood. "I insist. It's your turn to relax."

Nancy smiled and shook her head. "Nothing can change your

mind once it's made up, right?"

"You can say so." Eddie walked away with the tray. He got to the kitchen and rested the tray on the island's granite counter surface beside the sink. He opened the dishwasher door, pulled out the upper tray, and placed the cups inside one after another. He then grabbed a mug and was about to place it beside the cups when the lipstick smudge caught his eye—it was Chantal's. He froze as his mind suddenly went blank. Eddie couldn't think about what blocked him, something wasn't right, like déjà-vu. Somewhere in the back of his mind, the phrase about lipstick having to do with someone that had expensive tastes kept coming up...oh fuck...the wine glass at Theo's house. He looked at the smudge in front of him.

Shit, they were both the same color. Could Chantal be...naw...no way... but...

He had to get Jordyn.

He kept the mug with him as he left the kitchen, crept down the hallway, and stopped at the threshold that separated it from the living room. Eddie poked his head out slowly. Corey's arm was around Jordyn as they spoke to Smith. Eddie then looked at Chantal. She appeared to be calm and she was relaxed with her legs crossed. How could she have known Theo and not have shown any emotion at the mention of his death? Never mind that for now, he had to get a second opinion. "Jordyn?"

Jordyn turned her head as the others glanced at him. "What's up?"

"I need you for a second." Okay, he kept a straight enough face. No one should suspect anything.

Jordyn got up and came to him. She walked with him down the hallway. "What is it?"

Eddie shushed her with his index finger to his lips. He checked behind him once more, and then placed a hand on the small of her back to rush her into the kitchen.

Once inside, Jordyn turned around to face him, visibly anxious. "What's the matter?"

Eddie then showed her the lipstick smudge. "Check this out. What do you think?"

She looked at it and shrugged her shoulders. "So?"

"Haven't you seen this shade before?"

Jordyn took the mug and examined the smudge. "It's not a common shade."

"Smell it."

Jordyn looked at Eddie, clearly annoyed. "What's this all about? Why don't you just tell me?"

"Just smell it," Eddie whispered loudly.

Jordyn sighed, put the mug to her nose, and inhaled. Eddie noticed the change of expression in her face. She then looked away and paused. It was as though she were trying to place the scent.

"You recognize the smell, don't you?" asked Eddie. "Wouldn't you say that this lipstick belongs to someone with expensive tastes?"

Jordyn looked at him, her mouth agape. "Oh my God."

It hit her, and Eddie saw it in her eyes. "Doesn't this look like the same lipstick we saw on the wine glass at Theo's house?"

Jordyn covered her mouth with her hand as she turned to check the kitchen entrance. It appeared as though she feared that someone was eavesdropping. "Do you think that Chantal knew Theo?"

"I'd say that this is too much of a coincidence for her *not* to have known him."

"But this might *only* prove that she knew him, not that she killed him."

"And if she knew him, don't you think that she would've shown a bit more emotion when we talked about discovering Theo's body? Whether she was an acquaintance or just a fuck friend, I think she would've."

"If Chantal was having any type of affair with Theo, I can understand why she'd keep it a secret. If she told Smith about it, then he's under no obligation to tell us since she has a right to privacy."

"I'm not talking about disclosure, I'm talking about reactions. She didn't even flinch when I went into detail about how Theo's head was twisted halfway around his neck. Everyone else did."

Jordyn shook her head as though she was in disbelief. "Okay, maybe she didn't have a normal reaction. But even if you're right about Theo setting you up, how does this prove that she's involved in any way? And what would she have to gain from it?"

Eddie held his head with both hands as he walked away. "I don't know. It doesn't make sense." He passed Jordyn as he paced back in front of her. *Think, damn it! You're onto something. Don't let it go. What else did Bevins say that night?* He walked past Jordyn again when it came to him. He stopped pacing and turned to Jordyn. "Hold on, there's something else. On the night that Bevins died, he told me that there were things that he was involved in that even Serge Lamont didn't even know about. *This* could be one of those things."

"An affair between her and Theo?" Jordyn almost chuckled. "And you think that because Bevins knew about this that she wanted him dead as well?"

"Well...it's—"

"She couldn't have had anything to do with Bevins' murder. She was at the cemetery tonight when Mercier and Nuttal were being arrested. Why didn't they expose her then?"

"Maybe she wasn't involved in his murder, but it doesn't mean that Bevins didn't know *other* things about her that she didn't want anyone to know. This comes back to my point about her husband not knowing about everything that Bevins knew. Hence, Mercier and Nuttal would've been in the dark."

Jordyn didn't say anything but remained silent as though she were putting everything into perspective.

"What do we have so far?" asked Eddie rhetorically. "A Governor and a maledom—both murdered. Their one connection is Chantal."

Jordyn then pointed a finger at him. "But where do *you* fit in?"

"I don't know. Maybe I don't fit in. Don't forget, I wasn't originally supposed to meet Bevins. Theo was."

"And what if he didn't break his leg?" continued Jordyn. "He would've been killed along with Bevins, unless he got lucky like you did."

"True. It only makes you wonder what else was in those files, doesn't it?" said Eddie.

"Which we no longer have. Shit. Why the fuck couldn't Bevins have made backup copies?"

Eddie leaned against the countertop beside the sink, let his elbows fall on the surface, and let his head drop down into his hands. Now Jordyn was the one pacing up and down.

Hold a sec, backup copies? He raised his head and looked at Jordyn. "What makes you think that Bevins didn't have backup copies of those files?"

Jordyn shook her head and flung her arms out. "I don't know. Maybe he does. But where would they be?"

"I'd like to know too." A voice came from the doorway.

Eddie and Jordyn turned and saw Smith walk into the kitchen.

"I'm so glad you're here," said Jordyn. "Eddie and I have been talking. We think that there was more info in those files than we thought."

Smith raised an eyebrow as he stopped in front of the island. "Oh really, what kind?"

Jordyn then lowered her voice. "Stuff that could probably explain why Theo was killed." She then picked up Chantal's coffee mug and showed Smith the lipstick smudge. "This is a very close match to the lipstick smudge that we saw on a wine glass at Theo's place a few nights ago."

"We believe that Chantal knew him," said Eddie.

Smith shrugged his shoulders. "So what if she knew him?"

"She could've killed him, and there might be something in those files that could prove why she did it," Eddie answered.

Smith took the mug from Jordyn, examined the smudge, and then held it out in front of him. "This is a common shade. I'm sure there are thousands that are similar. This doesn't prove that Chantal was ever around Theo's house or that she even knew him."

"But what are the chances that the same shade shows up in such a short time, that just happens to be in the home of a murder victim?" asked Eddie.

"They even smell the same," added Jordyn. "I know this shade, and it's not cheap."

"Are you just going to ignore all of this?" asked Eddie.

Smith sighed. "And do you have the wine glass with the lipstick on it?"

"Of course not," Jordyn answered. "But we—"

"Then there's no proof." Smith put the mug back onto the counter.

Eddie watched as Jordyn and Smith went back at it over and over. It was like watching tennis players hitting the ball back and forth to each other. Why didn't Smith want to listen? Didn't they have their own specialists that could comb through Theo's house and find some kind of DNA evidence, like saliva, a hair strand, or something that would prove that Chantal was in his house last week? When he looked at Jordyn, she appeared to get more and more frustrated as she spoke louder. He was sure that the others in the living room would be able to hear them, but Smith didn't seem to care.

"Listen," Eddie said, coming between both of them. He then turned to Smith. "Bevins told me that there were things that he knew of that even Serge wasn't aware of. Is it possible—"

"You've already gone over this with me before." Smith interrupted, clearly losing his temper. "Bevins was drunk and he offered you a drink that you couldn't handle, you even spilled the drink onto the table when you started coughing. Blah, blah, blah."

"Spilled the drink when I started coughing? When did that—" suddenly he remembered. "Okay, yes, I drank the drink a bit...too fast." Something was wrong and Eddie sensed it immediately. *Hold on a sec. I never told Smith that I started coughing after sipping the beverage.*

"So there's nothing that you can do?" asked Jordyn. "Is that what you're telling us?"

Smith answered her, but Eddie didn't hear a word he said. It was as though what was said between he and Jordyn was nothing more than background noise similar to being in a crowded room. There was no way that Smith could've known about him spilling his drink...unless he was there. And the more he looked at Smith, the more he wanted to grab Jordyn by the hand and run for the nearest exit—yelling to Corey and Nancy to do the same. But he knew that was a lost cause.

As Jordyn continued to argue with him, Eddie put a hand on

her shoulder—stopping her in mid-sentence. "I think you should let it go."

"Like hell I'm going to let this go. Fuck, he has the whole goddamn RCMP at his disposal—"

"Jordyn," Eddie said sharply. His eyes were closed as he said this. She stopped yelling instantly. "Don't bother, because he ain't going to investigate stuff that he already knows." He then looked at Smith who had a smirk grow at the corner of his mouth. "Ain't that right?"

Jordyn, much calmer, turned to Eddie. "What are you talking about?"

Eddie kept staring Smith in the eyes. Smith didn't let go of the stare, and it convinced Eddie even more that he was onto something. "I never told you that I choked after sipping the drink that Bevins offered me—never told you that I spilled it, either—nobody did. How'd you know about that?"

From his peripheral vision, Eddie saw Jordyn look away from him towards Smith. At this point, she must have been wondering about the same thing as well. But by the way she grabbed his forearm and pulled herself closer to him, he knew what she was thinking—and it was most likely the same thing that scared him. Smith still didn't answer. "You're in on it too, aren't you? No wonder Corey thought you looked familiar. He must have seen you in the hotel lobby while he was waiting for me."

Smith's smirk grew into a smile as he leaned against the counter, crossing his arms.

Eddie took Jordyn by the hand and she began to squeeze it. Lord, his palms were already sweaty. "You had Bevins' room bugged, didn't you? You must have hidden the bug in the floral vase, which would've been damaged when I accidentally spilled the drink onto it when I bumped the table. And this has everything to do with those files, doesn't it?"

Smith slowly began to circle the island counter to the opposite side, eventually to come up behind Eddie and Jordyn. Both of them turned around slowly where they stood—Jordyn slowly inching her way behind Eddie—as they kept Smith in front of them.

"You're a clever young man," Smith nodded with pursed lips. It wasn't a look of disapproval, but more of one of approval. "I said too much and *you* caught it. Not many people would've."

"I've been told that I tend to notice stuff," said Eddie.

"What do you want from us?" Jordyn said with a shortness of breath. Although Smith completely circled the island countertop, he kept walking slowly towards them. Eddie and Jordyn found themselves walking backwards—maintaining a buffer zone between them.

"For now," said Smith as he closed the dishwasher. "I just want you to walk back to the living room and join everyone." He then lifted his jacket, exposing his service revolver, and patted it. "I'm sure you can both do that, can't you?"

Chapter 24

Eddie felt that there had to be some backup files. Smith must have thought so too. It must be what he was trying to find out when he questioned them. Jordyn was in front of him as they walked back to the living room—with both their hands held up. Nancy, Corey, and Chantal were in the middle of a conversation when they appeared. Eddie noticed how both Nancy and Corey's eyes dilated when they walked in.

Nancy looked at Chantal, then back at him. "What's going on?"

Chantal stood and turned to Smith. "Did they say anything else?"

"Not yet," he answered.

Corey stood, but Smith was quick to draw his service revolver, pointing it at him and prompting Nancy to shriek.

"Sit down."

Corey's hands shot up without saying a word. He kept them up, as he slowly sat, not taking his eyes off the gun.

Smith then shoved Eddie towards Corey with his other hand— causing him to bump into Jordyn as he stumbled forward.

Nancy turned to Smith. She didn't say anything at first as though she were dumbfounded. "I don't understand. Are they under arrest?"

"Not really," Chantal answered.

Nancy turned to Chantal. "What do you mean, not really?"

"Go ahead and tell her," said Eddie to Chantal. "I wouldn't also mind knowing why you killed Theo after you both set me up."

Nancy's jaw dropped. "What?" She looked back at Chantal. "Is this true?"

Chantal didn't answer, but smiled as she moved away from Nancy and approached the couch where Eddie, Jordyn, and Corey sat. She kept her eye on Eddie as Smith stood behind, keeping his sidearm visible. She put a foot up on the coffee table and leaned forward. "Let's cut to the chase. How'd you know I knew Master Tiger?"

Eddie glanced at Smith, who crossed his arms and raised an eyebrow, as though to prompt him to answer her question. He looked back at Chantal. "Your lipstick gave you away."

"Did it?" She turned to look at Smith, and then back at him. "What else have you figured out?"

Eddie looked at Nancy. She looked as though she'd lost some color to her face, as she remained frozen where she stood. He then looked back at Chantal. "I can only guess at this point."

"Enlighten us," said Chantal.

"You just referred Theo as Master Tiger. You were one of his clients, weren't you?" He then glanced at Smith briefly. "Or was *he* involved in your threesomes."

Nancy looked at both Chantal and Smith and slowly sank back into her chair. "Oh my God. Chantal."

Chantal looked over at Nancy. "Oh come on, where's your sense of adventure?"

"But why did you kill Theo?" asked Jordyn.

"'Cause he knew too much, said Corey as he looked at Smith. "They probably killed the computer nerd too—the one that supposedly hung himself."

Chantal took her foot off the table. "*They* were liabilities, if you must know." She then turned to Nancy. "So was your husband."

"But you didn't kill my husband," said Nancy.

"No, it was Mercier, under my husband's orders. You can't imagine how that affected my plans."

"*Your* plans?" asked Nancy.

"You heard me." Chantal sighed as she turned and walked away from Nancy. "Allow me to start from the beginning. Borealest used to perform well. So well, that my husband, along with his friends, including the Governor, were able to easily embezzle money. In order to stay under the radar of the provincial regulators, Lamont hired Fischer—the computer expert—to falsify client reports and also create false receipts to hide any missing money from auditors. It didn't take long for me to figure out that company funds were being diverted to a ghost account in which Lamont, Bevins, and his friends were taking a cut. So I did some extra digging. Interestingly, I found out that Fisher was taking an extra cut for himself. I figured, why can't *I* get a cut? That's when I blackmailed him. As a result, I found out about everyone that was involved, including Tony. As for Master Tiger, he was just my boy toy. And he also has a special talent for getting dirty little secrets out of people."

"No wonder you killed him. He spanked the truth out of you," said Eddie.

"No and yes," said Chantal. "He knew about what I was doing, and about my affair with Inspector Smith. By chance, I managed to get a peek at his client list one evening and saw that Tony was one of them. I couldn't believe the coincidence."

"Let me guess," said Nancy. "You decided that you could blackmail my husband also. You figured that you could destroy his political career and his marriage with what you knew about him."

"Actually," Smith said. "I did the blackmailing."

"Precisely," said Chantal. "I couldn't take the chance at showing my face around him. Or else I ran the risk of him telling my husband. He went along with it for a while until he decided that he would no longer cooperate. I feared that he was going to go public. That's when I needed Master Tiger to bait him into coming to the hotel."

"With the hidden microphone in the vase, I'd know precisely when to surprise them." said Smith.

"I agreed to give Theo a huge cut, which he accepted," said Chantal. "Unfortunately for us he broke his leg while entertaining a very overweight client of his." Chantal then walked up to Eddie and his friends. "That's where you guys came in."

"That's why you set me up?" Eddie said. "So you could lure the Governor to the hotel. Theo didn't even know what he was getting into. Fuck, he didn't even realize that he was setting me up to be killed."

Corey turned to Eddie. "It's like she said. He was just a boy toy to her. Nothing more than bait for Governor Bevins."

Chantal smirked as she looked at Eddie. "Tony has a thing for young black guys."

"So do you, apparently," said Eddie.

Chantal shrugged her shoulders before she turned to Nancy. "I know you're not too happy to hear that."

Eddie couldn't help but look at Nancy. A few minutes earlier she had appeared to be in shock. Now, he saw the rage build, starting with the narrowing of her eyes.

Chantal chuckled as she turned back to Eddie. "I can't believe this. You did all of this just to get some book of yours published?" She then leaned closer to him. "I hate to be the bearer of bad news, but you're never going to be an author. I'm sorry."

"You ain't sorry," said Eddie. "You killed Theo, and you would've killed me too."

"As I mentioned earlier, Master Tiger was a liability," said Chantal. "I couldn't take any chances. And although we were ready to dispose of you also, we couldn't do so then. While you were with Tony, we had an unexpected surprise."

"You went and spilled your drink and destroyed the bug," said Smith. "I still managed to catch bits and pieces and heard something about hidden evidence that could implicate everyone. I was about to head upstairs, demand to know where this evidence was, and then pop a few bullets into both of you. Then Mercier and Nuttal walked into the lobby, which screwed things up."

Chantal turned to Nancy. "You're husband's made quite a few enemies over the past few weeks, hasn't he?"

Smith walked closer to Eddie. "Fortunately I already had Mercier's number. I was able to reach him to give him the anonymous tip that scared both him and his partner off, but only after they murdered Bevins. I came to kill you that night. Ironically, I ended up saving your life."

Corey then turned to Smith, pointing a finger. "I knew I saw you before. You were in the hotel lobby while I was waiting on Eddie. You were out of uniform, reading some magazine."

"Yes, that was me. But you guys already had hotel security chasing you—another inconvenience. So I lost you that evening."

"Yeah, you did," said Eddie. "But since you were already there you were able to swipe the bug from Bevins' suite before the real police showed up."

Smith smiled. "I knew that as long as I could get to you guys before Mercier did, I could make sure that Tony's hidden evidence never surfaced."

"This also put us on the defensive," said Chantal. "So we eliminated Fischer. We knew that a scandal involving Borealest was imminent. It was just a matter of time."

"Making it look like a suicide was the best way," said Smith.

"But the hardcopy files are gone," said Chantal. "But where there are hardcopies, there are backups." She then turned to Nancy. "Isn't that right?"

"I don't know anything about those files. If I did then both of you would be in jail," Nancy refuted.

"You have a point." Chantal then turned back to Eddie. "But something tells me that you may know."

"Yeah, it's back in his other house in New Hampshire," said Eddie.

Chantal chuckled. "Don't lie to me. I think that Tony, in his drunken state, must have told you something."

"He did," said Eddie. "It was at the cemetery. You saw it for yourself. The files were burnt up."

The slap that he got to his face stung him. Chantal then held up a finger in front of him. "Don't fuck with me. I know that Tony told you where they are. I want those files."

"He just told you that he doesn't know," said Nancy. "What more do you want?"

"Then I guess we don't have anything to lose, do we." Chantal reached over, grabbed Jordyn's arm, and yanked her up.

Corey was about to leap out and stop her until there was loud *bang*. Nancy and Jordyn screamed while Eddie jumped to the side, falling into the arm of the couch while he watched Corey fall to the ground—screaming and clutching his right foot.

Smith turned to Eddie and yelled. "You want to do something

stupid like your friend and I'll do the same to you."

Somewhere in the house, Darwin II barked furiously. Corey still wailed as he lay on his side.

"Will you just shut up?" Chantal screamed to Corey.

Eddie wanted to assist Corey badly but knew that Smith wouldn't allow it. Corey still held on to his foot as he struggled to quiet down. But the agony was all over his face.

Jordyn turned to Smith. "Eddie's just been cleared of murder. Everyone who was at the cemetery tonight knows that he's innocent, clearing the rest of us. How are you going to explain our deaths?"

Smith curved his mouth to the side, sighed, and then turned to Jordyn. "Let's see. Considering what Eddie knew, Serge Lamont didn't take any chances and hired a hit man to deal with you in the event Mercier and Nuttal failed. How does that sound?"

"Listen," Nancy shrieked. "I can pay you whatever you want. Please, just don't hurt them."

Chantal shook her head with a smile. "I think not."

"We don't need your money, woman," said Smith. "I'm no stranger to making witnesses and evidence disappear. I know a few powerful families who owe me a favor."

"What kind of favor?" asked Nancy.

"I'll keep it simple. You bring us the files, we let you live under the condition that you don't tell anyone what happened this evening," Smith then looked at Eddie, Corey, Jordyn, and then back at Nancy. "But if any of you pull a fast one, I'll call in that favor. You'll all be hunted down one after the next. So will your families. I don't think I need to tell you what'll happen to you if you don't bring me those files."

Chantal then shoved Jordyn over to Smith, who caught her, spun her around, and pointed the gun to her head while eying Eddie.

"Are you sure you don't know where the backups are?" asked Smith. "Because something tells me that you're about to remember in about ten seconds before I start finishing each of you off one by one. Starting with her. Ten."

"Don't do it. Please don't hurt her," cried Corey.

"Shut up," screamed Chantal.

"Nine," said Smith.

Shit, what else did Bevins say? He just spoke about Darwin's grave. He looked quickly at Nancy who had the same panicked look on her face. He then glanced at Jordyn as her breathing sped up and tears streamed from her eyes.

"Eight."

Corey was now looking at him with tears in his eyes. His eyes pleaded him to think of something.

Fuck, what was it that I missed?

"Seven."

Tony mentioned that everything was in Darwin's grave. He didn't give the combination to the safe. No, that couldn't be it. Eddie grabbed the side of his head with both hands as he bent over towards the floor.

"Six."

Eddie now heard his heart pounding in his chest and his throat getting dry to the point that it hurt him. There was too much commotion for him to think straight.

"Five."

"Eddie," said Corey. "Just say something. Don't let him kill my girl, please."

"I can't say because I don't know," he answered. He then sat up and yelled at Smith. "I don't know where they are. Just let her go, please."

"Four."

"What the fuck you want from me?" yelled Eddie. "How am I supposed to know something like this? I never knew the guy."

"Times ticking," said Chantal.

"Three."

Eddie cupped his hands over his mouth, then to his neck, as he began to lose control of his own breathing. Something was between his hands and neck, it was his necklace with the flash drive attached to it—a cold reminder of how all of this started. Everyone knew why he had this around his neck, even Tony Bevins...wait, Tony said that he once thought of the same thing too—keeping his work close to him...Darwin's grave.

"Two."

Jordyn was screaming now, but Eddie didn't hear the words. Darwin's grave...origin...Nancy said Darwin II had that written on his locket...holy shit. That's it!

In his excitement, Eddie jumped up from the couch with his hands out with his palms visible to Smith. "I know where the backup is. Just don't shoot her. I promise that I'll show you where they are."

Chantal raised a hand in front of Smith, signaling him to lower his gun. "Do you now?"

Eddie nodded his head.

Chantal took a step towards him. "As I said before, if you're fucking with me—"

"I swear, I'm not," said Eddie as he brought his hands closer together.

"How far do we have to go?" Smith said as he tightened his grip on Jordyn.

"Nowhere, they're in the house."

"Where?" asked Chantal.

Eddie turned to Nancy. "Go get Darwin."

Nancy replied with short quick nods as she looked at Chantal, who tilted her head once to the side, letting her know that it was all right to leave. Eddie watched her walk out of the living room and disappear into the hallway. Chantal followed her but stopped upon entering the hallway. A few seconds later, he heard high-pitched whining and claws scratching the floor.

Chantal stepped back and Darwin II appeared, standing on his hind legs still whining at Chantal, as though to play with her. Nancy struggled with Darwin II by pulling on his collar and dragged him inside the living room.

"If your dog even growls the wrong way I'll have him shot," threatened Chantal.

Nancy appeared to ignore her as she told Darwin II to sit. He obeyed.

Eddie walked up to Darwin, eyeing Smith as he passed him, only to get a menacing glare in return. He knelt down in front of Darwin II, who licked Eddie's face a few times.

"Darwin, stop it," said Nancy. Again, he obeyed.

Eddie looked at Darwin, who looked right back at him. His mouth hung open and Eddie felt his warm breath over his face. He was so obedient...to Nancy...damn...I can't let these two get a hold of what's inside this locket. He held Darwin's silver locket in his hand. *Yeah, it was big enough.* He flipped it over, and sure enough saw the word *ORIGIN* written on the back. From where he was, both Chantal and Smith were behind him. Only Nancy and Darwin II were in front of him. He looked up at Nancy. "Can you go get the laptop?" He then mouthed the words, *go long,* and winked at her once. If Darwin II was as protective of Nancy as she told him earlier, then the plan that he had in mind just might work, despite how risky it was.

Nancy nodded in return. He hoped that she understood. "Sure, I'll go get it." While she walked across the living room into the adjoining dining room, Eddie undid the locket from Darwin's collar. When Nancy reached the table where the laptop was, she turned around.

"What are you waiting for?" Chantal said to Nancy. "Pick it up and bring it here."

"I think that it's still recharging, and the cord isn't long enough for her to bring it over here." Eddie answered.

"Bullshit," Chantal answered. She then pointed a finger at Nancy. "Bring the damn laptop over here right now."

"Nancy," Eddie yelled as he tossed the locket at her. She caught it easily from where she stood about twelve to fifteen feet away. Eddie then stood and backed away out of Darwin's path.

Chantal then turned to him. "What the hell was that? Do you think this is funny?"

Eddie took one more step back. "This place has wireless internet. If you want the flash drive that's inside the locket, you'd better shoot Nancy before she uploads its contents to the web."

Smith then raised the gun in Nancy's direction. "I just might do—"

Smith didn't get a chance to finish his sentence before Darwin unleashed an angry growl and charged him, leaping in the air and catching his wrist in his jaws. The momentum threw Smith to the ground, screaming a flurry of curse words.

Smith's gun flew from his hand and slid across the floor. Chantal rushed to grab it, but not before Jordyn dove across the floor in an attempt to beat her to it.

Shit, Jordyn was no match for that woman. He then saw Corey—pulling himself up onto one foot using the arm of the couch. He wasn't in danger right now. When he looked back at Jordyn, both she and Chantal were fighting over the gun.

Just then a shot was fired. Eddie immediately dove to the floor as two more loud explosions shook the room. The gunshots did little to drown out Smith's screams, as Darwin maintained his grip on his wrist, dragging him across the floor.

Eddie lay on his stomach as he watched the two women struggle. Chantal was taller than Jordyn and would surely prevail. If it weren't for the damn gun he would've tackled Chantal already. Just then, they both turned so that their backs were to him. Now was his chance. He got up just as Chantal shoved Jordyn to the side, causing her to knock her head against the wall and fall to the floor.

Eddie locked his arms around Chantal from behind and jostled her, hoping to shake the gun from her hands. As she aggressively resisted, he felt her stomp down on his foot, causing him to lose his grip momentarily as she spun around and kicked him right in the balls. It took him everything not to collapse to the floor, knowing that she would put a bullet in his head the first chance she got.

Fuck that hurt. He threw an arm outward and caught her wrist just as she was about to take aim. Eddie saw a bright flash and heard the *bang*. He still held onto the same arm, preventing her from aiming towards him. But she beat him with the other, as he was repeatedly struck on the side of his head and face.

"Fuck, Eddie. Just hit the bitch already!" he heard Corey scream.

That's all that it took to wake him up. He formed a fist with his free hand and struck her directly in the nose. Chantal's head snapped back and she fell to the floor. The gun dropped a few feet away from her. Eddie was relieved that it didn't fire. Chantal moaned a bit, but she didn't appear to move. Not wanting to take any chances, Eddie rushed over and snatched the gun before Chantal could. He then looked over where Jordyn lay, as she began to come around.

"Eddie," he heard Nancy shriek as she pointed at him. "Your shoulder."

That's when Eddie realized that he had been shot, as blood had soaked right through the sleeve of his shirt. He looked back at Nancy, surprised. He hadn't even felt the bullet—obviously the adrenaline surge must have kept him upright long enough to defend himself. It didn't take long before he saw the room swirl, as the pain in his shoulder intensified to the point that it felt that it was on fire. His legs gave away at the same time that his head got heavy. The room flipped over and he felt his head hit a hard surface. The pain that he normally would've felt from his head striking the ground was nothing compared to what he felt in his arm. He heard frantic cries, probably from Smith, but he also heard Nancy yelling something...something to do with an ambulance, he wasn't sure. It wasn't too long after, that he looked up into Nancy's gaze as she kept repeating the words: "Hang on, Eddie. Please hang on."

Then everything went dark.

Chapter 25

Sherbrooke, Quebec. Present Day

The first thing Eddie saw when he opened his eyes were the two large floral bouquets on the table in front of his bed. A few rays of sunlight brightened the room also. When he tried to sit up he felt a sharp pain in his left shoulder. *Shit, what the hell.* That's when he noticed the sling his arm was in.

"Sup, bro? You're finally up?"

Eddie turned to see Corey lying in the bed next to his. His foot was in a cast and was elevated slightly. "Where are we?"

"In Sherbrooke," Corey answered. "Two ambulances came and got us last night, except you had already passed out. The EMTs said that you were lucky that the bullet passed right through and that there wouldn't be any permanent damage."

Eddie nodded in the direction of Corey's leg. "How about you?"

Corey waved downward in the direction of his foot. "Shit, this ain't nothing. I'll walk again. We should both be out of here later on this afternoon."

Thank God for that. He reached for his necklace with the flash drive. It was gone. He looked to his left and saw it on the table beside his bed. He turned over in his bed slightly so that he could reach it with his opposite arm. It took a few attempts, but he eventually got it. He then slid it over his head, held the flash drive in his hand and gazed at it. He still couldn't believe that he went through this entire ordeal over a novel.

"Check this out," said Corey as he tossed a newspaper onto his lap. "We made the front page."

Eddie picked up the paper and turned it over to the front page. The bold-print headline read, *Prime Suspects Cleared in Governor's Murder.* Underneath the smaller bold-print read, *Conspiracy unraveled involving Borealest CEO Serge Lamont, wife, and RCMP and SPVM detectives.* Underneath the headline were headshots of him and Corey, and a larger picture of Serge Lamont seen struggling with police.

"If you think that's something," said Corey, "check the next five pages."

Eddie flipped through them and saw large photographs of Serge and Chantal Lamont, Smith, Mercier, and Nuttal. "They're all getting their asses thrown in jail."

"Hey guys." It was Jordyn followed by Nancy as they both came in the room.

"What's up, baby," said Corey as Jordyn came over and kissed him.

Nancy came to the foot of Eddie's bed and patted him on the leg. "How are you feeling now?"

"I feel like crap."

"You'll be fine." She then glanced at the newspaper in his hand. "I see that you've read the paper."

"Not really, just looked at the pictures and the headlines."

"All I can say is that it's a brave thing that you did. I just wish you hadn't encouraged that sociopath to point his gun at me."

"I knew that Darwin would've attacked him. You told me before that he'd automatically attack anyone who appears hostile towards you. I figured that the only way to do it was to trick Smith into pointing his gun towards you."

"Still, you didn't know for sure, did you?"

"I had faith. I just can't figure out how Smith of all people would've been involved in something like this."

"What can I say other than, the man was clever," said Nancy. "Read the paper when you get a chance. You'll see that the RCMP is now focusing their attention on him for his potential involvement with organized crime. Corrupt investigators like him aren't born overnight. If you ask me, both he and Chantal were made for each other."

"I guess so," said Eddie.

Nancy smiled. "How did you figure out that the backup copy of those files was hidden in the locket on Darwin's collar?"

Eddie then took his flash drive and held it up for her to see. "I showed this to your husband and told him what's on it. He told me that he had done the same thing once. Last night at the cemetery, you said that *origin* was engraved on Darwin's locket. So, I put two and two together. I doubt anyone would walk up to Darwin and try to steal his locket, unless they wanted to lose a hand."

"That's true. Anyhow, while you guys were fighting, I removed the flash drive, uploaded the files as an email attachment and sent it straight to the RCMP. In fact, I got a chance to read some of it."

"What did it say?"

"It's practically the Holy Grail for the prosecution. Everyone that's involved in the scandal is mentioned. I'm guessing that there's more in there that Chantal didn't want out in the open that could implicate both her and her lover. But they'll also have two murder charges to answer for."

"Allo tout le monde." *Hello everyone.* Eddie looked up and saw a nurse's assistant pushing a wheelchair. "Bonjour, Eddie. Ca va mieux, mon cher?" *Hello, Eddie. You're feeling better, my dear?* She was a petite young woman who appeared to be in her mid thirties. "I want to take you outside dee room for a bit." The nurse's assistant said this last sentence in English but with a heavy French-Canadian accent.

"Sure, where are you taking me exactly?" asked Eddie.

"Just down dee hall to the chapel."

What was there to see in the chapel? He decided not to ask her, as she helped him off the bed and into the chair.

"Don't worry," said Nancy. "I'll be close by."

Eddie said goodbye to Jordyn and Corey as the nurse's assistant rolled him into the hallway.

"My name is Giselle. I'm so excited to meet you in person."

The corridor was crowded, filled with hospital staff and some patients. Come to think of it, they were all staring at him. It was as though everyone knew who he was.

"Don't be intimidated. Word gets around quick here in dis hospital. It's not every day we have two heroes as patients."

"Cut it out, I ain't no hero."

"You're being modest," said Giselle as they came to a set of double doors. Eddie was turned around in order to face the other way, and Giselle wheeled him backwards into the chapel. As he was rolled past the threshold, he watched the doors close automatically.

"Oh, I forgot to mention," said Giselle. "There's a surprise." She then spun his chair around. Whom he saw brought the biggest smile he'd had in days, and he felt the tears coming soon. He didn't even have time to react before Monica assaulted him with a choking hug. His father joined in right after.

"You two are going to kill that boy before he gets out of the hospital." Eddie heard Beverly, but couldn't see her.

Monica let go of him and went down on one knee. That's when he saw Beverly and his sister, Denise, both of them smiling.

Edward also got down on one knee. "The police called us last night. We all jumped in the car and came here as soon as they gave us the news."

"Who shot you?" asked Monica. "The police didn't want to say."

Eddie shook his head. "It doesn't matter who shot me or Corey. I just want to forget about the whole thing."

Denise laughed. "You were accused of murder a few days ago. Now you have a bullet hole in your shoulder and you helped expose one of the biggest corporate fraud scandals in history. How are you going to forget about that?"

"In a few days everyone will stop talking about us, hopefully. I don't need any more media attention. It nearly got me killed," replied Eddie.

"Don't worry yourself," said Beverly. "You'll get used to it soon."

"I hope you don't mean getting shot at," Eddie quipped.

"No, silly," said Beverly. "Everyone's going to want to know your story."

Edward turned to Eddie. "Them same news people that hung outside our house when they were saying that you shot a politician, guess where they are right now?"

Shit, they're outside.

"Speaking of which," said Denise. "What's this fetish thing you've picked up with whips, chains, and leather? We're going to have to talk."

"There's going to be a trial, son," Monica jumped in. "You're going to have to testify in court against these people."

"Are you ready for that?" asked Edward. "Make sure you let me know if somebody calls you on the phone, threatening you."

Eddie waved his palms downward, as though to tell everyone to calm down. "Guys, relax. I already know all of this—you don't have to remind me. I'm sure some RCMP officer's waiting outside to question me, and the rest of us about what went on last night."

"I want to know first," said Edward.

Beverly slapped Edward on the shoulder. "The police already told you that he's not to say too many details about what happened."

"This is my son, I ain't no stranger," Edward shot back.

"Don't you two start arguing now," said Monica.

Denise then tapped Beverly on the arm. "Come, let's go see Corey. I'm sure his aunt and the Rinaldis must have gotten here by now."

"If your father wasn't driving so recklessly on the highway he wouldn't have lost them." That was the last thing he heard from Beverly just as she and Denise left the chapel. Then it was just his parents, both down on a knee beside him, a hand on each leg.

"Look," Eddie started. This time he would get it out of his system once and for all. For hours he'd wanted his chance at this. Now he wouldn't screw it up. "I just wanted to apologize for last Thursday. I shouldn't have blasted you and taken off like that. I've learned my lesson."

His father took a deep breath and let it out. "I'm very proud of you."

What? "Why's that?"

"I'm proud of you for sticking to what you believe in. Your mother and I should be the ones apologizing—for not believing in you."

"We're both very sorry," said Monica. "You should thank your aunt Beverly for talking some sense into both of us. We never meant to hurt you. You must believe that."

"I believe you. It's okay," said Eddie. "We've all learned something from all of this."

"That's why we want to make things different from now on," said Monica as she nodded to Edward. He got up and went to the pew in front of the alter, reached behind it and lifted a large plastic bag.

"What's this?" Eddie asked.

Edward took out a box from inside the bag. It was gift-wrapped. He then placed it on Eddie's lap. The parcel had a big bow on it and it was large enough to rest on the handles of his wheelchair. There was also a card tucked under the bow. He took it out of its envelope and saw that it was addressed to him from his parents, Denise, and Beverly.

"Go ahead, open it. Consider it as an early Christmas present," said Monica anxiously.

Eddie motioned his head to his left arm in the sling. "I'll need a little help." He started to tear away the gift wrap with his other hand as both Monica and Edward helped. He didn't have to remove all of the paper to finally guess what the present was.

"Denise suggested this for you," said Edward.

"She figured that your old computer must be on its last legs," said Monica.

"So we stopped at the mall just as we got into town and we all pitched in to get you this," said Edward.

Eddie chuckled as he hugged the box. He didn't even look to see what kind of laptop it was. He knew they wouldn't settle for second best.

Monica brushed some fuzz from his eyebrow. "So?"

"I love it, thanks." He stretched out his free arm and both Monica and Edward assaulted him with another bone crushing hug. He couldn't believe that these were the same people he wanted to disown a few days ago. How could he have ever thought of doing something like that?

When his parents finally let him come up for air, he felt the familiar dryness and soreness at the back of his throat. It didn't take too long before Monica dug into her purse and took out some tissues.

"That's all right dear. You're safe again."

I'm not crying...it's just a few tears. It's no biggie.

There was a knock at the door. "May I come in?"

Eddie recognized Nancy's voice and didn't even have to turn his head.

"Come in," said Edward. Nancy walked in and introduced herself. The introductions were brief since they all recognized each other from seeing themselves on the news.

Nancy then noticed Eddie's new laptop. "I guess you're going to be busy for the next few days."

Eddie glanced at his present and looked back at her. "It'll make life easier. I needed a new computer anyways."

"Excellent," said Nancy. "By the way, I didn't tell you this before. But for a while after the ambulance carried you off, I held onto your necklace. I was very curious to read the first few pages of your manuscript just to see what your problems have been all this time. I hope that you don't mind."

"No, it's cool."

Nancy then explained to Eddie's parents about her past employment in the publishing industry. She then reached into her handbag and took out a few folded sheets of paper on which she had typed her notes. "To start, I have to say that the premise sounds interesting and your main character, Simeon Wolf, appears to be a strong character. I have a feeling that this potentially could be a good story, so I must complement you on a good read."

"Thanks," Eddie said.

"I took these notes down. Although I cannot read the minds of the acquisition editors that read the sample chapters that they requested, I think I have an idea why they were rejecting your work. I've detailed everything I saw in my notes, which I won't go over with you right now. However I should point out that once I help you to spot your errors, you'll be able to rewrite it to publication standards."

Did I hear her right? "Did you just say that you're going to help me rewrite my novel?"

"If that's all right with all of you," said Nancy as she looked at Eddie's parents, who looked down at Eddie.

"I think our son's mature enough to decide what he wants to do with his life," said Edward.

Eddie's smile grew wide as he looked back at Nancy. "I'd love for you to help me. But is this going to be a career change for you?"

Nancy brushed a lock of her hair from over her eye. "I did a lot of thinking last night. Heavens, I couldn't even sleep while Jordyn and I waited for both you and Corey out in the waiting area. You've actually inspired me to go back to what I love doing."

"You're going to work in publishing again?" asked Edward.

"Not yet," Nancy replied. "I'd rather start out by being Eddie's writing coach for the time being."

Edward turned to Monica. "Get out the check book." He then looked at Nancy. "How much you charge?"

"Don't worry. It's on the house," said Nancy with a laugh as she looked at Eddie. "It's the least that I can do." She then patted him on the shoulder.

Eddie reached and held her hand as he looked at her. "Thanks, for everything."

Nancy returned the smile. "No, thank *you*. I'll see you outside." She then left.

Edward walked behind Eddie, grabbed the wheelchair handles, and spun Eddie around. "Let's go back to your room and see your troublemaking friends."

Monica walked ahead and held the door open for them. She then joined her husband as they both took a side and pushed Eddie. The number of people in the hall appeared to have increased. They all noticed when he was there with his parents, and automatically went to the sides where they lined up. Somewhere up ahead someone started clapping. Like a contagion, it spread to the next few people until eventually the entire hallway applauded.

Even though he appreciated it, he held his head down in embarrassment. That's when he saw the flash drive hanging outside his gown. Like a magnet, his hand was drawn to it. Once he had it he couldn't let it go, as the only thought that came to him, was that his parents finally wanted to hear what he had to say. Even though he knew the rest of the world wanted to hear his story, just having his parents' blessing was even more gratifying.

Chapter 26

Corey and Jordyn took an encore bow as they stood beside the baby grand piano. Eddie leaned against a pillar near the front entrance at the back of the audience as he watched. Jordyn finally did it. And Eddie smiled as he marveled at the new coffee shop he helped her purchase on Saint Denis Street in Le Plateau Mont-Royal borough of Montreal. It wasn't a big coffee shop, but it could hold over one hundred people once all of the chairs and tables were cleared away. And the place was complete with a small dais where guests could perform.

Corey, Jordyn, and Eddie had hired Flick to cater that evening, and the scent of Caribbean cuisine could be smelled blocks away. Seventeen months had passed since they left the Sherbrooke University Hospital that frigid Monday afternoon, to be bombarded by the media vultures the moment they left the building. But this was Eddie's time of year—spring. There wasn't any snow, nor slush, and there was no need for heavy boots and jackets.

When the applause died down, Eddie heard a woman call out his name just as Corey spoke to the audience through the mike.

"Mister Eddie."

Eddie turned to see three women—all appeared to at least five to ten years his senior—each holding a copy of his latest novel. It had been in bookstores for nearly two weeks and he was getting used to the *pop-in* autograph seekers.

Eddie took a pen out of his blazer pocket and signed all three.

He smiled as he turned around briefly to look at Jordyn and

Corey, who were each waving at him. Everyone had dogged him about what it was like to be the most wanted man in the country—from radio show hosts to the morning television hosts. Everyone was so fascinated by this, he couldn't figure out why. He thought they'd be more interested in knowing what it was like to have such a powerful adrenaline surge that he was able to still defend himself while he had a bullet wound. That question came up a few times, but nowhere close to the number of times as the other questions.

A few minutes had gone by as Eddie looked around him. He wasn't surprised that Nancy suggested that he put off his action/thriller novel for the time being while he focused on his current novel, *Thin Ice*. It made sense, since his adventures with Corey and Jordyn and the Borealest scandal were still fresh on everyone's minds. From what he read in the paper that morning, Serge Lamont faced over fifty-one charges from Quebec's top financial regulator, L'Autorité des Marchés Financiers, in addition to a minimum forty-year prison sentence. Thanks to the data that was contained on the flash drive that Darwin II had been carrying around, investigators were able to trace the two-hundred-and-twenty million dollar gap that wasn't declared in Borealest's books.

As for disgraced Detective Mercier, he cracked under pressure and testified against Serge Lamont in exchange for a lighter sentence. Not surprisingly, Smith did the same thing to Chantal Lamont. However it didn't change much for him considering that the RCMP was able to connect him to two unsolved cases that he helped to cover up. Many more were expected to come that would guarantee him a lifetime sentence.

The audacity of those people.

Now with *Thin Ice* available for sale online and in bookstores all over North America, Europe, and the Caribbean, and the nice advance that Nancy was able to negotiate with a renowned New York City publisher, he was able to help Jordyn purchase this coffee shop, going on a little over three months, now. Yesterday was the opening day which also doubled as a book signing for Eddie. After two days, the place was still packed. To his surprise, Eddie read in various online blurbs many former Borealest clients were among his fans—many who would have lost their life savings had the Lamonts not been caught when they were.

"What's up, bro? Or should I now say, *partner?*" Corey emerged from the crowd and gave Eddie their old-fashioned buddy hug. He then handed him a brown envelope.

Eddie took it, opened it, and took out a check written in his name for the amount of two thousand dollars. "What's this for?"

"That's the rent money that I owe you, plus interest."

"You didn't have to do this."

"Yes I did. You're my bro and my best friend. Jordyn and I wouldn't have made it this far without you." Corey then looked around him. "Look at this place. It's been packed since yesterday. Jordyn and I didn't end up closing until three in the morning. This is the shit, bro!"

Corey's head suddenly jerked forward as he grabbed the back of his head. Eddie turned to see Flick, dressed in an apron, and pointing a spatula at Corey.

"I know this ain't my restaurant. But I still don't want to hear any foul language. You understand me?"

"Yes we do," said Jordyn who approached them holding their son. "My husband still has to work on some bad habits around our son. Isn't that right?"

Corey and Jordyn—now husband and wife—was still something that Eddie had to get used to. Apparently Jordyn's father didn't give them a choice since the baby was on its way. The wedding wasn't anything fancy, just a small ceremony. Eddie was Corey's best man. There were a handful of other guests which included Nancy, his parents, Corey's aunt, and Jordyn's parents. The traditional wedding with the five hundred or so guests that Jordyn's father wanted to have, would be held later on in the summer.

Eddie turned to Corey. "You're a father now...you've got to watch your mouth around baby Malcolm from now on."

"Yeah, I know," said Corey as he turned to Flick. "Where's Robert, I didn't see him among the catering staff."

"My son's busy managing the restaurant," Flick answered.

"That's right," said Jordyn. "How's everything going?" She referred to the bigger space that Flick moved his restaurant to that could easily hold three times the amount of clients compared to the basement that he used for his previous place.

"Things couldn't be better," Flick answered. "Business picked up last year while you all were on the run from those wicked people. My previous location was packed all weekend with people crowding in front of the TV. I kept on running out of alcohol. The crowds died down a bit after, but I had more delivery orders that kept coming in. I had to hire some more youngsters just to keep up with them." He then turned to Eddie. "Since you mentioned the name of my restaurant in your book, my restaurant's always been busy and my debts are about to be all paid off." He then gave two friendly, but slightly hard, pats on his cheek. "Keep up the good work." He walked back to the kitchen.

"Excuse me."

They all turned to see a middle aged couple looking at Corey. The man spoke with a French accent. Eddie knew that it wasn't a Quebec accent, but it had to be one of European origin.

"We're on vacation from Belgium and we thought we recognized you," said the man.

"Oui, oui," said the woman. "We saw you on the internet on that Canadian Idol show."

Eddie looked at Corey and saw the smile drop off his face. *Shit Corey, don't lose your cool. Not now.* He looked at Corey's fist that was beginning to clench.

"I just wanted to say," the man continued. "That my wife and I saw you play the piano while you sang and we absolutely loved it. We feel so honored to meet you in person."

Eddie saw the surprised look on Corey's face. He could only sigh with relief.

The wife took out a digital camera and gave it to Eddie. "Do you mind taking a picture of us?" She then giggled. "Our children will be so jealous."

Eddie took a step back and snapped the photo.

"Merci beaucoup," said the wife. The Belgian then turned to Corey. "So, do you ever regret not getting the record deal?"

Corey turned to Jordyn and took Malcolm from her. While holding him he put his other arm around Jordyn. "No, the record deal doesn't mean much to me right now. I'm married, got a healthy little boy, and my best friend. I got my fans coming here to watch me play the piano and sing. I'm happy with what I've got."

Talk about a one-hundred-and-eighty degree turnaround. Just to think that last year he was flat broke on his ass, wasting his life away. Since Malcolm came, Corey's found a new purpose to move forward in life. Although they weren't roommates anymore, they managed to find two vacant apartments in a triplex that was four blocks away. Eddie had an entire two-bedroom apartment to himself—one that served as his bedroom and the other for his office where he was currently writing an outline for an upcoming novel. He had new furnishings complete with a high definition flat screen television that was complete with stereo-surround sound. Corey, Jordyn, and Malcolm were in a similar type of apartment directly across the stairwell.

"Hello, everyone."

Eddie turned and saw Nancy Bevins, carrying a Madison Avenue Tote bag. She was as stylish as ever.

"Parking's a nightmare in this neighborhood. I can't believe how many reserved parking spaces there are. It's ridiculous."

Nancy gave Eddie a peck on each cheek. She then did the same for the others.

"How long ago did you get back into town?" Eddie asked.

"About an hour ago. The flight from New York wasn't too bad."

Two months before, Nancy told Eddie that she was trying to negotiate a deal for his Simeon Wolf novel to publishers. She was also handling ten other authors.

"Congratulations on making the bestseller's list here in Canada. That's very rare for a new author."

"Thanks," Eddie replied. Corey and Jordyn patted him on the back.

"It's a good thing that you did," said Nancy as she reached inside her Tote bag, took out an envelope, and handed it to Eddie.

"I tried to push for more. I even used your celebrity status to help negotiate for something higher. But this is all they're going to offer for now. If you write a sequel, I might be able to negotiate for more."

Eddie paused as he glanced once at Corey, and then at Jordyn—

who both smiled at him while glancing at the envelope. He opened it, took out and unfolded the paper, then read it. It was just a short paragraph and he ended up dropping the envelope on the ground as he reached and grabbed the flash drive around his neck as his jaw dropped.

Eddie handed the paper to Corey as Jordyn looked at it with him. Both their eyes bulged a few seconds later.

"Damn, Eddie," said Corey. "That's four digits short of being a phone number."

The End

About the Author

Prior to becoming a writer, Russell Brooks considers himself fortunate that he had the opportunity to be an Indiana Hoosier Track Champion and Canadian Track Team member in both the 100 and 200 metres. It was during Brooks's travels across Canada, the United States, and Europe that he came up with his story ideas and created outlines for his future thrillers.

Russell's B.S. in Biology from Indiana University helped him to write his first spy thriller in the Ridley Fox/Nita Parris Spy Series, *Pandora's Succession*, followed by the short-story collection of *Unsavory Delicacies*. The latest addition to the spy series is *The Demeter Code*. So far, it appears that this series is far from over. The standalone thriller, *Chill Run*, was released afterwards.

Although Brooks's goal is to keep readers in suspense by writing edge-of-your-seat and page-turning thrillers, Russell may occasionally dash off a short story, entertain viewers with dramatic readings or play his violin.

Russell Brooks currently lives in Montreal, Quebec.

Also from Russell Brooks

The Ridley Fox/Nita Parris Series

Pandora's Succession
Unsavory Delicacies
(eBook only)
The Demeter Code

The Eddie Barrow Series

Chill Run
Coming Soon!
Jam Run

Find out more about Russell at:
www.russellparkway.com